At The Flood

By
K.J.RABANE

Taken at the Flood

Copyright © 2013 K.J.Rabane
All rights reserved.

Taken at the Flood

Dedication.
To The Tiny Writers.

Taken at the Flood

Acknowledgements
Many thanks go to Retired Police Sergeant Alan Lloyd, Nona Evans and Frank.

Taken at the Flood

Table of Contents

Beginning
Chapter 1 — Chapter 2
Chapter 3 — Chapter 4
Chapter 5 — Chapter 6
Chapter 7 — Chapter 8
Chapter 9 — Chapter 10
Chapter 11 — Chapter 12
Chapter 13 — Chapter 14
Chapter 15 — Chapter 16
Chapter 17 — Chapter 18
Chapter 19 — Chapter 20
Chapter 21 — Chapter 22
Chapter 23 — Chapter 24
Chapter 25 — Chapter 26
Chapter 27 — Chapter 28
Chapter 29 — Chapter 30
Chapter 31 — Chapter 32
Chapter 33 — Chapter 34
Chapter 35 — Chapter 36
Chapter 37 — Chapter 38
Chapter 39 — Chapter 40
Chapter 41 — Chapter 42
Epilogue

Taken at the Flood

Taken at the Flood

Prologue

She opens the package addressed to her and removes the journal. There is no doubt it's from the Englishman, or that he posted the money through her letterbox earlier.

Pushing stray strands of pale blonde hair behind her ears, she climbs the stairs to her room, takes the journal outside to the balcony, and places it on the rusty iron table. The autumn sun stokes her skin, as she smells the approach of winter in the crisp morning air spilling into the walled Tuscan town from the surrounding fields.

It's rare that she has time to herself and not attending to the needs of others. The last few months have been a nightmare. Her letters have remained unanswered. She has to know why and what has happened, waiting and wondering is driving her crazy.

Picking up the journal, she opens it to the first page, somehow knowing that it will hold the answer to the question, which has troubled her to the exclusion of all else. Perhaps it will give her peace. It can't be worse than living each day wondering. She takes a deep breath and begins to read.

Chapter 1

We were in Venice, Evelyn and I, eating pasta at a restaurant near the Rialto Bridge. We were in love. It was a perfect day. Sunlight dappled the water of the Grand Canal and my wife smiled contentedly. We got drunk on Chianti and toasted the rest of our life together, with the confidence of youth, certain that it would be a long one.

"Stay here, wait for me, there's something I need to do. I won't be long – promise."

She leaned across the table, her short curly hair brushing my cheek. I smelled her perfume as her lips touched mine then watched her hips swaying enticingly as she walked up the steps to the bridge.

Refilling my glass, I drank the wine whilst relaxing in the warmth of the mid-day sun, the sights and sounds of the Venetian landscape, an intoxicating mixture, as I waited for Evelyn to return. Below me gondoliers drifted past, their painted poles slicing through the silvered surface of the canal like knives through butter. I closed my eyes and sighed with contentment, as a tenor voice caught my attention. Squinting into the sun, I saw a colourfully decorated gondola slip into view as it passed under the bridge. Its shiny hull was painted black with red and gold flowers at intervals.

Taken at the Flood

Sitting in the prow were a young couple. The young man looked about my own age, the girl younger, twenty-ish, her head covered by a cream sun hat. As they passed below my seat, the girl removed her hat and I saw a glorious cascade of pale blonde hair fall to her shoulders. I opened my eyes wider, alert now. She was laughing at her companion and looked up at the restaurant at the same moment as I leaned forward from my seat. Our eyes met for the briefest of moments but it was enough to alter the course of my life.

"Close your eyes, my darling." Evelyn's hands caught mine and I felt a small box thrust into my palm. "Now you can open them."

She waited expectantly.

"What's this?" I asked. "What have you been up to now?"

She couldn't contain her excitement. "Open it, hurry up!"

I unwrapped the shiny gold paper to reveal a small black jeweller's box. Inside lay a gold signet ring with my initials engraved on the front in high relief and inscribed in tiny letters inside the band were the words, *Thank you E.*

I drew her on to my lap and kissed her.

"Whatever for?" I asked.

"For loving me," she answered and kissed my mouth.

Chapter 2

My parents, who had supported me throughout my difficult teenage years filled with madcap ideas and inventions, did not live to see my computer business succeed. They were travelling to New York to spend Christmas with my brother and his wife. I dropped them off at Heathrow Airport at four o'clock on the 21st of December and that was the last time I saw them. I remember embracing them both, handing over the Christmas gifts that Evelyn had packed for my brother's family, and telling them that we would ring them all on Christmas morning. As I walked away, I heard the announcement

"Would passengers booked on Pan Am flight 103 from Frankfurt to New York please make their way to the departure lounge."

My mother turned and waved. When she reached the gate, I blew her a kiss.

There was sleet in the air. I drew my coat around me and bent to open the car door. The wind was blowing hard against my face as I struggled to turn the key in the lock. Then I drove to my office. I had the radio tuned to the Classic F.M. station and Tchaikovsky's violin concerto kept me company above the howling of the wind. I'd told Evelyn earlier not to expect me much before nine, as the project I was working on was nearing completion and I needed to make up the missing hours, which would be lost whilst driving my parents to Heathrow.

I remember arriving back at my office at six thirty. The security guard was sitting at his desk in the foyer; he raised his eyes from his newspaper as I opened the glass doors from the street. He had the radio on and I could hear a Country and Western station playing a Willie Nelson song.

"I'll be in my office for a while, Walter," I said.

"Your parents get off all right, did they, sir?" He looked up. "I can feel the temperature dropping. I expect it will be bitter in New York. No doubt they'll be in for a white Christmas."

I agreed then pressed the lift button. My office was pleasantly warm after the chill of the evening air. I hung up my overcoat and as I passed the computer console, pressed the 'on' button on the monitor, made a cup of hot chocolate from the machine and settled down to work on a problem that I knew, with a little persistence, I could solve.

The internal telephone on my desk rang. I glanced at my watch. It was five past nine and the solution was within my grasp. I picked up the receiver at the same time as I switched off my computer. It was Walter. He sounded agitated.

"I've been listening to the nine o'clock news on my radio," he began.

"Yes?" I prompted, hearing the hesitation in his voice and his rapid intake of breath.

"There's been a plane crash somewhere in Scotland. The plane took off from Heathrow this evening, bound for New York."

The room spun for a moment.

"Mr Hope, Mr Hope, you OK?"

"Oh, God, no. I'm sorry, Walter, my external phone is ringing."

It was Evelyn." Darling have you heard the news?" She started to cry.

She'd been close to my parents and I needed to comfort her, needed to be doing something positive to stop myself from thinking. "I'm on my way," I said, trying to block the news from my mind in order to function rationally but I don't remember much of the drive home, except that the radio kept repeating details of a crash over the town of Lockerbie.

However, I do remember thinking that I'd never heard of the place. How was I to know that the events of 21st December 1988 would soon rob the inhabitants of that Scottish town of their former anonymity during the years that were to follow? The bombing, of a passenger plane, resulting in massive casualties both from within the aircraft and on the ground, was to become headlines all around the world as terrorism raised its ugly head.

Taken at the Flood

Driving home, all I could think about was how the disaster was going to affect my own life and that of my family. Evelyn was waiting for me and we comforted each other during the grim weeks ahead, until time blurred the edges of our memory.

Ironically, soon after the crash, my business started to make money. Softcell Computer Operating Systems was my baby. I always believed that one-day it would make my fortune. Nevertheless, it started slowly as I gradually beat off my competitors one by one, whilst refining my programmes until they were unique. The legacy my parents left me provided the funds I needed at that crucial time, until I had built up enough business to risk a takeover of Macropower, my biggest rival. I made my first million, and the rest is history. My only sorrow was that my parents didn't live to see it.

Throughout those early years Evelyn supported me without complaint. She bore with stoicism my constant absences when I'd been promoting my products, never once complaining, accepting the decision not to start a family until I'd made a success of my career. When success came, it was bigger than either of us had anticipated. Softcell shares rocketed on the open market and before we'd come down to earth, a reporter from the business section of one of the country's leading broadsheets was interviewing me. Television current affairs programmes followed, as I became known as one of Britain's finest young entrepreneurs.

Our holiday in Venice was a fond memory of a time before media madness entered our lives and, if I was to think of it at all, I always saw myself sitting alone near the Rialto Bridge looking into a stranger's eyes.

Chapter 3

Evelyn's voice penetrated a particularly sensual dream one morning, with the words, "Darling, you awake?"

Her naked body moulded into my back as she bent over and nuzzled my ear.

"Mm" I grunted dragging myself awake from a dream, the details of which escaped like a rapidly dissolving mist.

"What would you say, if I said, I think it's time to start a family?"

"Now?" I asked turning over to face her.

"Mmm, now would do nicely," she replied sliding her leg over mine.

Evelyn's first false alarm happened three months later. "We've done it! You're going to be a father," she announced patting her stomach.

I booked Giorgio's to celebrate. It was the Greek restaurant where we'd first met, she working as a waitress, during her gap year, before she started a college course, and me with my parents celebrating my twenty-first birthday and the birth of Softcell.

The restaurant was fully booked but Giorgio said that he could always find a place for his favourite people. This type of response was nothing new. It was like that all the time now, success seeming to open up all sorts of doors both metaphorically and physically.

Taken at the Flood

The table turned out to be the best the restaurant had to offer. It stood on a raised wooden floor overlooking the street. I remember ordering a bottle of Dom Perignon and we drank to our health and that of our unborn child, Evelyn taking care to drink only one small glass, half of which she left untouched. I smiled at her sensitivity; she was starting to take care of our baby even before it was born.

"What are you smiling at?"

"Nothing much. I suppose I just can't hide my happiness." I replied as she reached across the table and stroked my hand.

Afterwards, I wasn't sure whether it was the effects of the champagne, or whether it was my imagination. Evelyn was talking about how wonderful our lives were going to be when I noticed a car stopping in traffic in the street outside the window. The traffic lights were showing red and, as the car waited for the lights to change, I saw her again. The hair, the unusual eyes; she was watching us. She saw me looking at her and stared back, without a hint of recognition.

"Darling, what is it?"

"What?"

"You look as if you've seen a ghost." She glanced over her shoulder to see what had attracted my attention but the street outside was

Taken at the Flood

empty, the lights having changed and the traffic moved on.

Three days later I spent the day comforting Evelyn when it appeared that there was not going to be a baby after all. I tried to spend as much time as I could with her; owning one of Britain's largest computer software businesses had its advantages. The business was progressing satisfactorily without me and I could afford to spend some time with my wife.

We decided to look for somewhere to live in the country but not too far away from London. I suppose, if I could turn back the hands of time, that was the moment I should have chosen it to stop, for then the horror had not yet begun.

Chapter 4

Looking back through the years, I try to remember the exact moment she came into my life. Not the fleeting glimpses of her face in a crowd, I'd experienced ever since Venice, but actual contact, awareness, conversation. Ironically it was Evelyn who brought her to me.

We lived in the city. Our house was small but in a fashionable area. It was not the sort of place we'd envisaged sharing with a young family. Evelyn's false pregnancy made us think seriously about moving and we spent most days in estate agents offices discussing the merits of one property over another. Our prerequisite was somewhere where our child could run and play in safety and breathe air unpolluted by the fumes of city traffic. We needed space.

Over the following weeks, we looked at several possible properties in the country, most of which were expensive, rambling affairs with elaborate security systems and not another house in sight. Then one afternoon in mid April we saw it; the house on River Road.

We arranged to meet the estate agent at two o'clock. He'd given me directions and said he'd be waiting for us with the key, as the house was unoccupied. It was a beautiful spring afternoon, the trees were in bud and sunshine dappled the surface of the river as we drove along River Road. It was uninspiringly named River House and I knew Evelyn would want to think up a new name if we bought it. However, as things turned out the house was never re-named. Even now, I doubt whether Mrs Bates will change its name, and River House it will always remain.

Matt Hawkins, of Hawkins and Butler Estate Agents, was waiting for us as promised, the smoke from his hastily extinguished cigarette hanging in blue clouds above his head. Waving us through the gates, he followed us up the pebbled driveway to the house, our tyres crunching on the gravel as we drew to a halt outside a pair of oak doors studded in wrought ironwork.

"Mr and Mrs Hope, lovely afternoon, just right for viewing a property at its best, I always think."

He was a wiry young man with thinning hair who seemed unable to keep still. He bounded up the stone steps to the front door and inserted the key in the lock, standing back for us to pass through into the hallway. It was a modestly sized property, if you compared it with the ones we'd viewed recently, but we fell in love with it immediately. I have always felt that houses emit a kind of aura; you can tell whether the previous occupants have been happy or sad there. Emotions and traumas linger in the walls and hang like cobwebs clinging to the past whilst waiting to absorb the present. No such atmosphere lingered in River House.

The hallway led into a large reception room of elegant proportions, which I guessed my wife would enjoy furnishing. The view through two large French doors was of the garden, at the bottom of which lay the river, its surface shimmering and calm in the still afternoon. A set of double glass doors led to a conservatory with a high ceiling, strung with an intricate arrangement of louvered blinds. To the right of the hallway lay the dining room, study, large kitchen, utility room and back porch. On the upper floor were five bedrooms leading off a landing. The main bedroom overlooked the back of the house with doors leading to a balcony. Evelyn gasped, "Oh darling look at the view. Isn't it splendid!"

The river shone like polished pewter in the sunshine, its surface unruffled and still. At the bottom of the garden lay a small jetty and a path leading through woodland, which was bursting with buds. I drew fresh country air into my lungs and squeezed Evelyn's hand and feeling her return the pressure, knew that we had found our house.

River House stood in two and a half acres of ground on the banks of a tributary of the Thames. The garden comprised a neatly trimmed lawn leading to the river, bordered by flowerbeds beginning to bud and to the right of which was a shrubbery. A solid stonewall enclosed the property. On the opposite side of the lawn stood a large wooded area and I noticed around the curve of the river, just discernible through the trees, were the roofs of two houses. In summer, I doubted whether they would be visible, the view possibly obscured by thick foliage but it was comforting to know our longed-for child would be within a short drive of neighbours, who might have children of their own. Ready-made playmates leapt into my mind as insubstantial as the child I was sure we would make. After assessing the potential of the house and gardens, we walked back hand in hand, up the lawn to the French doors where Matt Hawkins stood clipboard in hand.

"Well?" he enquired, shifting his weight from one foot to the other as he waited expectantly for our reply.

"Darling, I think we can put Mr Hawkins out of his misery, don't you?" Evelyn said.

"I knew you'd like it. A lovely property and I hope you'll both be very happy in your new home." He closed the cover on his clipboard and sighed contentedly.

"I'm sure we shall, Mr Hawkins, as I told you, on the telephone, if we liked the property we'll meet the asking price and top any other offers you may receive during our negotiations."

"Now, when can we move in?" Evelyn asked, hardly able to contain her pleasure.

The estate agent confirmed that, as soon as the paperwork was completed, we could take up residence, adding, he didn't envisage any delays.

In the event the whole process took no more than a few weeks and during the second week in May, we moved into River House, Evelyn insisting there was no need to wait until the place was redecorated, as she loved it just the way it was. I remember laughing at her and telling her that was why I loved her, 'just the way *she* was'. We ended up in our king-sized bed, half filled packing cases littering the floor, blissfully content and unaware that our removal to our 'dream house' in the country was destined to destroy us both.

Chapter 5

The light was beginning to fade; the subliminal flickering from my computer monitor making my eyes ache. The new programme was not working. I stared at the black screen and scratched the back of my head. Yesterday, it had worked perfectly. Twice today I had managed to complete without interruption but ever since I had hit trouble. Just as I was sure it would work out, a large red cross appeared in the centre of the screen with the words DATA ERROR flashing at intervals, until the whole programme crashed around my ears once again. Painstakingly slowly, I started to rebuild and analyse the components once more, until Evelyn's car drew to a halt on the driveway beneath my study window. She looked up and waved. I went to meet her to help carry the mountain of packages she was already unloading from the boot. She'd been shopping in the city and I knew what to expect from such a trip.

She could hardly contain her excitement, "I've got news!" she yelled in my ear, "I'm pregnant."

I put my arms around her and held her close, afraid she was jumping the gun again. She noticed my guarded expression and held my face in her hands.

Taken at the Flood

"It's all right, I took a sample to Gordon last week and went to see him today to get the results. He confirmed it. I *am* pregnant."

Gordon Marchant was our GP I felt her body relax against mine, as a wave of intense happiness swept over me. "That's fantastic news. River House has been waiting for a baby; not just any baby, our baby." I spun her round and our laughter filled the air.

The following Friday we attended a preliminary meeting with Lucas Bennett, the obstetrician, who would be looking after Evelyn throughout her pregnancy. Gordon had advised us that he was the top man in his field and I saw no reason to doubt his judgement. At the end of the visit, he made an appointment for us to return in a few weeks time in order to conduct the initial scan.

Spring was in the air and in our steps as we walked back to the car and drove to River House.

During the following week, Evelyn returned, from yet another afternoon shopping trip, with even more news. "You'll never guess who I met today," she said, as I placed the inevitable mound of carrier bags on the kitchen table and started back for more.

"Wait a second, go and sit in the study and I'll bring you a hot drink. Then you can tell me all about it." I closed the boot of her car and drove it into the garage, then made coffee for us both and joined her in my study. She was standing at my desk.

"Trouble?" A line of meaningless codes flashed at intervals on the screen in front of her.

"Nothing I can't handle," I answered sounding more positive than I felt. "Now tell me all about this mysterious person you met in town."

She sat on the couch and patted the space alongside her. Like an obedient puppy, I sat beside her and she cuddled into me, stretching her legs over my knees for me to massage her toes. "Do you remember me telling you about my friend Josie Rawlingson? We'd been friends at school and were really close."

"I do."

"Well, after leaving school, Josie went to work in Switzerland. I haven't seen or heard from her for years, except for the odd Christmas and Birthday card usually sent from far flung places, until today." She sipped her coffee and I waited for her to continue. "I was in 'Harvey Nicks' at the perfume counter when I heard someone say 'Evelyn Wallis, it is you isn't it?' I felt a hand placed on my shoulder and there was Josie. Apparently she's married someone in banking and has done very well for herself."

"Oh good," I muttered becoming bored with the exploits of Josie Rawlingson and a chance encounter, as it was unlikely we would ever meet. But, my sarcasm did not escape my wife's notice.

"Before you switch off completely, I've also discovered who our neighbours are; the ones living in the houses we can see through the trees."

My interest mildly reawakened, I waited for her explanation. Evelyn was enjoying herself now and made me wait, sipping her coffee and reaching for a biscuit, playing to her audience and increasing the suspense.

"OK, you've got my full attention, who?" I asked in exasperation.

"Josie and her husband Henry live in one."

"Really?"

"And Mr and Mrs Lucas Bennett live in the other."

"Good heavens, you mean Bennett your obstetrician? What a coincidence!"

"My feelings exactly. Convenient wouldn't you say?" She took my hand and placed it firmly over her abdomen

"Perhaps not quite so convenient for Mr Bennett," I said.

Evelyn stretched her legs and sighed. "Josie is hoping to arrange a get-together soon, so we'll have a chance to meet the neighbours."

"There can't be many of those surely."

"No, well, actually it will be just us and Mr and Mrs Bennett. I hope it won't be too dreary for you.

Taken at the Flood

I groaned. Bennett was approaching sixty and I couldn't think he and I would have much in common, other than my wife's pregnancy, which would be a subject I would naturally wish to avoid, outside his consulting rooms. I knew what it felt like to be approached at a party, by some computer enthusiast with no other topic of conversation. I could only hope Josie's husband would be nearer my own age and we would be able to find some common ground between us.

The following week we received an invitation from the house through the trees. Josie rang, spoke to Evelyn and the party was arranged for Saturday night.

It was a warm night and I stood by the window and watched Evelyn dressing. She was wearing a red satin dress with some sort of flimsy chiffon overskirt, which hid the, non-existent, swelling of her abdomen – the one she insisted was most definitely there. I thought she looked radiant. Her curly dark hair shone as brightly as the diamond earrings I'd bought her in Tiffany's when 'Softcell Systems' had secured our first large contract in the States.

"Bit pretentious to insist on a black tie do for the neighbours, don't you think?" I pointed out, whilst struggling with my tie.

"Here, let me." She gently pushed my hand aside. "Not if you knew Josie. She loves entertaining, loves showing off. Everything has to be just right. She was always the same, even when we were young. The difference is now she has married a man with money and can afford to indulge her whims." She smiled up at me. "When we were children, she always said she would marry a millionaire, she never mentioned love. Whilst I, I'll have you know, insisted I would never marry for money, only for love."

I kissed the top of her head as she patted my perfectly knotted bow tie. I had a strong feeling tonight was going to be a disaster. To me Josie sounded a pretentious individual and I'd already anticipated that her husband was bound to be a pompous bore. But I kept my thoughts to myself, hoping I'd be able to see 'the something' in Josie that had made her one of my wife's childhood friends. I decided to trust Evelyn's natural good sense; after all, she had chosen me to be her husband.

"I wonder what Mrs Bennett will be like? I said, helping her on with her coat.

The ever-thoughtful Josie had arranged for their car to pick us up at seven thirty. I thought it was kind of her, especially as it was only a short drive to their house, but apparently, she'd insisted so I could have a drink and relax. Perhaps Josie wasn't going to be too pretentious after all.

The Dangerfields' house was no larger than ours, the grounds not as pleasantly landscaped,

Taken at the Flood

but somehow it seemed grander, more impressive. The large electronically operated gates swung open as we arrived, revealing a red brick paved driveway. The chauffeur opened the car door for us and we walked the short distance to a doorway, above which stood a lantern throwing a welcoming glow over the porch.

Josie opened the door, her dark hair elaborately piled up on top of her head. She threw her arms around my wife. "Darlings so glad you could come. Nice to meet you at last," she said, hugging me and air-kissing my cheek. So, this was Josie. Not at all what I had imagined. I was pleasantly surprised.

Inside the house, the furnishings were a sumptuous mixture of good taste and plenty of money, which do not necessarily always go together. It appeared we were the first to arrive.

The evening was destined to be full of surprises. Not only was Josie nothing like I had imagined, neither was her husband. Henry Dangerfield was a good-looking man a little older than I, with a shock of curly dark hair, a pleasant smile and seated in a wheelchair. He shook my hand and asked what I would like to drink then pressed a button on the arm of his chair and glided over to a well-stocked bar in the corner of the room. Josie was talking to my wife and I thought I heard the words 'riding accident'.

Taken at the Flood

"How are you settling in at River House? Bit of a change from the city, I should imagine." Henry handed me a generous tumbler of whiskey.

"You could say that, although I must admit I enjoy spending as much time as possible working from home now, less stress - you know how it is."

"Thank God for computers, eh?" He had a pleasant smile "They have been a life saver for me. They are a means by which I can keep tabs on what's happening, without having to move from my chair, which under the circumstances…" His voice trailed off and I felt it necessary to make some sort of comment.

"Have you been using your chair for long?" Banal, I bit my lip, what sort of crass remark was that? Henry Dangerfield, sensing my embarrassment, smiled again.

"I had an accident some years ago at a polo match."

"I'm sorry."

He smiled, "No need, I met Josie at a polo match actually. She was with my brother's girlfriend, they'd come to watch us play."

Henry, watching the two women, raised his glass in Josie's direction. I remained silent, unable to adequately express my sympathy for the man sitting in front of me. Then the doorbell rang.

Taken at the Flood

"You must excuse me, that must be Lucas and Leonora," Henry said, propelling his chair into the hallway to greet his guests.

Lucas Bennett entered the room alone. I recognised the tall, slightly overweight figure, with the thick head of snow-white hair, from our recent visit to his clinic. He walked towards me his hand outstretched in greeting.

"Good to see you again," he said, his handshake firm and slightly chill from the evening air and I thought maybe he and his wife had walked from their house, the gates of which we'd passed at the bottom of the Dangerfields' drive.

From the hallway, I heard the sound of voices, Henry's deep and resonant and a woman's light and pleasant with just the hint of an accent, which I tried to place without success. I had my back to them and heard the sound of Henry's wheelchair gliding across the wooden floor behind me as Lucas Bennett raised his hand.

"Ah, Leonora my dear, come and meet our new neighbour."

I was unprepared and my face must have shown it. I had expected to see a woman in her late fifties, slightly plump, hair going grey. I turned and my mouth fell open in surprise - it was the girl in the gondola, her pale blonde hair shining in the light from the Dangerfields' massive chandelier. In a voice unable to

Taken at the Flood

disguise a hint of boredom in its timbre, she said, "How do you do?"

Taken at the Flood

Chapter 6

Closing my mouth, I stammered a reply as her hand, as cold as a witch's claw, slipped inside my own. I remember little of the rest of the conversation that evening. I know I spent most of the time listening, or appearing to, contributing only when not to would have caused embarrassment. Evelyn sparkled, spicing up mundane remarks with wit and good humour.

I found Henry Dangerfield to be an amusing and amenable host and felt drawn to this unassuming man who coped so admirably with his disability. His wife Josie was the perfect hostess and I thought I could see a glimpse of the strength of personality she kept hidden beneath a charming surface. However, to say that I was impervious to Leonora Bennett's obvious attributes would be a lie. The incongruous pairing, of the eminent obstetrician who was old enough to be her father and the fey young girl who spoke little but whose presence it was impossible to ignore, remained an enigma.

During the evening, I noticed both my wife and Josie trying to draw Leonora into their conversation. They suggested she join them on a shopping trip the following week but I felt the whole time she stood apart, assessing the situation, unwilling to commit to relationships, which might bore her. At the time I felt it was youthful immaturity, which made her hold back until she was sure of us and that in itself held an appeal all of its own.

It was a strange evening. During dinner, I sat opposite Leonora with Josie on my left and Evelyn on my right. Henry and Lucas sat either side of Leonora. The conversation was light, the food delicious but I felt unable to relax in her company and yet part of me wanted to stay watching her face, even though her incredible eyes did not seek mine and I don't remember her speaking directly to me all evening.

After dinner, the women took a tour of the house. Josie wanted to show Evelyn some fabric she had bought for the bedroom curtains. Henry handed around the port and cigars and I found myself asking, "Where did you and your wife meet, Lucas?"

To my surprise, he started to laugh. "Don't mind me. You see most people have a shock when they see Leo. I can see it in their eyes; they wonder what she sees in me. You are a little more subtle, my friend, but the question is there just the same."

I tried to protest but knew that to do so would only make things worse.

"I met her in Italy, as a matter of fact. We were staying in the same hotel and her luggage had gone astray. I helped her out and it rather developed from there. Even now, I can't believe my luck when I wake up every morning next to such a perfect creature."

He raised his glass to his lips.

"I thought I could detect the faint traces of an accent. Does your wife visit Italy often?" I asked.

"She has an elderly relative living in Tuscany. Leo speaks fluent Italian but when I met her she was without her luggage in which she'd packed her travellers cheques. She was completely at a loss. Her vulnerability was very appealing, as you can imagine. Her intention had been to stay in the hotel for a short holiday before visiting her aunt who lived in a small village in the back of beyond. Not the sort of place to be of much interest to a young woman apparently but she said she felt it her duty to visit as often as she could, as she was her only relative."

"Really? What happened to your wife's parents?" I asked.

"Leo doesn't like to talk about it but I gather it was some sort of accident when she was thirteen, after which she lived with her aunt in Italy until she was eighteen. Then she came to England to work as a nanny but it didn't work out. I later discovered that she'd spent some time working as a receptionist in Great Ormond Street. We have hospital life in common, you see."

"Yes I can see that must be useful."

Taken at the Flood

He looked at me over the rim of his glass assessing if I was being sarcastic. He decided I wasn't and continued, "It wasn't all we had in common as it turned out. Leonora liked watching football. She'd followed her local Italian team when she was growing up and when in London followed West Ham. As Henry knows, I have been a lifelong supporter and one thing led to another. Even so, I was really taken aback when I found out she was interested in my body as well as my mind!"

Henry spluttered, "Succinctly put if I may say so."

"Well wouldn't you have been shocked? I know she's young enough to be my daughter and maybe that was half the attraction for her. Initially, I think she looked upon me as a kind of father figure. Not now, mind you. I think we have progressed in our relationship, grown together, if you get my drift?"

"What are you three looking so guilty about?" Josie, followed by our wives, entered the room. She kissed the top of her husband's head. "Time for coffee and cognac I think."

As the evening drew to a close, I decided I liked Josie and Henry Dangerfield and was pleased they were our neighbours: as for the Bennetts, well that remained to be seen.

Later, at home, I removed my tie and walked into the bedroom where Evelyn was slipping out of her dress and into a cream silk dressing gown.

"What did you think of Leonora Bennett? I noticed your jaw dropped a mile when you saw her." She stretched her legs across my lap and wiggled her toes, a signal for me to rub her aching feet. Then, not waiting for my reply, said, "You were obviously as shocked as me. She must be at least thirty years younger than Lucas. I thought at first that his wife had been unable to come and he'd brought his daughter instead."

"Quite." I laughed, easing the tension that was building up behind my eyes.

"She's lovely though, isn't she?" Evelyn persisted.

"I suppose she is, yes, though not as lovely as my beautiful pregnant wife. By the way I must say I was surprised you didn't tell anyone you were pregnant."

She closed her eyes and laid her head contentedly against my shoulder. "I want to keep it a secret for a while. I suppose I'm superstitious. We'll tell them after the scan."

Her eyes closed and she fell asleep, her breath soft against my cheek. I lifted her gently in my arms, carried her over to the bed and covered her with the silk coverlet. Afterwards, I showered, slid into bed alongside my sleeping wife and closed my eyes but was unable to remove the image of Leonora Bennett from

Taken at the Flood

spilling into my dreams. My sleep was disturbed by visions of her blonde hair floating behind her as she slid out of my view and out of my reach.

Chapter 7

"There, how do I look? And if you say fat you can wash your own shirts in future, buddy!"

Her curly hair gleamed and there was a healthy glow about her, pregnancy had made my lovely wife bloom. "You look beautiful as I'm sure Mr Lucas Bennett will appreciate."

She pushed my shoulder with the palm of her hand as she walked in front of me towards the car.

During the drive to the private maternity clinic on the outskirts of town, Evelyn was quiet, then suddenly blurted out, "You are happy about the pregnancy aren't you?"

"What silly thoughts are going round in your head now? You know I couldn't be happier," I replied. "Don't have any doubts, just sit back and relax, close your eyes."

She closed one eye and looked at me out of the corner of the other. "I know why you want me to close my eyes. You don't fool me, buster. Once I am soundly asleep, you can put your foot down without me nagging you. Don't worry, I'll be a good girl and obey my master, just this once mark you."

I patted her knee and put my foot down harder on the accelerator.

Taken at the Flood

Bennett met us in the doorway of his consulting rooms and led us into a clinically bright room where white painted walls held framed prints of cornflowers. His desk was the focal point and facing him were two upright leather chairs in which we sat. After commenting on how pleased he was that we were to be neighbours and how he and his wife had enjoyed the party, he went on to discuss Evelyn's pregnancy and what we could expect during the following weeks. Then he showed her into an examination room accompanied by a nurse.

When Evelyn emerged some moments later, she explained she had to drink a pint of water and hold it for an hour, at the end of which we should return for the scan assessment. Lucas smiled and placed a hand on my shoulder. "Nurse will show you to our waiting area where you'll find some refreshments," he said, showing us out of the examination room.

The waiting area was equipped in a manner only to be expected of a clinic charging such exorbitant fees. The elegant furnishings and casement windows overlooked an immaculate lawn and shrubbery and a selection of piped classical music drifted around us like a soothing wind. Evelyn raised her eyebrows at me as a waitress, dressed in a mint green dress and crisp white apron, brought a large bottle of water and a measured glass for my wife and a cup of black filtered coffee for me.

Taken at the Flood

The scan being completed, we returned to Lucas's consulting room where he assured us everything was as it should be and that my wife's pregnancy was progressing satisfactorily. He said it was unlikely there should be any problem and he would see us when the next scan was due, stressing that if we needed to contact him about any concerns we might have, we should ring him.

Afterwards, we sat in our car in the car park of the maternity clinic, the branches of the beech trees a stark reminder that although it was spring, summer was not about to make an early appearance. We watched the daffodil heads nodding in the breeze as if agreeing with us, as we gazed in wonder at the first grainy photographs of our baby.

"Lucas said it should be possible to tell the sex at the next scan appointment, depending on how clear the image is. I said I knew already and was certain it was going to be a boy. He laughed and said it was good that I was so certain but I might be disappointed," Evelyn's words came out in a rush.

"Would you?"

"Be disappointed? No of course not! We're expecting a baby and that's all that matters. I'll be thrilled, whatever the sex. I just have a strong feeling I'm carrying a boy."

Taken at the Flood

During the early weeks of Evelyn's pregnancy, I frequently worked from home. I was in the process of developing a new programme, which I hoped would compete against my biggest rival, Microbytes, for the twelve to twenty portion of the consumer market. The initial set up had worked surprisingly well and I was starting to feel the adrenaline coursing through my body, as I anticipated the finished product. My enthusiasm was short-lived though, as the longer I worked on refining the programme, the more snags I encountered.

That morning I'd been working in my study ever since Evelyn left earlier. I'd kissed her goodbye and made some joke about not spending too much, assuming she and Josie were shopping in town and had been too preoccupied with my programme analysis to concentrate fully on what she was saying as she left the house. However, I did manage to wave to her from my study window, as her car crunched on the gravel driveway and disappeared around the bend, before returning to my computer screen.

The sun was low in the sky casting shadows across my desktop. I stretched out an arm and flicked the switch on the desk lamp at the same time as ERROR flashed on my monitor for the fifth time in the past hour. I slid my chair away from the desk, beads of perspiration breaking out on my forehead, as I leaned back my hands behind my head, legs stretched out in front of me staring at the ceiling. Then my glance fell on the clock on the wall and saw that the hands were sliding around to six thirty. I sat bolt upright in my chair. Where was Evelyn? She'd been out all day. I tried to recall what she'd said to me when she left but it was no use. I cursed myself for being so absorbed in my work that I couldn't remember. By seven o'clock I was beginning to feel uneasy. Picking up the telephone, I dialled the Dangerfields' number.

"Josie, hi. Is Evelyn with you?"

I heard her sharp intake of breath, "She's not home then?"

"No. I know it sounds odd but I'm not really sure where she said she was going when she left this morning."

Josie's sigh spoke volumes. "You men. You're all the same. She's been shopping with me in town. But, I left her walking to her car at about four. I had a dental appointment so I stayed in town until Henry picked me up and we drove back together." She hesitated, obviously having glanced at the time. "I can see why you're worried though. It's getting late and she should have been back by now. Perhaps she's met someone, forgotten the time. Yes that must be it." She was trying to sound reassuring but I felt her unease. "Anyway, if she doesn't turn up soon, ring us and we'll come over."

"Thanks, I'm sure there'll be a simple explanation. I'll be in touch."

Sounding more positive than I felt, I replaced the receiver and picked up the telephone directory. Running my finger down the yellow pages under the heading Hospitals, I began to dial the nearest casualty department. The telephonist's voice was repeating a series of well-used phrases ending in an enquiry as to which department I required when I heard the gravel crunching sound of Evelyn's tyres, as she drew up outside the front door. Slamming the phone down, I rushed into the hallway.

"Darling, I'm so sorry, I know I'm late. I can see by your face you've been worried. I should have let you know, I wish I had but the time just flew."

"I tried ringing your mobile."

She hung her head looking up at me through thick coal black lashes. "The battery is flat."

My anger dissipated. I tilted her chin up with the end of my finger and kissed the tip of her nose. "Thank God you're OK. If you'd been any later I would have started to ring around the hospitals."

Her eyes strayed to the yellow pages open on my desk and she put her arms around my neck. "I really am sorry."

"Go and sit down and I'll unload the boot," I said with undisguised relief.

"What an angel I've married," she replied kicking off her shoes and walking into the living room.

I made a hot drink for us both, mine liberally laced with brandy. I had to admit I'd been worried, my mind an easy prey to the twin terrors of fear and concern, neither of which had fully left me, even though Evelyn was home safely.

We were sitting in front of a roaring log fire cradling our coffee mugs in our hands when she began telling me about her day. "I picked up Josie as planned this morning and drove into the city. We shopped, had lunch in Fortnum and Mason's and in the afternoon we caught a cab to Covent Garden where we bought a few bits and pieces in the market. You know how I love markets?"

I nodded.

"Then around half three, we stopped for coffee and afterwards took a cab to where I'd parked the car. Josie left me to go to the dentist's and just as I was about to open the car door, I heard someone calling my name." She paused, tucking her legs under her. I was well aware that her pause had been for dramatic effect but I said nothing and waited for her to continue. "It was Leonora. She had a flat tyre. She was waiting for the AA recovery vehicle to arrive to fix it. I thought she looked a little distraught so I waited with her for the repairman

Taken at the Flood

to arrive. Then she suggested we have a coffee until her car was ready. I tried ringing you but found there was no response from my mobile. Leonora said not to worry, as she was sure we wouldn't be long."

I sighed, and she looked at me over the rim of her coffee mug. "I know, don't look like that. Leo chatted to the man about payment and said that when he'd finished replacing the tyre he could leave. She said she'd be picking the car up later."

"What happened to the quick cup of coffee then?"

"Do you know the funny thing is I can't answer that question. The time passed so quickly. Leo is marvellous company. You should have heard the story about her meeting with Lucas. I thought I'd split my sides."

"Really?"

For some reason I was beginning to resent Leonora Bennett for entertaining my wife so fully she'd forgotten about me and, for a fraction of a second, wondered if I was interpreting my feelings correctly. Did my resentment spring from the fact that I was jealous of the time Evelyn had spent that afternoon sitting opposite the girl with the sapphire blue eyes?

"The café served food," she said, as she continued to explain the reason for her absence.

Taken at the Flood

"I was feeling hungry by then and Leonora had ordered a smoked salmon salad, which looked delicious. And, as you now know, our quick coffee turned into a light meal."

"How can I complain about that, sweetheart? After all you are eating for two!" I couldn't stay mad at her for long and the brandy had succeeded in dispelling my earlier feelings of unease.

I stretched out an arm, hooked the yellow pages with the tips of my fingers, until it was close enough to reach, found the 'Fast Food' section, and ordered a meal from our favourite take-away. The flames from the fire made Evelyn's cheeks glow and I slipped my arm around her shoulders as a feeling of contentment grew inside me. My business was thriving; we were expecting our first baby and we were in love. Self-satisfaction is always a dangerous indulgence and at that moment, I felt we were invincible. There was nothing to suggest that our happiness would ever be threatened, no demons hovered waiting to destroy our peace.

Later, as I stacked the remains of our take-away meal in the waste disposal unit, I whistled tunelessly to myself, unaware that the foundations of my stable life had started to crumble from the moment Leonora Bennett had slipped her cold hand into mine.

"Darling, come and rub my back will you?"

Taken at the Flood

I was smiling when I entered the room and found my wife lying naked on her stomach on the sheepskin rug in front of the fire, golden flames of firelight licking her soft skin. Business first, pleasure afterwards, I mused as I began to massage her aching back with slow sensuous movements, a precursor of the delight to come.

Chapter 8

Afterwards, it seemed my wife 'bumped into' Leonora with increasing frequency. Their relationship developed extremely quickly and it seemed to me at the expense of those closest to Evelyn.

It was eight o'clock in the morning and I'd been working in my study since six. The solution to a recent problem was within my grasp and I couldn't stay in bed a moment longer as my brain was busy formulating equations requiring a larger brain capacity than my own. I'd been careful not to wake Evelyn, as I crept quietly down the stairs to my study and switched on my computer. From then on, I lost all sense of time.

"Been up long?" She was standing in the doorway, her silk robe open to reveal the slight swelling underneath her nightdress.

"Since six. I tried not to wake you."

"You didn't, the Dangerfields' dog did. I could hear it barking somewhere in the woodland. Josie must be up early. She really has no consideration for other people. Leonora mentioned as much when I met her in the village, yesterday."

I turned to face her. The remark was not of the kind I was used to hearing from my tolerant wife. Besides Josie and she had been friends since their schooldays. I would have thought she could have made up her own mind about her without Leonora's input.

Coffee?" she asked.

"Yes please, but stay where you are and I'll make us one. You look all in."

"Thanks!"

"You know what I mean." I laughed

"Sure but you are probably right. I think I'll ring Sassoon's later. My hair could do with a trim. I always feel better when my hair is right."

"I'll run you into town if you like. I could pop into the office whilst I wait for you."

She hesitated.

"No. It's OK, really. I know you are in the middle of things here and besides Leo did mention yesterday that she might try to get an appointment with Felix today. I told her to mention my name. We could go together. I'll ring her later."

"Well, if you're sure. I must admit another day working on this should tie it up nicely," I said.

"Good. That's settled then," she replied, adding, "Don't get up, carry on with your work; I'll make coffee for us both then I'll go and have my shower."

Later that morning, after Evelyn had left for town, the telephone rang; it was Josie. "How's Evelyn keeping?" she asked.

"She's fine. She's not here I'm afraid. I think she's at the hairdressers in town."

Taken at the Flood

"Don't worry. I wanted to speak to you, anyway. I haven't seen much of her lately and I wondered…? Do you know if I'd offended her in some way? Has she said anything to you?"

I felt uncomfortable, knowing that Leonora was taking up so much of Evelyn's time. But I truthfully reassured Josie that as far as I knew it was not the case and ended by suggesting we all get together again soon.

It was mid afternoon, a grey murky sky threatening rain to follow. The view from my study window across the drive to the woodland was obscured by the formation of a thick mist, through which I saw the headlights of my wife's car as she drew up. I waited for her to open the door and then went to meet her in the hallway. Before I knew what was happening a bundle of fur, with what seemed to be exceedingly large feet, engulfed me. The feet rested on my chest and a wet tongue slobbered at my neck.

"Good gracious. What have you been up to now? Whose dog is this?" I asked struggling to stay upright.

"It's ours and his name is Tinker," she stated perfunctorily, adding, "He is gorgeous isn't he? You don't mind do you, darling?"

"I didn't know you wanted a dog." I watched her stroking its head. Gorgeous was not the adjective readily spinging to mind when describing the bundle of damp fur looking adoringly up at my wife. He was, I supposed, a golden Labrador cross but crossed with what was anyone's guess.

"I thought you were going to the hairdressers?"

"Don't look so annoyed. I did, but I met Leo and as we chatted, the subject of pets came up and before I knew it we were at Battersea dogs' home. We both fell in love with Tinker. Leonora would have taken him but she has an allergy to dog hairs. So, I said we would take him and she could help me take him for a walk occasionally.

"I might have guessed Leonora would be at the bottom of this. Oh, by the way, Josie telephoned. She's afraid she's done something to upset you. She's missing your company, sweetheart."

She looked shamefaced for a moment.

"I'll give her a ring sometime soon. I promise."

"Good. Now let's see if we can find a place for Tinker to sleep because, amenable though I am, I refuse to share a bed with that mutt."

Later, lying in bed, with Tinker's head on my chest, Evelyn said, "Thanks for being so understanding about the dog. We had a great day today. Leo is so kind. Do you know, I forgot to get my iron tablets and she took my prescription from me saying that she would go to the chemists and pop them over tomorrow morning."

Taken at the Flood

"That was good of her," I agreed, pushing Tinker's tongue out of my face.

The next day I went to London for a meeting with my office manager Alan Henderson. Alan and I had been friends for many years. He'd been one of the first people I had employed once Softcell was up and running and I counted myself extremely lucky in finding him. He'd been fresh out of school with excellent A level grades in maths and computer science but wasn't keen to go to University. He'd had enough of studying and wanted to get out into the world. As profits soared, Alan rose from programmer to office manager until acquiring the title Chief Business Manager with a commensurate salary, every pound of which he'd earned through hard work and loyalty to the company.

The purpose of this current meeting was to discuss my proposed visit to New York in order to promote my new computer software package. We were both excited about the project, which was beginning to look as if it might be our biggest seller yet but were unwilling to jump the gun.

Alan was waiting in the boardroom with Joseph Little and Charles Conroy, junior directors. Together we were the driving force behind Softcell's recent successes. Alice Baines, my secretary, had her pad at the ready to take the minutes of the meeting, her faded fair hair drawn back severely into a bun at the nape of her neck.

I, as MD, chaired the meeting and began by making a brief summary of my intentions. "Good morning everyone. As you know Softcell has produced a package which we hope will be another winner for us in the States. The working title of this latest piece of software is *Gorgon*. My objective is to produce further packages incorporating some of the features in *Gorgon* and extending them. The titles for these proposed packages will all incorporate names from Greek mythology. I feel we are on the brink of breaking into the market in the States in a big way and *Gorgon* is hopefully just the start." I turned to Alan. " You have the details of my meeting in New York on Friday with you. Perhaps you could put everyone in the picture."

Alan Henderson coughed, stood up and spent the next half hour explaining what we expecting to achieve over the coming months. At the end of the meeting, I followed him into his office.

"Could I ask a favour?"

"You don't have to ask. I'll keep an eye on Evelyn for you."

I smiled, knowing I could rely on him one hundred per cent and had no qualms about leaving my wife in his care.

Taken at the Flood

The next morning I began filling my overnight case in preparation for the New York trip. I intended to be away for three nights. My flight on Concorde was booked for ten thirty the next day and I hoped, if my visit went well, I would be home as scheduled early on Monday morning.

A car was due to pick me up at eight. I dressed in my dressing room so as not to disturb Evelyn then bent over the bed to kiss her cheek. We had said our farewells the previous night and I wanted her to rest, as she had started to feel sick in the mornings. She opened her eyes and slipped her hands around my neck.

"You weren't thinking of leaving without waking me?"

"Of course not." I lied and, as an afterthought, added, "Alan said he'd give you a ring and I'm to tell you if you need anything at all he is only at the end of the telephone. His mobile number is in the book in the hall."

"Don't worry. I forgot to tell you, Leonora is coming to stay in the guestroom whilst you are away. We're looking forward to lots of girlie chats without the men around."

"Thanks, I can see I'm going to be missed. Why don't you give Josie a ring as well?"

There was a pause.

"I may, but I don't think Leo is too keen on Josie."

Taken at the Flood

Evelyn had long since taken to calling her Leo, the name Lucas used and which, for some reason, made me feel uneasy. I wondered why she hadn't mentioned before that she was intending to have company whilst I was away. I thought it unlikely she would have forgotten but last night we did have other things on our minds, which resulted in an early night. Maybe I was becoming paranoid, I thought, closing the front door and walking towards the waiting car.

Just as the car slid around the bend in the drive, I thought I caught sight of a woman walking through the woodland separating the Dangerfields' property from our own. It was probably Josie walking the dogs but I was almost sure I could see a curtain of blonde hair lifting from the walker's shoulders as she disappeared behind a tree.

Chapter 9

The trees in Central Park were bursting with buds, their stark branches softening as green shoots opened in the spring sunshine. From my room in the Plaza Hotel, I could see across the Park where couples sat together enjoying a lunchtime break from their offices, whilst burying their faces in scarves, coat collars turned up against the wind. Picking up my briefcase containing *Gorgon,* I left the room for my afternoon appointment with Maxwell Hutton, chief executive of Megacells, the largest computer company next to Microbytes in the United States.

A silver and glass tube carried me up the outside of the building to the Head Office of Megacells, and deposited me on the top floor. As the lift opened, two portly men in pinstriped suits waited until I passed them then entered the lift behind me. They were carrying large manila folders bulging with spreadsheets. I anticipated that *Gorgon* had some strong opposition but was confident what we had to offer was so revolutionary it would beat off any competition. Therefore, it was with a purposeful stride, I walked towards the door at the end of the corridor.

"Come right on in!" A female voice with a South American accent replied to my knock. Once inside, I saw that the owner of the voice was sitting behind a desk filing her nails, her orange hair piled up in curls on top of her head. I noticed the cursor blinking on the computer screen in front of her and wondered if she'd find the time to complete her task.

"Mr Hutton will see you now, sir."

She nodded in the direction of the inner door behind which Maxwell Hutton sat with his junior executive Larry Manders. The latter was young and eager, determination oozing out of every pore. He reminded me of Alan when I'd first employed him. Maxwell Hutton was a man in his early fifties, balding and running to fat. He heaved his heavy frame out of his chair and reached over the desk to shake my hand. "Good to see you again," he said, his breath wheezing asthmatically. "Larry and I have been discussing your submission and I must say we are looking forward to hearing more."

In the corner of the room, I noticed a long table set against the wall, on top of which, stood a bank of computer screens, switched on, and ready to go. I knew my assumption, as I'd left the lift, had been correct. The monitors had been used recently, in fact I could almost feel the heat of a freshly vacated body as I sat in the chair and opened my briefcase.

Both men remained silent as I explained the intricacies of our product. They watched as I attached my PSD to the USB hub on the modem beneath the monitor and waited until the

Taken at the Flood

introduction to the package in bright eye-catching colours flashed up on the screen. As the colours faded, I took them slowly through the programme. The only sound in the room was Maxwell Hutton's wheezing chest.

The finale to the programme was spectacular, as I had intended it to be. I turned on the swivel chair to face them, waiting for some sort of reaction and met Hutton's inscrutable face. However, I wasn't fooled. I knew he was holding his enthusiasm in check, thinking ahead as to how much I would accept and how little he could get away with before I packed up my briefcase and beat a hasty retreat to offer my product elsewhere. Manders was harder to read but I had caught the glint in his eye and the almost imperceptible twitching of the corners of his mouth. He was busting a gut in an attempt to appear impassive.

"Am I to understand this is to be the first of a proposed series?" Hutton was bending towards the screen whilst stroking his chin.

"The second is already nearing completion with a blueprint for a third," I replied, removing my portable storage device from the hub.

Hutton's hand shot out. "Congratulations, we are more than willing and ready to run with this. We'll talk over the finer points tomorrow but I can assure you Mr Hope, you will not be disappointed with our negotiations. Megacells wants *Gorgon* and we are prepared to pay for it!"

It was more than I'd expected. I'd supposed there would have been a less than positive response, a hesitation on behalf of Hutton not to play his hand too early. Nevertheless, I could feel the frisson as I shook his hand, seeing the pounds rolling into my bank account at the same moment I knew he was seeing the dollars rolling into his. *Gorgon* and its offspring were in the running to make a fortune for us both. I felt my heart skip a beat then palpate wildly and couldn't wait to tell Evelyn the good news. Our baby's future was secure. We were about to enter a golden era.

Before leaving, I contacted my legal advisors in London to brief their New York office, and arranged for a representative to join me for negotiations with Hutton the next day. Hutton agreed to this and made his own similar arrangement for legal representation. I said I'd return at two, the following afternoon, to discuss the finer points of the contract and we parted company.

"Hope springs eternal." I chuckled as the lift slipped to the ground floor. My face stretched into a wide grin, I raised my head and breathed in the sharp New York air.

At the reception desk in the Plaza, I ordered a bottle of Dom Perignon to be sent to room 336. I had reason to celebrate but no one to join in

Taken at the Flood

my celebration. However, I knew I could share my good news with Evelyn, as soon as I reached the privacy of my room.

Sitting alone in the luxurious surroundings of my hotel room overlooking Central Park, I watched the evening shadows threading ghostly patterns through the trees, and with champagne glass in hand I lifted the receiver. The ringing tone continued unanswered and I felt my spirits sink. I was about to set down the phone when a breathless voice answered. "Hullo?"

It was Leonora.

"Hullo, it's me. Is Evelyn there?"

"No she's out."

The words were sharp and to the point and as no explanation as to her whereabouts was forthcoming, I said, "She's all right is she?"

"Evelyn's fine. I'll tell her you called."

I suddenly felt angry.

"I'll ring back," I replied curtly, slamming down the receiver and leaving my glass to discharge its bubbles untouched. My excitement had dissipated with the bubbles so I decided to soak in the bath, have an early night and ring Evelyn again before I turned in.

At eleven o'clock, I turned off the television and rang again. I guessed it would be teatime at home. This time she answered the phone. "Darling, I've been so worried. How did you get on? Did they like *Gorgon?*"

"They did. Why were you worried? Didn't Leonora tell you that I'd telephoned earlier?"

To be fair, I hadn't asked her to do so and it did rather occur to me I'd said I would ring back. But, I thought it odd she hadn't told her I'd rung. "Anyway," I continued, "sit down. I've lots to tell you."

We talked for the next hour. Her excitement matching my own and I couldn't wait to hold her in my arms and share our good fortune. I told her it would be unlikely I could return home the following day, as it would take a further day or two for my legal team to chew over the finer points in the contract before I could sign. I promised I'd be home as soon as I could.

"I love you," she said, her voice a distant promise, as we said our good-byes.

The following morning I awoke, as room service was delivering my breakfast, the first faint beams of spring sunlight filtering through the heavy damask curtains. After breakfast, I showered, dressed and walked into the crisp morning air. Shoppers idled on Fifth Avenue, well-dressed women spilled out of taxis then disappeared through the doors of department stores, their counterparts emerging carrying armfuls of carrier bags bearing the names of Gucci, Armani, Prada and many more, which meant nothing to me. Evelyn would be in her

Taken at the Flood

element, I thought, as I walked down Fifth Avenue towards Tiffany's.

The revolving doors deposited me inside the building where Audrey Hepburn had breakfasted and I made my way to the third floor where diamonds glittered under strategically placed spotlights. Engagement rings sat in trays waiting patiently for the wealthy to whisk them away. I glanced around at the shoppers most of whom were window-shopping, their jaws dropping at the glittering array of expensive gems.

Then my eyes fell on a glass case containing a solitary diamond necklace on a black velvet tray. A fine gold chain supported a square cut diamond, which flashed with yellow fire, the overhead spotlight catching its facets and splaying its rays into a thousand dimensions. I knew Evelyn would love it as much as I would enjoy hanging it around her neck. The assistant gift-wrapped the necklace in a box, covered it in shiny silver paper and tied it with a silver and black bow. This she placed it in a small turquoise cardboard carrier bearing the store's logo. I slipped the package into my briefcase and went to meet Harvey Anderson of Anderson, Beckett and Woodvine, the law firm representing Softcell.

Harvey and I had become friends over the years and when he was in London he usually gave me a call and we would meet up for drinks.

Taken at the Flood

As we walked the short distance from Harvey's office to Megacells Head Office, he said, "Evelyn OK?"

"Fine," I replied unwilling for some reason to tell him of her pregnancy. On the few occasions that they'd met, I had the distinct impression he didn't approve of my wife. His antagonism was understated and he was always polite but I'd picked up on it nevertheless.

The afternoon meeting with Maxwell Hutton and his legal team went well. Harvey was satisfied with the contract at first glance but both sides agreed he would scrutinise it in more detail that evening after which, if everything was in order, I would sign *Gorgon* and its future over to Megacells.

I shook hands with Hutton and he slapped me on the back. "I look forward to doing business with you in the future, son. And don't forget we have first refusal on any follow up packages."

Somehow I managed to book a seat on Concorde at the last minute, for the next day and rang home to speak to my wife. She picked up the phone and I heard laughter on the other end.

"You sound as if you're having a good time. I'm beginning to feel quite jealous," I teased her.

"Hullo, darling. There is nothing for you to be jealous about. It's just Leo. Now when are you coming home?"

Taken at the Flood

"Everything wrapped up here earlier than I'd anticipated. I'll be home tomorrow. I should be there about four. Then we can celebrate *Gorgon's* success together."

From my seat on the aircraft, I watched the New York skyline disappear below me, anticipating the joy of spending a financially secure future with my lovely wife and our baby. It is a mistake to wallow in self-satisfaction, even for a short time. Luckily, none of us is aware of what life has in store otherwise living would become an intolerable journey. For if I had known, what awaited me on my return from New York, I should not have been so complacent.

Chapter 10

The door flew open and Evelyn threw her arms around my neck at the same time as Tinker licked my hand with his large slobbering tongue.

"What a welcome. I must go away more often," I said.

"You most certainly must not. I couldn't stand the strain." Evelyn pulled me into the hall and kissed me hard on my mouth.

"Has your guest left?" I asked, when I had breath left to speak. I looked over her shoulder half expecting to see Leonora standing in the hallway.

"Yes, first thing this morning. She had a phone call from her aunt in Tuscany yesterday and arranged to fly out today. It was all very sudden. Her elderly aunt is ill and wanted to see her urgently," Evelyn said, slipping her arm around my waist and leading me into the conservatory. "I've laid a meal for us in here. Sit down and relax and tell me all about New York."

Later, when we were in bed, Tinker lying on a blanket at our feet, I said, "It was kind of Leonora to keep you company. " Trying to keep my voice even, I added, "What did the two of you get up to?"

"We went shopping in town, all the usual things. But mostly we just 'chilled out' as Leo

Taken at the Flood

put it. She is such fun. She had me in fits of laughter. One day she mimicked Josie's voice so well, I thought Josie was actually in the room. She also fussed around me like a mother hen making sure I took my iron tablets which she put out for me every morning."

At the mention of shopping, I remembered the necklace, which was still in my briefcase. I jumped out of bed promising to return before she missed me.

"Here it is. I don't know how I forgot to give you this immediately. It must have been the thrill of seeing you and wanting you so much."

She carefully untied the bow and opened the lid of the black velvet box.

"Oh this is just too much!" she exclaimed, holding the chain over her hand, allowing the diamond to hang between her fingers. As she twisted the chain, it caught the light from the bedside lamp. The fire deep inside the gem sparkled with a bright golden light, which splayed out over her wrist.

"You like it?"

"Like it? I absolutely adore it. Who wouldn't?"

She held the chain up for me to fasten it around her neck. The diamond rested above the swelling of her breasts and I found it impossible to take my eyes off either.

Taken at the Flood

Looking back that was the last moment I could truly say we were both completely happy. The morning horror had not yet begun.

The wind in the trees outside our window woke me or it may have been Tinker rushing around on the landing. The dog was uneasy, perhaps it was the wind or maybe it was something else, a kind of sixth sense, an innate feeling something was wrong. My wife's side of the bed was empty.

"Evelyn?" The door to our bathroom stood ajar. I padded across the carpet, the thick pile caressing my toes and tickling the soles of my feet. Tapping on the door, I whispered, "You OK, darling?"

"Mm," her answer was indistinct. I pushed the door open to see her sitting on the side of the bath, her head hanging over the sink.

"Morning sickness?"

"No, not exactly."

She raised her head and there were tears streaking her face. She was holding her side with her right hand. I crossed the floor, the marble as cold under my feet as the chill that was settling around my heart. I sat beside her and put my arm around her shoulders. "What is it?"

"I don't know. I'm frightened. I'm bleeding."

Her tearful eyes looked up at me, set in a face as white as the marble under my feet.

"I'll ring Lucas," I said, rushing to the phone in the bedroom.

Lucas answered and after I'd explained said, "I'll be right there. Make sure she keeps her feet up. Don't let her get out of bed. Try not to worry, it might be nothing."

I carried Evelyn back to bed, made a hot drink because I didn't know what else to do, and waited for Lucas to arrive. The five minutes he took seemed like hours during which neither of us spoke, afraid to say the words that might make it real.

I opened the door and Lucas took the stairs two at a time, ahead of me, saying, "Make yourself a stiff drink. You look as though you could do with it. I'll see to Evelyn. I'll call if I need you."

The brandy hit the back of my throat and thawed out the numb feeling creeping through my body. After what seemed like forever, I heard footsteps on the stairs. His face told me all I needed to know. The sympathetic expression he gave to his more unfortunate patients was there, this time for me.

"How is she?" I asked, the futility of the question hitting me as soon as the words left my lips.

"Not good, I'm afraid. She wants to see you. Phone me if you need anything."

He was holding a zipped plastic bag.

Taken at the Flood

"I'll send this to histology for examination but I doubt they'll find anything. There's usually no recognisable reason why these things happen. Sometimes it's nature's way of sorting out problems that might occur later in the pregnancy." He patted my arm, his manner at once professional and detached. "I know it's of no consolation to you now but believe me I've seen this happen many times and it in no way hinders patients from producing trouble free pregnancies in the future. I'll leave you to comfort your wife and, as I said before, you know where to find me."

I thanked him mechanically and when he'd gone, I stopped at the foot of the stairs and drew in a deep breath. What could I say to my wife that would make it better? I knew there was nothing. Dragging my feet up the staircase, I somehow reached the top and our bedroom door. She lay in bed, her face as ghostly white as the pillowslip beneath her dark hair. Damp curls clung to her forehead. Lucas had given her a sedative and she looked at me though heavy-lidded eyes as I sat beside her and held her hand in my own.

"I'm so sorry." The tears squeezed under her closed lids and slipped down her cheeks. Her silent sobs racked her whole body. I climbed onto the bed and cradled her in my arms. We wept together, our tears mingling as they slid onto the bed cover.

Taken at the Flood

Exhausted by grief and aided by the sedatives, she finally slept. I waited to follow but lay staring at the ceiling, listening to Evelyn's breathing until dawn crept feebly through the blinds.

It was midsummer; two months had passed since the miscarriage. I'd thrown myself into work but I was worried about Evelyn, as she didn't seem to be able to move on with her life. She never smiled, hardly ever left the house, however much I coaxed, and to make matters worse Leonora had not returned from Italy. She had written to express her deep sympathy at our loss but explained, as her aunt was not at all well, she didn't think it would be possible to return home for a while.

I was in the bedroom dressing one morning when I heard the telephone ring and reaching for it, I realised Evelyn had picked up the extension in the kitchen. I should have replaced the receiver but hesitated and to my shame listened to the conversation. I argued that it was because I was worried about her.

"It's kind of you, Josie, but I don't think so."

I heard my wife replying to her friend's invitation. I sighed and quietly put down the phone. It was no use, Josie was trying to help but I had the distinct impression the only person Evelyn wanted to see was Leonora.

Taken at the Flood

It was odd because, the day after I had eavesdropped on Evelyn and Josie's telephone conversation, Leonora returned from Tuscany. It was a beautiful summer evening. We were sitting in the garden, a table bearing a bottle of wine and two glasses standing between us. Her glass was virtually untouched. I lay back in the lounger and closed my eyes. The summer scents were all around us. In the distance we could hear the hum of a motorboat making its way up river and the sound of laughter from an on-board party in full swing. I opened my eyes and looked at my wife. She was staring into the distance in the direction of the woodland, which was now green with thick foliage. Suddenly her expressionless face broke into a wide grin and she stood up, more animated than I'd seen her for months. I had a glimpse then of the old Evelyn and it warmed my heart.

"Leo!" she shrieked.

Leonora emerged from the trees, at the bottom of the garden, looking tanned and lovely in a white cotton dress, her long fair hair hanging loose about her shoulders. Tinker, who had been lying under my chair, growled.

"Down boy. It's only Leonora," I patted his head but he would not be still. He bounded off down the lawn followed by Evelyn. They both reached Leonora at the same time. The women hugged each other, as Tinker prowled around them sniffing at the interloper in a proprietary manner.

I went into the kitchen to fetch another wineglass and when I returned I saw they were in deep conversation and oblivious of my presence.

"How is your aunt, Leonora?" I asked, as I filled her glass. She looked up at me a guarded expression in her pale blue eyes. "Well at present, thank you."

"What exactly is the matter with her?" I persisted and glimpsed a flash of annoyance on Evelyn's face.

"Difficult to explain exactly," she said, keeping her eyes fixed on her hands, which were resting in her lap. "She is old and gets frightened. I feel I have to go to her at these times."

"I'm sorry to hear that. I expect having a doctor in the family helps. Lucas must be a great comfort to her."

She hesitated before replying. "My aunt does not encourage visitors. She sees no one but me. Lucas understands." She turned away in a dismissive manner and I could see she did not welcome any further attempts at conversation from me.

Soon after, I left them, explaining that I had some work to catch up on in my study. I looked back through the French doors leading into the garden. They sat together like naughty schoolchildren intent on some devious plan. The impression lingered, long after Leonora had left. She'd insisted on walking home through the woods alone. I tried to dissuade her but she assured me she had a torch and could see perfectly well. Evelyn and I stood at the edge of the lawn and watched her go. She refused my offer to walk with her, kissed Evelyn and said she would see her in the morning. From our bedroom window, I watched the pinpricks of light flashing through the trees as she followed the river path.

Later, when Evelyn had showered, she joined me in bed but my attempts at conversation were met with a cold shoulder both metaphorically and physically as she turned her back towards me. It became obvious that I was unable to break the close bond, which had developed between my wife and Leonora. Part of me did not wish to try, as it pleased me to think at least she was starting to enjoy herself. My only sorrow was she had completely excluded me from sharing in her renewed happiness.

Throughout the summer, Leonora was a frequent visitor at River House and as I was busy developing the basis for *Gorgon's* successor I hardly noticed how much time my wife and she spent together. In some ways, it took the pressure, of keeping Evelyn happy, from my shoulders but during the times we shared together, I noticed her conversation was strained and she seemed unable to look directly at me, without her eyes brimming with unshed tears. I began to dread seeing that look and so buried myself even deeper in my work.

"Darling!"

I was staring at the screen unable to believe the programme I'd been working on was at last a viable proposition. It was an additional component to some software Softcell had sold to a German company some years before. They had requested an update with some additional features, which I gave assurances, would be no problem, but for weeks, the picture on my screen had disintegrated before my eyes as the programme refused to remain stable. However, success was within my grasp, the commands were responding, the picture remained static repeatedly without crashing.

"*Darling*!" exasperation dripped like ice from her tongue.

Evelyn was standing in the doorway. The September weather had turned cold and she was dressed in a cream wool coat and high brown leather boots. I thought she looked adorable.

"I'm just letting you know, I'll be spending the day in town with Leo."

I tried to hide my surprise. She hadn't been to town since the miscarriage, in fact, she'd hardly left the house or its grounds.

"Excellent idea. Don't hurry back, enjoy yourself." I crossed the room and kissed her gently on her cheek, avoiding her newly painted mouth.

I watched from the window as she drove out of sight. Then rang Alan Henderson and told him to get in contact with Dieter in Germany to let him know we were ready to update his system. As I put the phone down, the front doorbell rang. It was Josie.

"Come in, good to see you," I said.

"I don't want to distract you from your work but needed some fresh air and, as I haven't seen you both for some time, the walk took me in your direction and bingo! Henry is in town today and so I thought it a good opportunity to come and see you. Although I must admit the fresh air is a little fresher than I'd anticipated."

I assured her she was a welcome interruption and besides I'd finished work for the day adding, "Evelyn's not about, I'm afraid. She's in town with Leonora."

I showed her into the conservatory then poured coffee for us both and sat opposite her. A fine mist was rising from the surface of the river and creeping up the lawn towards the house. Outside, the trees were starting to turn colour in preparation for the winter. Soon we would be able to see the rooftops of the two neighbouring properties through the trees. I noticed Josie was frowning into her cup.

Taken at the Flood

"It's good to see Evelyn has started to go out again. Her condition has been very worrying. Henry and I felt for you, seeing her in such a state couldn't have been easy. I have tried to get her to come over."

She looked out over the mist-covered lawn and I took her hand in mine. "I know you have Josie and I appreciate it but it would seem that it has to come from her, no amount of coaxing from me has made the slightest difference. It has been very frustrating for us all."

She was immediately sympathetic, making all the right kind of responses. We talked about mutual friends, holidays and the weather and, as she rose to leave, said, "Now Evelyn is feeling better maybe we could have a night out together, the four of us, perhaps a meal in town or the theatre?"

I noticed there was no mention of the Bennetts in Josie's invitation. "Yes I'd like that. I'll get her to give you a ring."

Evelyn never did ring Josie. For some reason the invitation did not appeal to her. I made some excuse to Josie and Henry, which sounded lame even to my ears.

Sometime later, Dieter Brandt requested I visit him in person to discuss the adaptation to their software. He worked for a large hospital complex in Munich. He said, if Evelyn and I would like to spend a few days with him and his wife, we would be more than welcome.

She was brushing her dark curls, her reflection in the dressing table mirror looking back at me, as I lay propped up on the pillows with my address book open on the coverlet.

"You know I spoke to Dieter, yesterday, darling? Well, he asked if we would like to spend a short holiday with him and Gerda. I need to see him about some software updates anyway. What do you think?"

She turned towards me, her face expressionless. I continued, not waiting for her reply. "I know it's work for me but it shouldn't take long, it's very straightforward and then we could spend some of the time sightseeing, perhaps take a trip to Innsbruck to do some shopping."

"It's too soon. You go. I don't feel up to travelling yet."

Swinging her legs around, she continued to brush her hair leaving me looking at her reflection once more.

Anger and frustration boiled up inside me. "We have to get on with our lives. There is nothing to stop us trying for another baby. It will help to put all this behind us - to make a new start."

Slowly she replaced the hairbrush in the silver tray on the dressing table. Her shoulders drooped and I could see tears glistening on her

Taken at the Flood

cheek reflected in the mirror. To my shame and sorrow, I could not go to her. Could not comfort her, my own grief and unhappiness intervening and preventing me from giving her the compassion I would have shown to a stranger and yet could not give to my wife. The painful memory still slices through me. If I had only known then that the future for us both was already mapped out and there was nothing we could do to stop it from happening.

Chapter 11

Dieter and his wife Gerda were perfect hosts and expressed genuine concern that Evelyn's health had not allowed her to visit them. The morning after I arrived in Munich, Dieter drove me to a nursing home on the outskirts of the city where his firm had installed the computer hardware.

The road out of the city gradually climbed upwards and I could smell the freshness in the air as we left the pollutants of the city far below us. Evergreen trees, their tops dusted with a light sprinkling of frost, lined the roadside as we drove to the nursing home. In the distance, I could see the outline of red pan tiles forming the roof of the building, and I understood the benefit of positioning it in such a location, for as we drove in through the wrought iron gates at the end of the drive, a spectacular vista opened out before us. Above, snow-capped mountains rose majestically forming a semi-circle beneath which the ground fell away in slopes of rolling green pastures towards a village nestling in the foothills. The whole place spoke of luxury and I rightly assumed that the fees for recuperating in such a place would be steep.

The previous evening, Dieter and I had gone over the details of the update and now all that remained was to put it into practice and hope it would perform on the hardware he'd previously installed in the nursing home. As I'd anticipated there was no problem, the whole operation took little under two hours to complete and we had the rest of the day to spend at our leisure. Dieter suggested we drive down into the village, where he knew of a tavern that had a fine selection of German beers.

Inside the tavern, the air smelt of hops and fresh sawdust. Behind the bar, a ruddy-faced barman with a large belly raised his hand. "Herr Dieter, good to see you again."

He spoke in English, no doubt as a courtesy to me.

"Fritz, this is Mr Hope. He would like to sample a selection of your finest beers, if you please," Dieter said, as we sat at a table near the bar.

Two hours later, full of Fritz's beer and a lamb stew cooked by his wife, we left the tavern. I admit I was more than a little unsteady on my feet but noticed that Dieter was suffering from no such malady as we walked to the end of the narrow street on the corner of which stood a small jewellery shop.

"Won't be a moment," I mumbled and disappeared inside the shop. Behind the counter sat a thin middle-aged woman wearing half moon spectacles. I pointed to a tray in the window not knowing whether she spoke English or not.

Taken at the Flood

"This one, sir?" she asked, her perfectly rounded vowels making me feel foolish.

The rings were of the type usually known as eternity rings. Impulsively I chose a gold one studded with diamonds at intervals around its band.

"A wise choice if I may say so," the woman said, packing the ring in a small box and tying it with a gold ribbon.

I smiled. She'd made a very lucrative sale with the aid of Fritz's beer, I thought, as I left the shop and joined a bemused Dieter.

That evening, after dinner, Gerda left us to drink our branies and chat about old times. When we were younger, our paths had crossed at a conference, where one topic for discussion was the benefit, the new generation of computer systems could provide, in the workplace. We'd carried on discussing the merits of one system over another in the bar afterwards and had stayed in touch after the conference had finished. Our friendship proved to be beneficial in many ways, including the formation of strong financial and social bonds that had been mutually satisfying.

"We were sorry to hear your sad news," Dieter said, pouring the golden liquid into a crystal brandy bowl.

I smiled ruefully. "Thank you. We are trying to put it behind us and move on but unfortunately Evelyn is finding it difficult."

"You mentioned she is starting to go out again with this friend of hers?"

Dieter sat in the leather armchair opposite me, concern tracing fine lines on his fair skin.

"Leonora. Yes, though confidentially, that is part of the problem. I don't quite know what to make of Leonora. On the surface she has been good for Evelyn but I have this niggling doubt that her influence over my wife in not an altogether healthy one."

Dieter lit a cigar and offered me one, which I declined. He knew I'd given up the habit some years ago but was uncertain whether my resolve had weakened.

"What makes you say that?" he asked blowing perfect smoke rings high into the air.

"When I put it into words it sounds ridiculous. But lately, I've begun feel Evelyn is slipping away from me. I know the miscarriage unsettled us both but somehow I feel she is growing closer to Leonora at the expense of our relationship. She has even ditched her best friend Josie, for no particular reason, other than Leonora does not appear to like her."

Dieter frowned and tapped his cigar ash into the silver ashtray at his side. "I'd been about to say it sounded very much like jealousy on your part, my friend, but changed my mind when you mentioned she has dropped her friendship with her close companion. I'm not a psychologist but

Taken at the Flood

it does rather look as if this Leonora is exerting some sort of hold over your wife."

I sighed with relief and raised my glass to my lips thankful that he'd agreed I wasn't imagining things.

When I finally went to bed, the effects of Dieter's generosity with the brandy decanter taking its toll on my unsteady limbs, I realised it was too late to telephone Evelyn. It would have to wait until the following morning.

On waking, I felt reluctant to make the call, which I was sure would be answered in a voice, I would hardly recognise as belonging to my, once vivacious, wife. I waited until after breakfast and then sought the privacy of my bedroom.

"Hullo?" I spoke tentatively.

"Hullo, darling. How are you? And how are Dieter and Gerda? You did pass on my apologies? When will you be home? I've missed you so much and I have a little surprise in store for you."

Her voice was high pitched and excited. She was like the Evelyn I used to know. Maybe this was the turning point; perhaps things would be different now. I felt my spirits lift as I packed my case and later said my farewells to my hosts.

During the taxi ride from the airport to River Road, we hit the rush hour traffic. The taxicab crawled along the motorway hampered by the

Taken at the Flood

presence of patchy fog, which drifted across our path obscuring our vision and then drifted off to disperse over the fields bordering the road. Throughout the journey, I kept a picture of Evelyn in my mind. The Evelyn I used to know with the impish grin and gleaming dark curls. The road to River House was thick with fog drifting up from the riverbed. The trees, naked, devoid, as they were of their summer foliage, rose up like spectres as we reached the wrought iron gates leading to the driveway.

I paid the driver and picked up my case as the car disappeared around the bend in the drive. But before I'd reached the steps leading up to the front door, it was thrown open. I gasped. Evelyn said she had a surprise for me but nothing could prepare me for the nature of her revelation. I hardly recognised the face, which greeted me, framed by short, sleek, white-blonde hair.

She threw her arms around my neck. "Well what do you think?"

She broke away and spun around fluffing up her straightened hair with the tips of her fingers.

"I don't know what to say," I began, trying to hide my horrified reaction, "You look so different."

"Leo and I went into town and she suggested I have a make over. I've always loved her hair and she said why didn't I go blonde and, well, I thought you might like it. I've noticed that you find Leo attractive. Well what man wouldn't? I thought you'd be pleased!"

A glimpse of the old Evelyn showed then. She looked like a little girl seeking approval. I slid my arm around her waist.

"Of course I like it, but you must understand - I love you as you are. I don't want you to be a copy of Leonora. I agree she is attractive but it's you I love, every bit of you."

She leant her head against my shoulder. I couldn't find the words to tell her how much I detested the transformation. My wife had disappeared and I could only hope I could persuade her to revert to her former self, without hurting her feelings.

After dinner, my new wife looked up at me through thick black eyelashes. I saw a glimpse of smouldering sensuality burning in her heavily made up eyes and reacted, as any man would to her suggestion that we have an early night, by following her trail of underwear up the stairs and along the landing to our bedroom. She lay on the bed, naked, her blonde hair resting against scarlet silk sheets which I was certain I hadn't seen before.

"I want you so much," she said, running a scarlet painted fingernail across my chest and circling my nipple.

Our lovemaking was nothing like I'd experienced before. Part of me felt the thrill of being with a 'new woman' but part of me longed to find the 'old' one. I felt all the intensity of making love to a stranger, without the pleasure of being with the woman I loved.

Afterwards, as we lay side by side, our passion spent, Evelyn talked constantly about Leo. She hardly slept all night and seemed overtaken by a nervous, excitable, energy, which I would have liked to attribute to her pleasure at my return. However, her frenetic manner made me wonder if she were riding on the wave of some drug induced 'high'. This thought I hastily buried in my sub-conscious. I was worried enough without looking for trouble. But I could not rid myself of the feeling that during my absence some stranger had spirited away my wife leaving in her place a clone, like some crazy Stepford wife on speed.

All too soon I was to discover my analogy was not so very far from the truth but it was too late to alter the course of events. With hindsight I should have made a desperate attempt to divert of the torrent that was about to engulf us. But hindsight, by its very definition, is wisdom after the event and I was still waiting for it all to happen.

Chapter 12

The week after I returned from Germany, Evelyn developed a heavy cold. She was running a temperature and her body was wracked by coughing fits which left her weak.

I rang Alan Henderson. "It's me. How are things going?"

"Fine, Boss. No problems this end, everything's ticking over nicely."

"I'm glad to hear it. I need to spend some time at home. Evelyn's not well and I thought it might be an opportunity to take a few weeks off. Maybe do some gardening ready for the winter, walk the dog you know the sort of thing. I'm going to keep away from my study for at least three weeks, rest my brain and spoil myself."

"Sounds good to me. I'll keep in touch, enjoy yourself."

After making sure Evelyn was tucked up in bed with a hot drink and a pile of magazines, I let myself out of the back door with Tinker scampering about excitedly at my heels. The October air was crisp and clear and I took a deep breath whilst flexing my muscles in an attempt to relax. The past few months had depressed my spirits and I needed a lift. I heard the flapping of wings overhead and looking up saw ducks flying in formation above my head. Tinker jumped high into the air as I reached the river path at the bottom of our garden.

"Down boy, you'll never make it, even you can't jump that high."

Barking excitedly, he bounded ahead of me into the woodland bordering the path. I followed as he went deeper into the trees, his nose pressed to the ground sniffing the earth before he raised his head and scampered out of sight.

"Tinker, here boy," I called, unable to see or hear him. Then from the depths of the trees, I saw a figure emerge.

"Hullo. I thought it might be Evelyn."

Leonora stood in my path, a black wool coat reaching her ankles, her hair falling over her shoulders like a silken wave.

"Evelyn is in bed. She has a heavy cold," I explained, as I heard Tinker barking in the distance.

"Would you mind if I visited her?" She was looking over my shoulder, her eyes not meeting mine.

"Not at all. I'm sure she would welcome a visit. The back door is open."

"Thanks," she said, and was gone.

I followed in the direction of Tinker's excited bark and saw him with two dogs, which I recognised as belonging to Henry and Josie. They were licking each other and sniffing nether parts as they renewed their acquaintance. Then I heard the cracking of twigs nearby followed by heavy breathing as Josie parted the brambles and stumbled into my view.

"Oh, it's you! That explains why the dogs suddenly ran off." She held her hand to her side. "I'm out of condition, too much good living and not enough exercise." She smiled, as she leant against the bark of a tree. "How are you both?" she asked, once she'd caught her breath.

I felt uncomfortably aware that Evelyn and I had neglected our friendship with Henry and Josie and was determined to make amends. "I'm OK but Evelyn has a cold and is staying in bed. Though I'm glad I've bumped into you. I've decided to take a well-earned rest from work and was hoping you and Henry would come over for a meal one evening, what about a week tomorrow? That should give Evelyn enough time to recover. Make a note of it - let me know if it suits you both."

"No need. I can tell you now. Henry and I would be delighted. It's far too long since we've spent time together. We'll look forward to it."

"Good. See you at eight on the nineteenth then. Give my regards to Henry."

I called to Tinker and once more took the direction of the river path leading away from our house. I wasn't anxious to return whilst Leonora was visiting, as I had the oddest feeling I'd be intruding, a feeling, which I resented.

Tinker was happy to enjoy the extended walk and some time later both he and I returned to River House exhausted and content at having enjoyed the fresh air and each other's company.

Taken at the Flood

Opening the back door, I led Tinker to his food and bed in the utility room and kicking off my boots opened the door into the hall. I heard laughter coming from our bedroom and realised with a sinking heart that Leonora was still visiting.

"Darling, is that you?"

I'd been hoping to creep into my study unheard. "Coming," I answered, reluctantly.

I noticed two spots of colour on my wife's cheeks, as soon as I opened the door. She looked flushed and excited. Leonora was sitting on the side of the bed facing her. "Darling, Leo has been keeping me entertained in your absence."

"Yes I can see that," I answered, unable to keep the sarcasm out of my voice. I saw that Leonora didn't miss it, although Evelyn didn't appear to notice.

"A few moments ago I needed to use the bathroom and guess what? There was the most enormous spider sitting on the cold tap."

"Oh no!" I raised my arms in mock horror and she laughed.

"I know, I know."

"I expect by now Leonora is aware of the terror you have of the poor little creatures," I said, trying to make amends for my previous sarcasm.

"This one wasn't little. Was it Leo? Tell him."

Taken at the Flood

"No it wasn't little," Leonora answered, but she did not turn around and stayed with her back to me.

"Leo was so brave," Evelyn continued, "She came into the bathroom when I cried out and just bent down, picked it up in her hand and flushed it away."

"Saved me the honour, eh, Leonora?"

She shrugged and stood up, facing me at last. "It was nothing," she answered, her eyes meeting mine. "Anyway I must go, Lucas will be wondering where I am. I hope you'll soon be better," she patted the mound of bedclothes covering Evelyn's legs.

I recovered some of my good manners and showed her to the door, thanking her for her visit.

"It was my pleasure," she said. "Call me anytime Evelyn wants to see me."

I closed the door behind her and leaned against it. Why did I always feel disturbed in her presence?

When Leonora had gone, I carried two bowls of hot stew, which our new housekeeper, Mrs Bates, had left in the kitchen, up the stairs to our bedroom and sat at her bedside whilst we ate our meal.

"Who told you about Mrs Bates, darling? She's a real treasure. I don't know how we've managed without her."

"Josie. Mrs Bates is her housekeeper's friend. Apparently, she's a widow and the family she was with recently moved abroad so she was looking for employment." I took a deep breath. "By the way, talking about Josie, I met her in the woods today when I was out walking with Tinker."

Evelyn flicked over the front page of her magazine with her finger as I continued, "I've invited them for dinner this coming Saturday actually. I thought you'd be better by then. It will be nice to see them both again. What do you think? We could ask Mrs Bates to stay over and cook for us. I'm sure she wouldn't mind."

My wife's reaction took me completely by surprise. She flung the magazine down to the floor, inhaled deeply, her breath hissing through her teeth and with flashing eyes, she replied, "Mrs Bates may not mind, but I certainly do. What were you thinking of? Inviting people to our house, without even asking if I minded."

I looked at this person whom I no longer recognised, either in appearance or in demeanour, and my mouth dropped open. "I didn't think you'd mind for heaven's sake. Josie is *your* friend after all," I answered, trying to deflate her inexplicable anger.

"I don't want to see anyone, especially not Josie."

Her breathing had returned to normal but her eyes flashed with an unhealthy light.

"I don't understand. What has turned you against Josie? I wasn't aware you had quarrelled and I know she is unaware of any animosity existing between you."

"I don't want to talk about it. They're not welcome," she fumed.

Anger at her unreasonable manner welled up inside me; I'd come to the end of my tether. There was a limit to my patience, especially as I saw Evelyn isolating Josie in favour of Leonora. The unfairness of the situation and her unwillingness to explain drove me to reply, "As far as I am concerned, Evelyn, Henry and Josie *will* be coming to dinner next Saturday. And I will entertain them, with or without you. I hope you'll see sense and join us but make no mistake they *will* be coming," And with that I left our room and to my shame slept in the spare bedroom for the first time since our marriage

On the Friday before the proposed visit by the Dangerfields, Evelyn tapped at the door of my study. My resolve had crumbled since our disagreement, but although I'd returned to the marital bed, the atmosphere between us was frosty and I found working on a project was a way of putting some distance between us both.

"Darling." She stood in the doorway. The roots of her blonde hair were beginning to show dark against her scalp. "I'm sorry I was so pigheaded about tomorrow. I want you to know I'll help all I can."

I stood up, crossed the room and taking her by the shoulders bent and kissed her cheek. "It will be all right, I promise."

My father once told me, never make a promise that you couldn't keep. That was my mistake. How was I to know - it was simply a dinner party with old friends, what could go wrong?

Chapter 13

Mrs Bates arrived early on the Saturday morning, carrying a small travelling case, which she deposited in the bedroom at the end of the small corridor leading off our upstairs landing. During the week, she had filled the freezer with a selection of homemade dishes in preparation for the weekend. She'd insisted we leave all the arrangements to her.

Evelyn, finding she was at a loose end, said she was going to take Tinker out for a walk. When I suggested I join her, she replied, "No, don't worry, I thought I'd call in on Leonora. I know Lucas will be in town and she's on her own."

"Fine," I said, switching on my computer monitor. "I've plenty to get on with, see you later."

I was lost in concentration until I noticed it was nearly three o'clock. I heard Mrs Bates humming to herself in the kitchen and I remembered she had put a sandwich down on the desk earlier but I'd been so lost in my work I'd left it untouched, as was so often the case, once I started working on something.

Hastily making short shrift of the sandwich, I took the empty plate into the kitchen. "Have you seen my wife about, Mrs Bates?"

"No, sir. She's still out, I think."

Taken at the Flood

"Do you need any help?" I asked, as she opened the fridge door and removed a large casserole dish full of seafood.

"No thank you. Now don't concern yourself, Mr Hope, everything is running like clockwork."

"And you're sure you don't mind serving the meal?"

"Not at all. Now away with you and leave me to my dishes," she said, flapping a dishcloth aimed in my direction.

I couldn't relax. I thought of ringing Leonora but something stopped me for I didn't want it to look as if I was fussing. Evelyn knew when our guests were due to arrive and I'd have to trust her to return on time. Nevertheless, when the hands of the clock spun around to seven o'clock, I was beginning to think I'd have to entertain Henry and Josie without her.

I was in our bedroom changing when I heard the front door slam and the sound of footsteps running up the stairs. The door opened and Evelyn stood in the doorway. She was breathless as if she'd been running and was holding a carrier bag tightly under one arm. "I'm sorry I'm late. You go on down. I'll have a quick shower and change. Leo has let me borrow a dress. I'm sure you'll like it."

I noticed two spots of colour on her cheek; her speech was high pitched and she seemed excitable. The result of an afternoon spent in

Taken at the Flood

Leonora's company, I thought dismally, then decided that perhaps she was just looking forward to the evening, nothing more.

The doorbell rang as I reached the bottom of the stairs.

"Henry, Josie, come in. Glad you could make it. Evelyn won't be a moment. She's just changing," I said.

I ushered our guests into the sitting room, which led into the conservatory and poured our drinks. The river at the bottom of the garden sparkled in the moonlight. We could see the reflection of the trees lining the pathway like sentries.

"I love this house. The view from here is breath-taking," Josie said, walking to the window. She turned, as the sound of running feet met our ears, I think Josie was the first to gasp for she was facing the doorway and caught sight of her before either Henry or myself.

"Hullo everyone. Sorry I'm late. It's so good to see you, Henry. I've really missed you," Evelyn said rushing towards Henry, swinging his chair to face her and kissing him full on his lips.

Her blonde hair was seriously in need of repair. At least an inch of jet-black roots showed beneath a froth of spiked up fringe. Her makeup was heavy and didn't suit her delicate features but nothing had quite prepared us for that dress. It was black, what there was of it. The bodice opened in a deep V to the waist. Her breasts, struggling to remain inside the flimsy material covering them, looked as if they were about to escape as she bent to kiss Henry. The skirt of the dress was short with slits to either side, which opened as she teetered on impossibly high heels. Once more, I felt I was looking at a stranger.

"Pour me a gin and tonic would you, darling? Oh and go easy on the tonic."

I caught Josie's eye over the tufted top of Evelyn's hair as she bent once more in animated conversation with Henry. I raised an eyebrow, smiled as if everything was normal, and poured the gin into her glass.

The evening was a complete disaster. Every time Josie tried to engage Evelyn in conversation, she received one-word answers. It was obvious she was giving her friend 'the cold shoulder' and I felt Josie's embarrassment as acutely as I did my own at her behaviour. Poor Henry looked bewildered. His confusion, at my wife's conduct was plain to see.

Evelyn flirted outrageously with Henry all evening and he appeared to be at a loss to know how to deal with it. By the time Mrs Bates announced dinner was ready, my wife had downed three large G and T's and was beginning to slur her words. I was grateful the time had come for us to eat, in the hope that the food would lessen the effects of the gin.

Taken at the Flood

The meal was delicious Mrs Bates had excelled herself and we were effusive with our praise of her culinary skills, all of us that is except Evelyn. She picked at her food and complained that the meal was too rich for her digestion. However, I don't think Mrs Bates took any notice as the rest of us were heaping enough praises on her head for Evelyn's petulance to pass her by.

At the end of the meal, my wife hurried ahead of us to the sitting room and put some music on the stereo system. The CD she selected I'd not heard before. It was loud and to me appeared to be anything other than musical.

"Who *is* this?" I asked above the din.

"It's the 'Punkins'! Isn't it great? It's Leo's favourite group." She caught hold of my hand and drew me across our wooden floor, kicking off her high heels, which slid into a corner. Then she danced with me sliding her body provocatively against my thigh, as if we were alone. I held her at arm's length for Josie and Henry's sake as they were beginning to look more than a little uncomfortable. Then she let go of my arm and danced towards Henry and to my horror, I saw her catch hold of his wheelchair and spin him around full circle in time with the raucous beat. This she repeated until I saw Josie raise her hand to her face.

"Evelyn, that's enough," I said, pulling her away and steering her towards the couch. I removed the offending Punkins and put on a CD of swing music I knew Henry enjoyed, and tried to make light of the incident. "You'll wear Henry out with your enthusiasm, my love. At least let him digest his meal in peace. At the mention of food, Evelyn put her hand over her mouth, retched and rushed out of the room. We could hear the sound of her vomiting in the downstairs loo above the strains of Tony Bennett leaving his heart in San Francisco. At that moment, San Francisco was looking more and more appealing to me: anywhere other than watching our friends' embarrassment as they made their excuses to leave the disaster area, without making a difficult situation any worse.

"We hope Evelyn will be feeling better soon. Thank you for inviting us," Josie said, kissing my cheek. Henry just patted my arm as he left saying. "I'll ring you."

Later, when I had put her to bed, I sat in my study watching the stars burning in the night sky and wondering how I was going to put a stop to the unhealthy relationship, which had developed between Leonora and Evelyn, without either of them being aware of my involvement. My thoughts ran around in circles and the situation seemed impossible to rectify. I should have known I was wasting my time.

Taken at the Flood

The stars above looked down on me as if acknowledging my insignificance in the scheme of things.

Chapter 14

The day after the disastrous dinner party, Evelyn spent in bed recovering. She had an almighty hangover and her mood was depressed and uncommunicative. I tried to make her give some sort of explanation for her actions of the previous evening but all she would say was 'I'm sorry, I'm sorry' repeated in a monotone, devoid of either remorse or emotion. Hovering between extreme anger at her bizarre behaviour and concern for her mental state, I left the room and walked to the riverbank.

The telephone rang just after lunch. It was Josie thanking us for the evening. Uncertain how to proceed, she asked tentatively after Evelyn and finished by telling me that she and Henry were always there should I need them. Her concern rang alarm bells and I began to worry about my wife's health in earnest, deciding that when Lucas returned from Europe I would pay him a visit. Maybe he would have the answer, without me having to consult someone professionally.

During the following week, the weather worsened and I saw little of my wife. She was preoccupied with visiting Leonora on the pretence of keeping her company whilst Lucas was in Europe.

Taken at the Flood

Frost covered the trees in the woodland and the edges of the river froze solid near the bank. Tinker shivered when I opened the back door and seemed less than eager to join me on our regular walk. I huddled into the depths of my sheepskin coat and watched him bound off into the trees his nose pressed to the ground. At one point I thought I saw Josie with the dogs in the distance but she turned abruptly and made her way back towards her house when she saw Tinker.

When Thursday arrived, I found myself looking for an excuse to visit the office when coincidentally the telephone on my desk rang. It was Alan Henderson. "Sorry to bother you at home, Boss, but I wondered if you could spare some time to come in today. There's something I need to discuss with you."

I looked at my watch. "It's a bit late today. What about tomorrow?"

"Tomorrow's fine. See you about eleven?"

"Sure. I could make it today if it's desperately urgent?" I offered but he assured me that it could wait.

The next day, I awoke to the sound of Evelyn singing in the shower. I ran my fingers through my hair and sighed, it was a sound I hadn't heard for months. She seemed almost content. Maybe things were going to improve after all. Ever the eternal optimist, I dressed for work but events that day were set to change the habits of a lifetime.

Evelyn, emerging from the shower room her fresh, cleanly scrubbed, face at odds with her black-rooted bleached hair, looked in the mirror, saw my reflection looking back at her in the glass, and smiled. Tapping the top of her head she murmured, "My hair is badly in need of a colour. It's just as well Leo and I are booked in with Freddie today. If I leave it any longer I'll be back to my old colour."

"I didn't mind your old colour. Why don't you ask Freddie if he can colour it back?"

"You must be joking! Don't tell me you don't like my blonde bombshell look after all?"

Not wishing to hurt her feelings, I hedged my bets. "It's not that. I love you, whatever colour your hair is. I just thought it might be easier for you to let it go back to its normal colour that's all."

"It's no bother. Anyway Leo likes it."

She started to comb the wet hair forward and I noticed how long it had grown.

"So, you and Leonora are going into town. Are you making a day of it?" I asked.

"Of course. You don't mind, do you?"

"No, I'm going to the office for a while. So we'll meet up for dinner at eight? Take care driving, the roads look icy to me," I said, parting the bedroom curtains and peering through the frost-coated windowpane.

"I'll be careful, I promise. Oh by the way, I rang Leo yesterday to ask her to join us for dinner as Lucas is still away," she said, yawning.

I didn't turn around so she missed the expression on my face. Then I heard her say, "She can't make it though, Lucas is arriving home this evening."

Later, I helped her into her car and watched as she drove in the direction of the Bennetts' place, then followed in my car until the road forked and I joined the motorway slip road.

The side roads were icy but the motorway was clear and I arrived at my office in time to meet Alan at eleven o'clock. Alice put two cups of coffee on my desk as Alan and I got down to business.

"I thought you ought to see this," he said handing me a letter, headed 'Megacells' Computer Software. "As you can see it's from Maxwell Hutton. He said sales of *Gorgon* have gone through the roof and he's keen to have more of the same. He wants to know how long it will be before *Centaur* is complete and ready for production."

I put the letter down on my desktop and rubbed the palm of my hand over my chin. "So it's good news and bad news then."

"How much longer do you think?" Alan looked at me apprehensively.

Taken at the Flood

"I've had a bit on my plate recently, as you can imagine." Frowning at him, I said, "I can't see my way clear to finishing the finer points much before the end of December."

"Hutton wants it in the shops before Christmas." He looked at me over the top of his glasses. "How is Evelyn, by the way?"

"Not good, Alan, not good at all."

"I'm sorry but I guessed as much, that's why I wanted to talk to you today. This letter from Hutton only precipitated our discussion."

"Go on," I urged

"There's this chap, nephew of an old mate of mine. His name is Charles Thornley, known as Chip, only partly because of his interest in computers."

I smiled and Alan relaxed. "He's completed his degree but as yet hasn't found a job. I wondered if?"

"Excellent, get him on to *Centaur* straight away, as soon as possible. I trust your judgement as always. In fact it couldn't have come at a more appropriate time."

"Great, I'm sure he'll be an asset to us."

"That's good enough for me then," I said.

"I told Chip I'd speak to you today and I've arranged to meet him in the wine bar across the road at half five. Now it looks as though we have something to celebrate. Why don't you join us? I'm sure he'd appreciate hearing the good news from the main man."

Taken at the Flood

I hesitated but only for a second. I doubted if Evelyn would be home much before seven. "Sounds like a good idea to me. See you later. Now, while I'm here, I suppose I better do some work. Send Alice in would you please?"

Chip Thornley was tall and thin with a shaved head and an earring in one ear. He was keen and his enthusiasm reminded me of myself at his age, although there the analogy ceased, as I had conformed to the norm in appearance and dress, neither of which he seemed inclined to do. Although his appearance did nothing to advertise his reliability, I felt drawn to him. During our conversation, I had the strong feeling his loyalty would be unquestionable, which was why I felt able to trust him with *Centaur* without any misgivings.

Softcell had a more than adequate technology department staffed with analysts and programmers who, I had no doubt, would be competent enough to deal with most problems but *Centaur* required a visionary. *Gorgon* and its followers were special projects of mine and Alan Henderson knew of my sensitivity regarding their production, but even Alan could see I was struggling and couldn't possibly complete in time for the Christmas market. I trusted his judgement where Chip Thornley was concerned and my first meeting with him had done nothing to dispel that feeling

Taken at the Flood

The wine bar was full of office workers, Alan, Chip and I stood in a corner at the end of the bar discussing what we would be expecting from our new recruit.

I looked at my watch. "I must be going gentlemen. Chip it's good to have you on board. Alan will fill you in with all the details."

Alan Henderson walked to the door with me leaving Chip standing at the bar.

"What do you think?" he asked

"I like him. I think he could be just what we are looking for. Sorry to dash off. I'll give you a ring in the morning."

"No probs. Give my love to Evelyn," he said, closing the door behind me.

Outside, the cold air hit me full in the face and my breath burned in my chest leaving me panting for air. Snow flurries swirled in the light shed from the lamppost and I bent my head as my face began to sting. By the time I'd reached my car, there was a light dusting of snow on the bonnet and my fingers felt numb as I struggled with the already freezing lock.

The motorway was clear and the snow showers died away when I took the side road leading to the village. A fire engine passed me from the direction of the River Road, its blue light flashing in the gloom and I wondered if it had been called out on yet another false alarm. The fire alarms in our building at Softcell were always being set off accidentally and it was a source of embarrassment to me that we'd had to explain to the fire chief, on numerous occasions, that their assistance wasn't required.

I felt my tyres slide on a patch of black ice and turned my wheel in the direction of the skid, so that I remained pointing in the right direction. It was dark, and the side road which branched off to River Road, was unlit. All I had to guide me was the beam from my headlights. Glancing through the trees to the road, I saw everything appeared to be in darkness. I thought maybe there'd been a power cut.

It's easy to say I knew that something was wrong, now, but it's true the nearer I drove to River House, the stronger became my sense of unease. Icy rain began to fall and I switched on my windscreen wipers. The wind had strengthened and the trees at the side of the road rustled and shook their bare branches eerily in the darkness. I thought I saw our house lights as I turned a bend in the road and wondered how it was possible to see them so clearly at such a distance and if so the power cut had only affected the lights on River Road. As I approached, it looked as if Evelyn had left every light in the house on.

Our security gates stood wide open and behind them I could see the reason for the lights. Two police cars and an ambulance stood in my driveway, their blue lights flashing intermittently. The front door was ajar and I could see Mrs Bates with two uniformed police officers standing in the hall. She had been crying and I saw her dabbing her eyes with a teacloth. As I drew up and hurried out of my car, Lucas Bennett walked towards me.

"What's wrong?" I asked, dreading the reply.

"It's Evelyn. Look I want to speak to you before you go inside. There's been an accident."

I turned in the direction of the ambulance; there was a body on a stretcher. Two paramedics stood one each side of the back door to the vehicle. I took a step forward but Lucas placed a restraining hand on my arm. "No, please, let me tell you what happened first."

I felt an icy finger slide down my back and shuddered as he continued.

"Evelyn had just dropped Leonora off and had barely driven two hundred metres along River Road. A while later we heard a crash and rushed to the scene."

Drawing breath into my aching lungs, I felt the biting cold once more, this time sending its icy fingers towards my heart as I struggled to understand what Lucas was saying.

"By the time we reached her, we were too late. The car had crashed. She must have skidded on the ice and hit the lamppost. We looked to see if we could help but it was useless. The lamppost was lying across the bonnet and was thrust through the windscreen."

Lucas put his hand on my arm as a look of pure horror spread across my face. "I phoned the emergency services and afterwards followed them back here."

I watched him running his fingers through his grey hair, saying, "If it's any comfort, she wouldn't have suffered. It must have been over in an instant." Lucas bent his head, "I'm so sorry."

I started to walk towards the ambulance once more but he stepped in front of me.

"Come inside, Leonora is in the kitchen, she's still in shock but making hot sweet tea for everyone. There's nothing to be gained by seeing Evelyn now. Take my advice and wait until they call you for identification."

I tried to pull away from him but recognised the futility of my actions. What was I hoping to see? Evelyn had gone. What was the point? Lucas was right. Reluctantly I allowed myself to be steered past Mrs Bates, who howled when she saw me and buried her face deeper in her teacloth. Ignoring the two police officers, who were waiting to speak to me, I found myself deposited in the kitchen where Leonora stood in front of the kettle her face even whiter than normal. Lucas held out a chair and I felt my legs collapse as I sat down.

"Forget the tea, Leo. Pour a large brandy, please." Lucas instructed. "You're coming home with us tonight." I shook my head slowly,

Taken at the Flood

my mind refusing to accept what had happened." No use protesting. I want to keep an eye on you. I insist. Don't worry about the police, I'll have a word with them," he said, walking into the hallway.

It's impossible to recall the anguish I felt that day. Something in my subconscious refuses to allow me to feel the strength of emotion I felt then. I remember little of the next few days with the Bennetts. It seems I must have spent them in a drug-induced stupor. I do remember Lucas bringing me a daily paper one morning, when I was sitting in his kitchen staring out of the window with unseeing eyes. He put a cup of coffee and the morning paper down on the table in front of me before leaving for his consulting rooms. Leonora was in town shopping and I was alone.

I turned over the front page and saw a photograph of Evelyn and myself on the inside pages. It was taken some years previously when we'd attended a dinner where I'd been presented with the *Young Businessman of the Year award*. We were smiling and I was holding my trophy aloft for the cameras to get a good picture. Above the photograph was the headline DEATH OF MILLIONAIRE COMPUTER GIANT'S WIFE and below an account of the accident. I read on;-

Taken at the Flood

Beautiful Evelyn Hope, wife of the millionaire founder of 'Softcell Computer Operating Systems,' is dead. In a tragic accident on a side road near the village of Kings Datchet her car skidded in icy conditions.....

I let the newspaper fall to the floor, buried my face in my hands and there I remained until Leonora returned from her shopping. She made no comment when she entered the kitchen, quietly removed the paper and replaced the half-empty coffee cup with a tumbler containing a large measure of brandy. Then she left me alone with my grief and the stupefying effects of the golden spirit in the crystal glass for which I'd developed a fondness.

During the following weeks, I remember identifying my wife's body. The sanitised body with all traces of the bloodied cuts mercifully lessened gave me the distinct impression that she was just sleeping. I closed my eyes to the laceration that started under the hairline and slashed across her cheek.

The eternity ring I'd bought in Germany sparkled in the beam from the spotlight above the mortuary gurney. Her short dark hair curled around her face and I felt as if my heart would break - it was as it used to be. She'd been to the hairdressers earlier and I knew that she'd done it to please me. The poignancy of the situation tugged at my heartstrings in a way I would never have thought possible.

The inquest was brief and to the point. The coroner instructed the jury that, although Mrs Hope's body had contained a quantity of antidepressant drugs, it was clear she'd been prescribed them following her miscarriage some months before. He stressed that the amount in her bloodstream was not significant. The relevant line of enquiry had been followed and in his opinion, the pills were not a contributing factor to the incident on the River Road on Friday the 14th. However, the icy road conditions were another matter, as it appeared Mrs Hope had not refastened her seatbelt when she'd left her friend at her house earlier. Therefore, under the circumstances he concluded, his advice would be to consider a verdict of accidental death.

When the police returned Evelyn's belongings to me, I carried the sealed plastic bag towards the door leading to our basement, flicked on the light switch and went down the steps. Shelves ran from floor to ceiling. The previous owners of River House had been meticulously neat and it hadn't been difficult for us to follow their example. Each shelf contained a variety of plastic boxes labelled in Evelyn's sloping handwriting. At the end of the bottom shelf stood an unlabelled box, which I opened and dropped the plastic package inside with the rest of the things, too personal for me to look at. One day, I promised myself, I'd sort them out, when time had eased the pain of looking at reminders.

On the day of Evelyn's funeral, Mrs Bates was busy in the kitchen preparing food so that family and friends could return to River House after the service. The weather had deteriorated and Evelyn's parents were too elderly and infirm to travel. She'd been their 'surprise', a child born when both parents were in their forties. Her elder sister Sylvia and her family stayed overnight with Josie and Henry, as they were concerned their children's boisterous antics would disturb me. I felt swept along on a tide of events, arranged without my participation by family and friends anxious to spare me the trauma of dealing with the funeral.

Somehow, I managed to watch, stony faced, as they buried my wife. Nothing penetrated the wall I'd built around me and I watched as though I were somewhere else. The monotonous line of mourners, with their monochrome clothes, standing around the graveside made me wonder what she would have thought of it all.

Afterwards, when everyone was leaving I called to Evelyn's sister, "Sylvia." She followed me into my study. "I want you to have this."

The top drawer of my desk slid open to reveal the black velvet box containing the diamond necklace I'd bought on my New York

Taken at the Flood

trip. I removed it and handed it to her. Sylvia gasped as she opened the lid and raised her eyes to mine. "I couldn't," she said, holding the box in the palm of her hand.

"Please. I know Evelyn would have wanted you to have it and so do I."

She bent to kiss me and I smelled the same perfume Evelyn used to wear. With cheeks wet with tears we held each other for a moment, both trying to recapture a fragment of her that clung to us, ephemeral as the mist rising from the river at the bottom of the garden.

Later, I waved goodbye to Sylvia and her family and walked into the conservatory where all that was left for me was the view.

Chapter 15

The weeks passed and work was my salvation. I began to prepare the basis for my next project, which was *Minotaur,* a follow on from *Centaur,* which would be an advanced concept without appearing more complicated to use. Burying myself under a mountain of theoretical analysis, I found the distraction that stopped me from dwelling on my loss.

Returning to River House one evening, I became aware spring had arrived, its birth having occurred unnoticed. Buried somewhere in the depths of my grief, I'd missed the first crocus shooting up through the frost-speckled earth and with surprise saw a clump of daffodils nodding their heads as I entered the driveway. It was an uncomfortable reminder of the day Evelyn and I had first seen the house. The Christmas and New Year period too escaped my notice, as had the dreaded months of January and February.

Mrs Bates was waiting for me as I drew up. "Mr Hope, I'm glad you're home early. I wanted to see you before I left." She looked agitated and I noticed she was wearing her outdoor clothes.

"Left, Mrs Bates?"

"Yes, sir. My sister over at Kings Bentham has had a nasty fall and broken her leg. She lives all alone, now her Arthur has gone, and I wondered if you would mind if I took some time off to look after her. I've made sure the freezer is well stocked and…."

I stopped her in mid sentence, "Of course you must go, Mrs Bates. Take as long as you need. Don't worry about me, I'll be fine."

She buttoned up her coat and picked up a small case from the cloakroom. "There's a casserole in the oven, Mr Hope."

"Thank you. Now off you go. Do you want me to give you a lift to the station?"

"No thanks, I can hear Morton coming up the drive. I telephoned him as I heard your car coming through the gates."

Morton Phillips ran a taxi firm on the outskirts of the village, a stone's throw away from the entrance to our drive. I stood and watched from the doorway as his elderly black Rover saloon crept down the driveway to transport my housekeeper to her sister's house, then I went inside to sample my evening meal.

After I'd finished eating, I called to Tinker and closing the back door behind us, walked down the garden to the river path. The ground was damp underfoot but not excessively so. I'd neglected Tinker of late and had been glad of Mrs Bates's help. Now I was alone in the house, I'd have to make sure I gave him the care and attention he deserved.

Leaves were beginning to sprout on the trees and the river gently lapped against the bank on

Taken at the Flood

my right. Tinker trotted alongside me unwilling to run off into the undergrowth in case I disappeared. His tail wagged, as if thankful that at last it could behave as nature intended. From time to time he looked behind, making sure I was still there.

I began to feel my spirits lifting and took a deep breath relishing the fresh evening air and unable to quite believe I could spend more than a moment without thinking about Evelyn. It was getting dark as evening approached. Tinker was the first to hear the footsteps and smell the presence of the other dogs.

"Josie?" I said, as a figure approached from out of the trees.

"Good gracious, it *is* you," Josie exclaimed. "How are you, my dear?"

"Better, I think," I answered uncertainly.

"I'm so glad. We've missed you, you know, Henry and I. We wanted you to stay with us after Evelyn…"

"I know you did. It was.." I hesitated. " it was just that I didn't know what was happening at the time and Lucas, well Lucas, sort of took over. You know how it is."

She nodded and put her hand on my arm. "Anyway, it's good to see you. You must come over to see Henry some time soon. Please don't wait to be invited."

I thanked her and asked her if she'd seen anything of Lucas and Leonora lately.

Taken at the Flood

"They're on holiday. We don't see much of them now but I bumped into their cleaning lady in the village – they're away for a month I understand."

"Very nice, if you can spare the time," I said. "It's getting dark, I'll walk back to the house with you. I took her arm. Passing the Bennetts' place, which was in darkness, an owl suddenly hooted loudly above our heads and I felt Josie tighten her grip on my arm.

"Sorry." She laughed.

We walked on together in the gathering gloom until we reached the bottom of her garden and there I accepted her invitation of a nightcap. Henry was reading in an armchair in front of a roaring log fire. He looked up as we entered the room.

"What a lovely surprise. Sit down and tell me what you've been up to."

That night was the first time I felt a return to normality, after the horror of the past few months. Josie and Henry were amusing and entertaining company. No one mentioned Evelyn and I felt, although we had not spoken of her, she was still very much in our thoughts. That fact alone drew me even closer to them. The dear friends who had remained constant all through my wife's odd behaviour and who, even now, were trying to keep me on the straight and narrow.

115

Taken at the Flood

Henry insisted on driving me home and when I awoke the next morning, it was to a bedroom filled with sunlight and the knowledge that for once I had slept a dreamless sleep, undisturbed by the past.

A month had gone by when Mrs Bates telephoned to say her sister was still finding difficulty coping on her own and would I mind if she stayed on for a further couple of weeks. I told her to take as long as she felt it necessary and her job would be waiting for her whenever she decided to return. After assuring her I was coping, I replaced the receiver and realised I hadn't lied, I *was* coping. Time was gradually filling my life with purpose and the rest I kept locked away, unwilling to open the part, which was filled with thoughts of her.

Perhaps I'd been over optimistic because soon after, I returned home from my office to find the freezer was empty and the fridge and cupboards told the same sad story. It hadn't occurred to me that at some point I would have to go shopping. It was strange because as I searched amongst out of date tins of mince and baked beans for something palatable to eat, I felt as though someone was watching me. Out of the corner of my eye, I could have sworn I saw a flash of red pass the window. Then I heard the back door open.

"Hello?"

"Leonora! I thought you and Lucas were still away."

She was wearing a vivid red jumper and blue jeans and was carrying what looked and smelt like my dinner. In one hand, she held a key on a fine chain.

"I thought you might like some steak and kidney pie. I heard Mrs Bates had deserted you."

"You must be a mind reader. As you can see my cupboards are bare!"

She laughed a high-pitched tinkling sort of laugh I'd not heard before, put the pie into the oven and turned a few dials. Then she held out the key.

"I found this amongst my things. I'd forgotten about it. It's your back door key. Evelyn gave it to me. She was afraid she would lock herself out when you were in work and thought if I had a duplicate then there would be no problem."

"Oh, right," I said, wondering why Evelyn hadn't mentioned it before. She didn't move but stood looking at me with a steady gaze from eyes that were as blue as the river on a sunny day. "Would you like to join me in a drink before I sample your kind offer of dinner?" I asked.

I thought she was about to say yes but without taking her eyes from mine, she replied, "No, thank you. I must get back, perhaps

Taken at the Flood

another time? Your meal will be ready in thirty minutes. I've set the timer."

She backed out of the kitchen, her eyes still locked on mine, then closed the back door behind her.

I watched her cross the lawn and make for the river path, the breeze lifting the curtain of hair from her shoulders as she disappeared into the woodland. Then I stood there long after she'd dissolved into the mist, hovering over the river and spilling into the trees, until the pinging of the oven timer broke the spell.

Chapter 16

Minotaur was proving to be a more difficult proposition than I'd envisaged. Chip Thornley and I spent many fruitless hours closeted in my office discussing features and analysing components until we realised things were not going as planned.

"Chip, I think we need a break from *Minotaur* and its problems. We're getting nowhere fast with this, time to focus on other projects. Leave *Minotaur* to me and I'll take it back to basics and see what I can come up with. It's going to take time and I can use your expertise on other ventures."

Chip closed his laptop and shrugged. "I hate being defeated but I don't envy you unravelling the plot," he said.

"Luckily, Maxwell Hutton isn't on our backs at the moment. I spoke to him yesterday and he said they are more than satisfied with the sales from *Centaur,* which will hold him off for a while. Without rushing towards a deadline, I should be able to crack the problem and I think that the place to work on this is at home where there are no distractions," I closed my briefcase adding, "Tell Alan he can contact me on my mobile or at River House."

Summer arrived and with it Mrs Bates. Soon after the house smelled of cooking and furniture polish. Josie and Henry refused to let me wallow in isolation and were frequent visitors, often with kind invitations to lunch or dinner. When I failed to see them, they telephoned just to see if I was OK but I saw little of the Bennetts, after my housekeeper's return. I supposed Leonora had tired of keeping an eye on me and I knew Lucas was a busy man with little time for social chitchat, unless it was at a gathering accompanied by his wife. Being a single person again absolved me from the obligatory invitation to a 'couples evening' and I found it a relief not to have to make small talk with strangers. I'd not yet reached the time when well-meaning friends would seek to invite me to join them in situations where there would be an obviously unattached female lying in wait.

The summer months were hot and sticky and people were beginning to wish for rain. I heard them in the supermarket discussing the drought and bemoaning the fact that there was a hosepipe ban and their gardens were beginning to suffer. Even though Mrs Bates had returned, I found I enjoyed my visits to the supermarket with its bright lights and piped music. Mechanically filling the shopping trolley, I let my mind wander to the *Minotaur* project. For some reason the distraction seemed to work and I was able to return to my desk with fresh ideas. I think Mrs Bates thought I was mad. It was beyond her comprehension that a man would actually enjoy the chore of shopping. Nevertheless, she humoured me and allowed me to help when the fancy took me.

It was a hot afternoon in August, when the lawn had dried to a faded yellow and the flowers stood with their heads drooping searching for moisture, that I heard a car draw up on the gravel driveway and Henry calling out, "Hello, anyone about?"

I walked around to the front of the house as he was lowering himself into his wheelchair.

"Oh good, you are in residence I see. Wondered if you fancied a chat? I've brought a pack of cool beer with me. Josie said she'd walk over to drive me back later. How does that suit? If you'd rather work, you only have to say."

"Nonsense, let me push you around to the back garden as the ground is a bit uneven due to the dry weather. No doubt you'll be glad to know I've actually found some shade."

When we were seated in comfort, the cool beer slipping down our parched throats, Henry said, "You're looking better. Josie wondered if you were taking a holiday this year. If you want company you know where we are."

I suppose I'd been thinking about relationships and suddenly I wondered about Henry and Josie. "The first time we met you told me you and Josie hooked up at a polo match. How did that come about?

Taken at the Flood

Henry sat back in his chair, his face turned towards the sun.

"We started dating after the match, actually. She was a real live wire and I fell under her spell immediately. Six months later, I was playing a match in Buenos Aires. Josie was attending a conference in Geneva. The match was a gruelling fight and, although we fought hard, we were no competition for the Argentineans. I took a tumble and this was the result." Henry patted his legs.

It was the first time he'd discussed the details of his accident. It showed me our friendship had reached a stage where he felt comfortable enough to trust me with such a sensitive topic.

"By the time they'd driven me to the hospital, I was in excruciating pain. They X-rayed me, pumped me full of drugs and then decided to operate to relieve the pain. It was a delicate operation on the discs in the lumbar region. Didn't work I'm afraid.

"After the accident, I spoke to Josie and told her to get on with her life and forget about me but she wouldn't hear of it, told me not to be so selfish, if you please. I don't know where I'd be without her." He was serious, as he continued, "It was Josie who banished my depression, she who insisted we marry as soon as possible so she could keep an eye on me. Her words, not mine, and she's been doing it very effectively ever since." The humour was back in his voice.

"She arranged my work room so I could keep in touch with my office, sorted the house so I could get around without a problem and made me feel a man again. The woman is totally selfless. Who else would put up with an old crock like me?"

I sighed and changed the subject. "Henry, you and Josie are the kindest friends anyone could wish for. You're anything but an old crock and well you know it. You really don't have to worry about me. I'm managing very well on my own and trying hard to forget the past. And not to put too fine a point on it - you two have been the rocks I've clung to and saved me from drowning in my despair."

"Steady on," he laughed, opening another can and sliding it across the table towards me. "Personally, I was so sorry that Evelyn didn't make peace with Josie before…." He glanced up to see how I was taking his remark then continued, "We were very concerned during those last few months. Evelyn's behaviour seemed quite unlike her. We didn't comment too much at the time as we thought it was none of our business. Was it all to do with the miscarriage, do you think?"

I put my can down on the table between us and narrowed my eyes against the sun. "Impossible to say. At the time I thought it the most likely explanation but now I'm not so sure, her behaviour was at times both bizarre and disturbing."

"There's something on your mind?" Henry asked.

I looked out over the parched lawn to the river, lower now than during the winter months and saw a family of swans gliding by. It all seemed so peaceful that I hesitated to interrupt the tranquillity but he was waiting for my reply, his eyes fixed on me. "I don't quite know where to begin, Henry." I ran my fingers through my hair. "I think I first noticed a change in Evelyn before the miscarriage. She became excitable, where once she was always calm and relaxed. When we first met, I was the one who was quick to react to situations, quick to anger and respond with words. I envied and respected her self-control. It was one of the characteristics that had first attracted me to her, apart from her looks."

Henry nodded.

"I put the change in her behaviour down to her pregnancy and I suppose, afterwards, I put it down to her distress at losing our baby."

When I paused, Henry said, "That seems like a feasible explanation to me but I can see you are having second thoughts."

I nodded, "You see, at the inquest, I was surprised to find out that traces of drugs were found in Evelyn's body. I wasn't aware she was still taking the antidepressants. I said nothing at the time because the coroner stated that they were not a contributory factor but it did make me question whether they could have explained the changes in her behaviour. It disturbed me so much I made some enquiries and discovered, it was as I had thought, the tablets she'd been prescribed would have produced the opposite effect. I realise now that any fool would know antidepressants would do as the name implies but I had to make sure she hadn't experienced some sort of adverse reaction, which would account for the change in her."

"And what did you find?"

"The only thing I did find was, if alcohol was consumed whilst taking the tablets, the effects of the alcohol would become more powerful. For example one drink would act like two and she would become drunk much quicker than normal."

Henry looked thoughtfully into his glass, "That could explain the night we came to dinner before…" he left his sentence unfinished.

"Precisely, I also found that in some cases, judgement and dexterity could be impaired, which also explained some of the odd things that had happened in the weeks before the accident."

"Who prescribed the tablets?"

"Lucas."

"Didn't he monitor her? The little I know about such things leads me to believe tablets of that sort are potentially addictive. I remember watching a television programme on the subject some time ago. The women, who had taken them for prolonged periods, seemed to react like drug addicts when they stopped taking them. It was so horrific it made a lasting impression on me."

"Yes, but think about it, Henry. Evelyn was prescribed the tablets after the miscarriage and as far as I knew when she started to feel better, she stopped taking them. I had a chat with Lucas about it after the inquest and he said the only explanation might be that she had kept some tablets in reserve, in case she felt low. He tried to explain to me that it took a week or two for the tablets to take effect, so in actual fact she wouldn't have felt the benefit, unless she'd renewed her prescription and he assured me he hadn't done so."

Opening another can, Henry slid it across the table to me saying, "Well there's one sure thing you will never know exactly what was responsible for the change in Evelyn. Torturing yourself with possibilities will get you nowhere and only result in further distress. Try and put it all behind you and remember the happier times."

I leaned back in my chair and saw the swallows diving towards the treetops fluttering their wings and dipping their divided tails in the sunshine, whilst in the distance, I heard laughter coming from the deck of a cruiser further up river. "Do you know, Henry, I think you're right. Time to move on doesn't mean time to forget but time to remember the things that mattered. Moreover, I think the time has come to open the bottle of Dom Perignon, I bought for the birth of our baby. I'll give Josie a ring and ask her to join us, as it's a magnum."

Henry joined his laughter to mine and I thought how lucky I'd been to find such a good friend and neighbour."

Chapter 17

It rained throughout most of September that year. Dark, endless days filled with grey, dripping trees, waterlogged lawns and slippery paths. The philosophers in the supermarket now commented that at least the gardens could do with it. By the end of September, their views were not so strident. It made no difference to me; my days were spent closeted in my study trying to find my way through the complicated maze that was the *Minotaur* project, so the weather was not a consideration.

At the beginning of October, I was starting to see daylight and with it came an unexpected bonus in the shape of a new project. I'd been sitting at my desk in my study almost ready to shelve the concept as a hopeless proposition, when suddenly I unlocked the data, which resulted in stabilising my components. Realising where I'd been repeatedly failing, I made a search of the new files and noticed that hidden away in a minor file were the beginnings of a whole family of offshoot projects just waiting to be knocked into shape. I could hardly contain my excitement. *Minotaur* would be ready for the Christmas market and I had stimulating new possibilities awaiting future development.

The downpour of the previous month gave way to drizzle filled days. Tinker wasn't so keen to join me on our daily walks, as he disliked the

Taken at the Flood

damp muddy ground beneath his feet and shook his coat continually, showering me in a spray of fine mist. Mrs Bates spent more time with her sister during the day and with increasing frequency asked if I minded if she stayed the night at Kings Bentham. It was an arrangement that suited us both.

My excitement at discovering an answer to *Minotaur's* problems was hard to contain. I telephoned my office to speak to either Alan or Chip, only to be told by my secretary that they were both out of the office. Pacing the floor, restless at being unable to share my elation, I heard Tinker bark and walked into the kitchen. Looking out into the dismal misty rain, I saw a figure approached from the river path, her blonde hair hanging limply around her shoulders. It was Leonora. I rushed to open the back door.

"Good Lord, you're soaking," I exclaimed, pulling down a towel from the hook in the back porch. "Quickly, dry your hair or you'll catch your death of cold."

"You'd make someone a lovely wife," she replied, smiling up at me as she removed her wax jacket.

"It's good to see you. How is Lucas?" I asked, as I hadn't seen either of them for weeks.

"He's OK. Got a bit of a cold, which he insists is flu, but he's dragged himself into the surgery even though I suggested he should stay in bed." She shrugged. "So I thought I'd look in on you. See what you're up to."

It was the opportunity I'd been waiting for. I took her into my study and bored her with my success. I don't think she understood one word of it but she listened and asked all the right questions. "It sounds to me as though your breakthrough will mean your company will be in a secure financial proposition for the foreseeable future," she said, as I shut down my computer. "I'll tell Lucas to buy some shares." She smiled and I felt as if the whole day had been worth the effort.

"I'm sorry if I've bored you," I said. "It's just, I had to share my excitement with someone. And yes, you could say Softcell's future is most definitely secured. This morning has opened up enough avenues for growth and development to be pretty much 'in the bag' as they say. How would you and Lucas like to celebrate with me tonight? I'll book a table at *The Holly Tree* in Kings Bentham. What do you think?"

"Sounds great." She stood up. "I'll see you later then."

"Good, I'll ring Morton and we'll pick you up at eight."

The drizzle that had heralded Leonora's arrival earlier continued all day and, when Morton Phillips drew up in his taxi at five to eight, it had turned into a downpour. We drove

Taken at the Flood

to the Bennetts' house and I told Morton to keep his motor running, as I hurried up the steps to their front door. Leonora, who was buttoning up a black mackintosh over her dress, opened the door. She was alone. "You'll have to make do with just me, I'm afraid."

From somewhere upstairs I could hear Lucas coughing. A barking sound that seemed to catch in his throat.

"Look, if you'd rather stay with Lucas, I don't mind. He sounds really rough."

She closed the door behind her saying, "No, he insists I join in your celebrations. He'll be OK. I've made sure he has everything he needs."

The restaurant was quiet, the rain having kept people indoors. The waiter found us a table overlooking the river. We sat and watched the rain-dappled water spreading reflected lights from the restaurant outwards, into a hundred shimmering circles.

"I like the rain," she said, looking at me over the top of her champagne glass.

"Why?" I asked.

"It makes me feel secure. It reminds me of a time when I was little and my family were all at home because the rain had kept them indoors."

Knowing that tragedy had struck her family, I tactfully changed the subject. We talked of books, hobbies, past experiences and holidays.

Taken at the Flood

We did not talk of Evelyn. In fact, it occurred to me that, since her death, neither of us had mentioned her name. Maybe it was too painful, an unspoken bond drawing us together.

The evening passed in a flash. We toasted my success repeatedly and were both a little tipsy when the taxi drew up to take us home.

Neither of us spoke much on the homeward journey. But when we stopped outside her house, I felt her cool breath against my cheek and her lips brushing against mine for a fraction of a second, so I was hardly aware that she had kissed me. "Thank you for a lovely evening," she said, leaving the taxi and walking slowly up the steps to her front door. She turned her and waved as she reached the top step.

The next day, I telephoned to find out how Lucas was. Leonora answered, "Not good, I'm afraid, he coughed continually throughout the night. He thinks he has a chest infection. I'm going to get him some more antibiotics, later."

"Would you like me to pick them up for you?" I offered

"No, it's no trouble, thank you. But if you could come and sit with him for a while I'm sure he'd like it. I think he's bored.

The bedroom was warm but not overly so. Lucas was propped up against a mound of pillows and looked older than his years. His face

Taken at the Flood

was ashen and his eyes, bloodshot from coughing, were set in dark rimmed hollows. On his bedside table stood a glass of water and a variety of pill bottles. As I entered the room, he pointed to a seat near his bed.

"Leonora was on her way out when I arrived, she told me to come on up," I explained, as I slipped out of my coat.

"She's gone to the chemist's. I can't seem to get rid of this damned infection," he said, tapping his chest with the tips of his fingers. "The first course of antibiotics hasn't worked so Leo's gone to fetch some more."

He started to cough and I could see how he struggled to draw breath into his lungs.

"Don't try to talk, Lucas. I'll tell you all the news. You already know of my latest breakthrough with the *Minotaur* project."

He nodded and seemed to take an interest.

"Right, well, as I have a captive audience, I'll bore you with the rest of my news."

He looked pale but he managed a weak smile, so I tried to make my conversation light and engrossing. It seemed I didn't succeed because, after a while, I could see his eyelids drooping suggesting he was falling asleep. I stood up, slipped my overcoat over my shoulders and quietly left the room.

Leonora arrived as I closed the front door behind me. "He's asleep." I said, "I'll call again.

Taken at the Flood

Let me know how he is. Don't forget, if you are at all worried, you know where I am."

"Thanks, he should pick up when these take effect." She held up a white paper bag with the local chemist's name printed in blue letters above a green bottle. "It's unusual for Lucas not to recover quickly. He has remarkable stamina. Would you like me to run you home?" She was holding her car keys in her hand, hovering uncertainly over the lock.

"No thanks, I'll take the river path. At least it's stopped raining."

The river lapped gently against its bank and, as I followed the path to River House, I kept seeing Lucas's face. The change in him had been quite a shock. He had aged almost overnight. I failed to share Leonora's optimism that he would soon pick up; to me he looked very ill indeed. But I hoped I was mistaken, after all his wife knew him better than I did and she didn't appear to be unduly worried.

My anxiety increased, as over the next few weeks Lucas made little progress. His GP wanted to admit him to hospital for tests but he refused. He kept insisting it was just a stubborn bug that was taking a while to respond to treatment.

Almost exactly a year to the day after Evelyn's death, Lucas Bennett passed away in his sleep. I received a phone call from Leonora the next day. She'd called the doctor but Lucas was beyond his help. I sympathised and offered my support but she politely refused my offer. "Everything is in hand," she said.

The morning of Lucas's funeral dawned with a heavy fall of snow. I stood with Henry and Josie in the snow covered churchyard with the rest of Lucas's friends and colleagues and watched the fey young woman with the pale blonde hair bury her husband, her face as white as the flakes, which covered his coffin, as it slid into the grave at her feet.

The day after the funeral, I walked over to their house. A light dusting of snow covered the river path, which had frozen hard, so I walked through the woods, ice-covered branches snapping like gunshot under my feet.

When I reached the bottom of their garden, I saw the windows were shuttered on the upper storey and on the ground floor the curtains were drawn. Was it an observance of a mourning ritual perhaps? I knocked on the front door and waited. There was no answer. I walked around to the back of the house but every window was covered and no sound came from within. It was ten-thirty in the morning. Reluctantly, I retraced my steps through the frozen woodland back to River House but an uneasy feeling kept gnawing away at me.

The next day I called again but the telephone remained unanswered, until finally cutting in to

Lucas's voice asking the caller to leave a name and number and he would return the call. As I replaced the receiver for the third time that day, I thought ironically that Lucas Bennett would never be able to 'get back' to his callers again - his clear voice a reminder of the transient nature of life.

Henry and Josie had no idea what had happened to Leonora but I could see they thought it rather odd she hadn't mentioned her departure to me, as I had been a frequent caller at the house prior to Lucas's death. At the end of the following week, I was becoming concerned in case something had happened to her. Then on Saturday morning, I heard the clatter of the letterbox followed by Tinker's usual cacophony.

"Quiet boy, it's just the postman," I reassured him as I picked up the mail. Bills, circulars, a note in Mrs Bates's handwriting to tell me she would be returning from her sister's on the four-forty train, and a postcard.

The picture on the front of the postcard showed the towers of San Gimignano, a small town in Tuscany, surrounded by fields of large headed sunflowers nodding in the sunshine. I turned it over and in small neat handwriting were the words. *I will be away for some time, will contact you when I return. Thank you for your help. L*

Taken at the Flood

A feeling of relief swept over me dispelling my unease. I slid the postcard into the bottom drawer of my desk, where it lay forgotten until it played a major part in the events that were to come.

The weather worsened and now the talk in the supermarket was that we were likely to have a white Christmas.

Returning home one afternoon during the week before Christmas, I found Henry and Josie sitting in the conservatory talking to Mrs Bates. Apparently, in my absence, they'd been discussing my welfare during the forthcoming Christmas period.

"You will come and stay with us won't you?" Josie pleaded.

"Of course he will," Henry confirmed.

"My sister has asked me to stay but of course I told her my first consideration was to Mr Hope." Mrs Bates looked up expectantly. What could I say - that I wanted to be alone - that I didn't want to impose on anyone? Three faces searched mine for an answer.

"I would be delighted to spend Christmas with you both but on the understanding that I'll supply the drinks. I won't allow you to feed me without making some contribution to the festivities," I insisted.

Mrs Bates's audible sigh of relief joined Josie's pleasurable response to my acceptance

Taken at the Flood

of their invitation. "It will be lovely to have company, someone else to cook for. I'm so glad you'll be staying with us."

Her pleasure was genuine and disarming. I walked across the room to where she stood and kissed her cheek. "You're a paragon of virtue, Josie. I hope Henry appreciates you."

She smiled fondly at her husband and took his hand in hers. "Oh he does, he does," she said emphatically.

Christmas that year confirmed the pundits' predictions leaving the bookmaker's gutted as drizzle turned to ice and the countryside awoke to a dreamscape. Josie cooked a turkey lunch with flaming plum pudding for dessert. It reminded me of meals I'd shared with my parents when I was young. Afterwards, Henry and I filled the dishwasher whilst she relaxed, even though she insisted she couldn't let her guest work on such a day. It took all my powers of persuasion to assure her that she could.

Snow fell heavily covering the Dangerfields' lawn. Inside, Josie, Henry and I sat in front of a roaring log fire drinking brandy from crystal glasses that splayed a golden light over our mottled hands.

"That was a splendid lunch, Josie, my compliments to the chef."

She inclined her head in my direction in acknowledgement and refilled my glass as Henry raised his. "To good friends," he said.

"Good friends," we echoed his toast.

"I have a strong feeling the coming year is going to be a good one; a time to put the past behind us," Henry continued and I noticed a slight slurring of his words, the pre-lunch champagne and wine drunk during the meal, having taking their toll. I smiled fondly at him.

"I do hope so, Henry. The last two years are ones I'd prefer to forget."

He reached over and patted my arm, "Quite so old fellow, quite so," he said.

I noticed the sky outside the window darken as the showers increased. Henry's eyelids closed and before long he drifted into sleep. Josie moved her chair closer to mine. "How are you, really?" she asked, concern in her dark eyes.

"Better. I'm learning to live with it. You know I'll never forget her."

Josie sighed. "Me too," she said. "We used to be such good friends when we were young. I miss that. We were so close. She was such a live wire, always leading me into trouble of some kind or another. We even shared a boyfriend or two if I recall. I was so pleased to meet up with her again and couldn't wait to tell Henry how thrilled I was she'd moved into River House."

She stood up and walked over to the window peering out into the swirling drifts then sat down once more at my side and I saw her cheeks were damp. "At first, I thought she seemed like the same old Evelyn, but I was mistaken and as the weeks passed I found little that reminded me of my old friend."

"In what way had she changed?" I asked.

"She was much more highly strung than I remembered. You see I'd always envied her calm unruffled manner. She used to be so easy going."

I nodded in agreement, Josie's thoughts echoing my own.

"I began to look for reasons for the change in her and I'm afraid I put most of it down to Leonora's influence. Perhaps wrongly, who can say? Maybe I let my own prejudices colour my judgement. We will never know now."

"You don't think much of Leonora, do you?" I commented raising my glass to my lips.

"Let's just say we don't see eye to eye and leave it at that. It would be wrong of me to influence your opinion of her. All I would say is I felt as though I'd lost my friend many months before she died and it was something I found difficult to accept."

We were silent, each with our own memories. Henry grunted in his sleep and awoke with a start.

"Good Lord you two, cheer up. It's Christmas day. I suggest we plug in the old TV.

and pit our wits against that new computerised quiz our guest gave us for Christmas."

Henry's good humour lightened the mood and before long, we were laughing companionably as Christmas night fell. Outside, the snow had stopped, the sky was clear and stars twinkled in the frosty air. Silence lay around the house and its grounds, cushioned by the snowfall cradling us in an atmosphere of isolated contentment.

It was to be the first and last Christmas I spent with them both. Henry's optimistic toast for the coming year was fulfilled but not in quite the way he'd intended, when he'd raised his brandy glass aloft on that snowy Christmas afternoon.

Chapter 18

At the end of January, the editor of HI LIFE magazine contacted me. It seemed they were interested in doing a lifestyle spread for the magazine, complete with glossy photographs showing me at work and at home. At first I was surprised at the suggestion, contemplated giving an outright no as an answer, then after brief consideration changed my mind and accepted. The publicity would be good for Softcell, the money was a bonus and I could see no reason to refuse.

The photographer and reporter from the magazine met me in my office on a wet Thursday afternoon in the middle of February. The reporter was a lively young woman with a Knightsbridge accent who insisted on slanting the questions towards my love life and how I was managing being single. She was careful to avoid mentioning Evelyn but I sensed the topic remained hovering in the background.

I answered her questions, as truthfully as I could, whilst stressing there was no one special in my life and nothing of a romantic nature that could possible interest her readers.

When the interview ended, the photographer took photographs of me working at my computer, giving dictation to Alice Baines, and in conversation with my I.T. department. Before leaving, they arranged for us to meet again the

Taken at the Flood

following day at River House. The interviewer, whose name was Kate, explained she wanted to continue with photographs of my home and an in-depth conversation with me in that environment. Apparently each 'Lifestyle' piece was conducted in a similar manner. I accepted her explanation, having never to my knowledge delved into the pages of the magazine, although I had seen copies of it lying around when Evelyn was alive.

As I showered and dressed the following morning, I heard the sound of the vacuum cleaner drifting up from the floor below. Mrs Bates was cleaning the house from top to bottom in preparation for the visit. Fresh cut flowers adorned the hallway, sitting room and kitchen. There was even a small vase of snowdrops on my study windowsill.

The day dawned with no trace of the previous day's rain clouds remaining in a clear blue sky. The photographer suggested I sit in the conservatory with my back to the garden. Then he decided to take a few shots of me seated at my desk in the study before moving into the garden to photograph views of the house and the river.

Kate's questions were of a more personal nature this time. She wanted to know who had been responsible for the floral theme in the conservatory and the minimalist design of the kitchen and dining room. I gave perfunctory replies but I sensed her need to delve further into the life I'd shared with Evelyn. When she could see I wasn't going to satisfy the prurient nature of her readers, she switched off her tape machine and thanked me for the interview.

After they both left, I breathed a sigh of relief, my jaw aching from trying to smile without looking like a complete idiot and my muscles cramped from having to sit still for so long. I was beginning to realise the whole process had required more of me than I was prepared to give and had in fact earned the large sum of money the magazine was offering. Trying to look relaxed and casual had been more difficult than I'd anticipated.

During the first week of March I stood watching the daffodils bending back and forth in the strong wind blowing up the garden from the river, when Mrs Bates called to me from the kitchen. "Oh my word just look at this, sir." she exclaimed holding up the spring edition of HI LIFE magazine, complete with a glamorous picture of a well-known starlet on the cover. In one corner was a passport-sized photograph of myself above the words **Tycoon's riverside retreat. Full report - see page 5.** I opened the magazine with trepidation, to find the house looked very good indeed and as far as my photograph was concerned they had done the best of a bad job. But to my surprise Kate had made me sound like some sort of eligible prospect on the marriage market;-

The widower sits alone surrounded by peace and tranquillity with no one to share the fruits of his successs, except his faithful companion, a dog called Tinker.

The report of the interview sat under a photograph of me looking out at the garden with Tinker's head resting on my knee, a sorrowful expression in his dark brown eyes. I laughed out loud and to Mrs Bates's annoyance, tossed the magazine into the wastepaper basket. I later heard her remove it as I left the room to answer the telephone.

It was Josie. "Have you seen HI LIFE magazine?" she asked, unable to keep the excitement out of her voice.

I'd not mentioned my photo shoot to either of them, partly from a sense of embarrassment and partly because I thought it unlikely they would see the article anyway.

"I have indeed," I replied.

"I must say you look extremely handsome."

For the second time I laughed at the prospect. "It's miraculous what an airbrush and good lighting will do," I said.

"Nonsense, I think you'd better be prepared to receive a post-box full of letters from gold-digging females only too eager to share the 'fruits of your success'."

"God forbid," I replied

"Oh, I almost forgot; Henry wants to know if you'd like to go to Twickenham with him this weekend for the rugby international. He has acquired a spare ticket."

"Tell Henry, thanks. I'll pick him up at eleven on Saturday."

I doubted very much that Henry just happened to have a spare ticket. They were like gold to come by but my dear friend was still looking after my welfare and refusing to allow me to wallow in my hermitage. Although, after seeing the photographs of River House in the magazine, hermitage was perhaps the wrong word.

Josie's prediction turned out to be nearer the mark than I'm sure either of us had anticipated. Because, the week following the publication of the article, the first letters began to arrive and by the end of the week, I had a substantial pile waiting for my attention. Some contained photographs of women, in what I supposed were flattering poses, with accompanying letters, which if nothing else, did wonders for my ego. Others, were typewritten sheets of descriptive prose designed to whet my appetite for the undoubted pleasures that awaited me by arranging a meeting with their authors. At first I was vaguely amused but the larger the pile grew, the more I began to regret my willingness to put my life on display in what I now realised was an extremely popular magazine. The first

Taken at the Flood

letter I received from Switzerland made me also realise that the publication had a European network distribution, which fuelled my regret still further.

Leonora returned one sunny day in April, when I was sitting in the conservatory opening yet another pile of letters. The letters were arriving by the sack load now and I was getting to the stage where I thought it might be expedient to place them in the bin unopened but my curiosity got the better of me and I began systematically slitting the envelopes one by one. I was alone in the house except for Tinker, as Mrs Bates's sister was having one of her 'turns'. The faint aroma of recent baking wafted through the house from the direction of the kitchen, which was usually the case when Mrs Bates was preparing for her departure. She'd spent the morning baking and continued to assure me that the freezer was fully stocked, as I'd opened the taxi door and Morton Phillips had carried her away on a cloud of instructions, drifting like confetti in her wake.

I'd been reading the letters for some time before I was aware I was being watched. I looked up and there she was, standing outside the door to the conservatory, her pale blonde hair resting on the shoulders of her short beige fur jacket. She had been gently tapping the glass with her fingertips but I'd not heard her as I had turned up the volume on my sound system.

I opened the door. She raised her head, stood on tiptoes and kissed my cheek.

"Hullo," she said, as she slipped past me into the room. For a moment, I was speechless. "You don't seem very pleased to see me."

"I'm sorry," I replied. "It was just such a surprise seeing you standing there."

"I should have rung."

"No, no, not at all. When did you arrive?"

"Late last night." She removed her jacket and placed it over a chair.

"Is this a short visit? Or are you home for good?" I asked.

She looked at the pile of letters on the table and left my question unanswered.

"I see you seem to be extraordinarily popular, judging by your mail."

"Oh that," I laughed and went on to explain about the magazine article.

"I know," she said, as she sat opposite me. "I saw it. In fact, in a way, it's responsible for my being here."

"It is?" I queried, unable to think why that should be the case.

She picked up one of the opened letters attached to which was a photograph of a redhead in a bikini.

"And it looks as though I was just in time to save you from a fate worse than death!" she exclaimed and I heard again the tinkling laughter floating around her like a gossamer cloud.

It occurred to me then that Leonora often left a question unanswered, preferring to steer the conversation in a direction of her own making. So, I persevered with my former question. "Why should reading the magazine article precipitate your arrival?"

She hesitated, glanced at me briefly and said enigmatically, "I think the answer will become clearer in time."

I shrugged. I could see I was getting nowhere. "Anyway whatever the reason, it is good to see you. You will stay and help me eat the mound of steak and kidney pie Mrs Bates has left for me, won't you?"

"I thought you'd never ask," she replied standing up and holding her hand out towards me. "Point me in the direction of the pie and I'll make sure it's warmed up to perfection."

I laid the table in the dining room, whilst Leonora was busy in the kitchen and for some reason used the cutlery Evelyn and I kept for entertaining; it gleamed like gold in the light from the overhead chandelier. Then I went down to the basement and searched the wine store for my finest bottle. I felt in the mood to celebrate and realised that my spirits had lifted from the moment I'd looked up and seen Leonora standing outside.

Taken at the Flood

We ate the meal in companionable silence, after which we drank coffee in the sitting room and watched the moonlight turning the river to a thread of silver, slowly winding its way along the riverbank. Leonora stood up and walked across to the bar in the corner of the room. Evelyn and I had created a small games area alongside the bar, consisting of a roulette wheel, she'd bought for me after a holiday in Las Vegas, a card table and a carved chess set, I'd inherited from my parents. Leonora reappeared holding up an unopened pack of cards. "Do you play poker?" she asked.

I frowned. "I haven't played for years but I don't think I've forgotten the basics. I may be a bit rusty though."

"Excellent, so much the better." She smiled, tossing her hair over one shoulder.

I placed a small card table between us and held out my hand for the cards but she ignored me and after slowly removing the cellophane wrapper, kept her eyes glued to mine in a most disconcerting way. Then she took the pack in her right hand, tapped them on the surface of the table once, held the top of the pack with her thumbs and, with her fingertips lightly resting at each side, shuffled the cards as neatly as any croupier I'd seen during my stay in the gaming capital of the world.

I whistled softly, "Very impressive!"

Taken at the Flood

Her eyes still holding mine, she said softly, "Merely a trick I was taught many years ago."

I was to discover later her expertise in handling the cards, was not her only attribute. If we had been playing for money, instead of matchsticks, she would have made a killing.

"As you can see I was being honest, I'm a bit rusty, I'm afraid," I explained lamely, as I scooped up the cards and laid them on the table between us. She made no comment, as the clock above the fireplace struck midnight. I looked up shocked at how quickly the time had passed.

"I must go," she said, rushing away from me like Cinderella at the last stroke.

"I'll drive you home." I offered

"No, you've had too much to drink. It's no problem I'll walk back the way I came. Perhaps I could borrow a torch?"

"Nonsense, at least let me walk you home."

She nodded and as we walked into the kitchen, Tinker sauntered out of the utility room, sensing a walk might be in the air. Leonora patted his head and he nuzzled up against her leg.

"Tinker, here boy, leave Leonora alone," I commanded.

"It's all right, really," she said, patting her side as Tinker resumed his formed position.

I raised an eyebrow. "I thought you had an allergy to dogs?"

"Me? No, whatever made you think that?" she asked.

"Something I heard once. Maybe I was wrong." I frowned at the memory.

We didn't need the torch. The moon shone out of a star-studded sky bathing the ground in silvered light. It was a crisp April night and not a breath of wind stirred the surface of the river as we walked along the path. When we reached the bottom of her garden, the security lights came on bathing the lawn in bright light. Leonora turned to face me.

"Thanks for tonight. I really enjoyed myself."

"Me too," I said, mesmerised by her face shining ghostly white surrounded by a curtain of silver hair.

She turned away and before I knew it, she was standing at her back door, leaving me with a sinking feeling of loss. I think it had been in my mind that she might do as she had done previously and brushed her lips against mine, in a gesture of thanks. When it turned out not to be the case, I felt cheated and strangely disappointed. I waited until she disappeared through the doorway and turned on the kitchen light then retraced my steps but the beauty of the moonlit night failed to penetrate my thoughts as I made my solitary way home.

That night I tossed and turned in the large double bed, unable to remove the picture of Leonora from my mind. At six o'clock I decided

Taken at the Flood

enough was enough I would get up and work in my study. Assembling protocols, analysing data and structuring new software would focus my mind on something other than Leonora Bennett. For the first time in my life, I found work did not produce the necessary anaesthesia to numb my senses. I stared into my computer screen seeing nothing but her face, her moonlit hair and those eyes, which I knew had fascinated me ever since I first saw them in Venice, a lifetime ago.

I closed down my computer, called to Tinker and decided to walk through the woods to clear my head. It was early and as soon as we entered the path through the woods, Tinker saw a rabbit and raced off after it, like one of the hounds of hell. I sauntered behind knowing that before long I would meet up with him, probably having lost the trail, with his nose stuck in a burrow.

I'd walked further than usual and the woods opened out into fields bordered by trees covered in the green shoots of spring. A footpath led over the fields to the village of Kings Datchet and I saw a tall figure, two dogs at her heels, striding towards me from the direction of the village. I would have recognised Josie anywhere but as if in confirmation, I heard Tinker barking behind me as he recognised the dogs. He raced past me through the fence and along the path until he reached Josie, who looked up, saw me and increased her pace.

"Hullo you. Enjoying the spring sunshine?" she panted, her breath billowing around her in the frosty air.

"I am indeed. You look energetic."

"I've walked over to Kings Datchet. Henry's got a cold, poor thing. I've been to the chemist's for some cough medicine."

I sympathised and asked her to pass on my regards to Henry.

"You'll never guess who I saw in the chemist's?" Josie slipped her arm through mine and I helped her over the style.

"Leonora Bennett," I said.

"How? Oh you've spoiled my surprise. I must admit I didn't think we'd be seeing her again. I had it in mind she might put the house on the market and leave the area."

"What made you think that?" I asked falling into step alongside her as the dogs bounded off through the woodland.

"Oh I don't know. I suppose I've always had the feeling that she was more drawn to Italy than here. I know Lucas mentioned, on more than one occasion, he'd thought of retiring there. I think he felt it would please her if he suggested it. Poor Lucas, I still can't quite believe he's gone too."

We were silent for a while and then Josie asked, "When did you see Leonora?"

"She called over last night. I was reading through more of those letters and suddenly she was there, outside the conservatory. It gave me quite a shock."

"I can imagine. Had she seen the magazine article by any chance?" She stopped to catch her breath for a moment waiting for my reply.

"She had, as a matter of fact. Why do you ask?"

Josie gave me what my mother would have described as an 'old fashioned look', drew in her breath and started to walk on. "No special reason. I just wondered that's all."

We reached the river path to find the dogs standing over the body of a small shrew, looking up at us and eagerly awaiting congratulatory pats. "I must be off or Henry will wonder where I've got to. He's always like a bear with a sore head when he has a cold. Don't forget to pop over and see us when you have time?"

"I won't," I assured her and, calling Tinker, started to walk back to River House.

The telephone was ringing as I opened the back door. I picked up the kitchen extension. It was her. "Hi. Would you like to see if you can win back the matchsticks you lost last night?" she asked.

I didn't hesitate. "Try and stop me,"

"Good, my place at eight then."

My face was stretched into a wide grin as I replaced the receiver.

Taken at the Flood

That night was the start of it. She was waiting for me, dressed in a flowing white silk shift that took my breath away. Standing on tiptoe, she removed my coat from my shoulders and was so close I could smell her perfume and feel the warmth of her body through my shirt.

I can't quite remember what we ate; all I remember was her eyes. They seemed to bore into my soul. I think she let me win at cards but I can't be sure. I know I drank too much and so did she. We laughed a lot and flirted with each other and as the evening wore on, I became desperate to take her to bed, my desperation increasing as she kissed me goodnight. This time no mere brush of lips but a tender lingering pressure, her mouth slightly open, so I could taste her tongue. I held her close, feeling the softness of her body through the thin silk of her dress. I drew her even closer and kissed her with a passion that was threatening to explode within me but when we parted for air, I heard her say. "Goodnight, Mr Hope until the next time?"

I wanted to pick her up and carry her up the stairs to the bedroom but something in her expression held the assurance of much, much more for the future if I did not force the issue, so I held her hand up to my lips and kissed it gently. "Until the next time," I promised.

Chapter 19

The following morning I awoke with an excited feeling in the pit of my stomach, like childhood Christmas's when I'd scrambled from my bed to see if *'he'd'* come, but this was no Christmas morning and I was no longer a child. Waiting to see Leonora, to continue what I felt had begun the previous evening, was as frustrating as poking the brightly wrapped presents under the Christmas tree with the end of my finger until finally being allowed to open them.

I was pulling on my jeans, after taking a cold shower to restore my equilibrium, when the telephone rang. I rushed to the phone; it had to be her. "Sorry to bother you, Boss." It was Alan Henderson and my disappointment showed in the reflection staring back at me in the bedroom mirror. "Maxwell Hutton's been on the line from New York. He wants to see you, said he'd tried your house yesterday but couldn't get hold of you. He needs to discuss an urgent matter, something about a follow up to *Centaur*?"

"Damn. Can't you put him off?"

"'Fraid not. I did try my best but he was adamant."

"OK, OK. I'll ring him." I glanced at my bedside clock. It would be 2.30 a.m. in New York. "I'll leave it until this afternoon."

"I wouldn't, Boss. His last words were 'Tell him to ring me at home. I don't care what the time is. I want to see him over here on the next plane."

My heart sank. Megacells were our biggest distributor in the States and I didn't want to upset their Chief Executive. "Right, thanks, Alan. I'll get back to you," I said, as I replaced the receiver and dialled Hutton's number.

Alan hadn't exaggerated; he was insistent, saying he had to see me at once, there was a deal in the air and he had to get some first hand details from me before he could give his assurances that he could come up with the goods. This could be a very lucrative deal for both of us he stressed.

From then on, it was one mad rush. I had my secretary book the first available flight on Concorde from Heathrow, which turned out to be at one o'clock that day. I tried to ring Leonora but the phone kept ringing, without the satisfying click of the answer phone cutting in. It was a close thing but I managed to make the flight with minutes to spare.

Later, in my room at the Plaza, I slept soundly until my travel alarm woke me. I felt refreshed and ready for my meeting with Maxwell Hutton. I tried to ring Leonora again but there was still no reply from her number.

Taken at the Flood

Hutton was alone in his office when I arrived. *Minotaur* was completed and with a few minor last minute adjustments, I assured him, it would be ready for distribution. After I had apprised him of its capabilities, he leaned back in his chair and lit a fat cigar, a smile creasing his plump face. "Too big a deal to lose son. Had to see it for myself before going ahead."

He was content with the last of the *Gorgon* trilogy. It appeared the panic was over.

"There's something else I'd like you take a look at whilst I'm here," I said, removing *Minotaur* from my laptop. I slipped my PSD into a USB port and transferred the files. It was an outline of the new project with the working title *Andromeda*. I knew it to be a revolutionary concept so was unwilling to give too much away at its inception but even so Hutton seemed excited by the prospect of becoming our U.S. distributor. He was no fool and could see the potential immediately.

"I must point out," I stressed, "this concept is in its infancy. The first module will not be available much before the end of November."

"No problem," he said, shaking my hand across the desk. "This is better than I could have hoped for. I now have something I can work with and the prospect of another project in the making." He inhaled the smoke and coughed. "But I don't want you to run off back to England just at the moment, son. There are some people I want you to meet. I'm having a party on Friday and I'd like you to be there. I promise you it will be worth your while." He rose and walked around the desk to where I stood ready to leave then placed a friendly arm around my shoulder, the smoke from his cigar making my eyes water.

"You will say yes, now won't you? Louanne is dying to meet you. I've told her so much about my soft spoken English genius that she's insisting I don't take no for an answer."

What could I say? "I'll be delighted, see you the day after tomorrow," I said, backing out of his office in an effort to escape what I was afraid was going to turn out to be a bear hug.

That night I dreamed of Evelyn. She was standing in our garden at the edge of the river. She seemed to be floating just above the surface of the ground. She was trying to tell me something and was smiling, her arms outstretched. As I drew nearer she whispered, 'I'm happy for you. I loved Leo,' and with that her image dissolved. I awoke, the dream still vivid, and found I felt extraordinarily calm. My mind was clear, the future mapped out for me with an unusual clarity. I saw my life, as it could be with Leonora, and was impatient to begin the journey.

The feeling of elation persisted as I walked down Fifth Avenue. I had the day to myself, I was in New York and the spring sunshine was flooding Central Park with colour illuminating the shades of greens as effectively as floodlights on a football pitch. I turned up the collar of my coat against the cool breeze, which swept across the park and stood watching a young mother and toddler feeding the ducks. The young birds were crowding around them in eager anticipation, and it was the sound of their hungry cries that accompanied me as I walked through the park and out into Fifth Avenue where, as in another life, I'd headed for Tiffany's. This time I knew exactly what I was after. I took the escalator to the third floor and walked towards the counter holding trays of diamond rings.

The assistant nodded in my direction and I smiled. I was standing in front of a glass counter under which stood a raised plinth supporting just one ring. The diamond was large, square cut and burned with a pale blue fire, which emanated from its centre and splayed out as its facets caught the light. It was perfect. It matched the colour of her eyes exactly.

"See anything you like, sir?" the assistant asked, hopefully.

"Yes, this one." I pointed and saw the assistant hesitate.

"That is a very special diamond, if I may say so, sir." He looked at me uncertainly and I could see he was trying to assess whether I could be in the financial bracket, which would allow me to possess such a gem. He seemed unsure.

"It's for a very special lady," I said.

"Well in that case, may I suggest we have our security men stand by, as we remove it to enable you to inspect the ring at close quarters?" He held a chair for me to sit down and placed the ring in my hand. I held it up for inspection.

"It's beautiful. I'll take it."

The assistant coughed, discreetly showed me the price tag and waited. His anxious expression disappeared as I handed him my platinum card.

"Would sir like me to have it sent around to his hotel?"

I was about to say no that I'd take it but remembered this was New York, so I wrote down the number of my room at the Plaza and left feeling happy and contented.

I decided to walk for a while and for the first time noticed how bright everything seemed. The inhabitants of New York appeared a breed apart, smiling and chatting with each other as they passed me. I was looking at the world through a haze of happiness. The expression 'walking on air' was clear to me as I drifted on a cloud of euphoria towards my hotel.

When the ring arrived, I placed it in my room safe then later dressed for the Huttons' party without much enthusiasm. As I'd anticipated, the party was a boring affair and I couldn't wait to make my excuses to leave. At the first opportunity, I thanked my hosts, promised to keep in touch and left by yellow cab for the sanctuary of my hotel room.

Closing the door behind me, I walked to the bed and picked up the phone from the bedside table in order to ring Leonora. At last, I heard her pick up the receiver.

"It's me. I've tried to ring you before but you must have been out. Did you get my message about New York, your answer phone cut out the second time I rang?"

Once more, she ignored my question.

"God, I've missed you," she said, in a breathless voice.

"I'll be home as soon as I can," I promised and put down the receiver to ring the airport. I was in luck there was a spare seat on a flight leaving in four hours' time. I hurriedly pushed my clothes into my case and checked out of the hotel, the ring in the inside pocket of my overcoat. Inside the cab taking me to the airport, I told the taxi driver to hurry. I was anxious for my new life was about to begin.

The flight and taxi ride home seemed endless, although in fact both Concorde and my awaiting car made good time. Throughout the journey, I kept seeing Leonora, as I had last seen her, standing in her garden bathed in moonlight.

When I reached River House, I opened the front door and walked through into the kitchen to wash my hands. There was someone sitting in the back porch. I could see the outline of a figure against the glass. The house was quiet and the kitchen in darkness. I felt a stirring of unease as I gingerly opened the door and Leonora fell backwards into the room. She'd been leaning against the glass and I suspected she'd been waiting for some time.

I took her in my arms and kissed her with all the pent up passion within me exploding with a force that surprised us both. She laughed nervously. "Oh good, you've missed me too."

Then I picked her up and carried her gently upstairs to the bedroom. I could feel her hair brushing against my arms and smell the damp rising from her clothes.

Removing her wax jacket, jumper and jeans with trembling hands, I kissed her like a drowning man grasping at a life raft then in desperation tore off my clothes and led her into the shower room. We made love in the shower, the water spilling around and over our bodies as we urgently satisfied our desires.

Later, in bed, sliding beneath cool silk sheets, I took her to me gently, caressing every part of her with such tenderness that is only possible when both love and lust are satisfied in one glorious moment. Her skin was as soft as the dew on the grass and at her touch my body reacted as if I'd been stroked by a thousand fingertips, each one intent on finding the places that pleasured me the most. It is impossible to

Taken at the Flood

find the words to adequately describe how it felt making love with Leonora; if I were a poet then maybe, I'd stand a chance.

Comparisons, I know, are odious and I wouldn't dream of comparing what Evelyn and I shared to my present situation but that night I felt as if I'd experienced true ecstasy for the first time in my life.

Afterwards, she sighed, her blonde hair fanning over my chest, her warm breath rippling over me as she gently tugged the hair at the nape of my neck until our lips met once more. "I was afraid I'd imagined the other night and when I couldn't find you I thought you'd left because you couldn't bear to be with me," she said, looking up at me.

"So you didn't get my message?"

"There's something wrong with the answer phone. I was trying to record a new message and the tape must have jammed. I couldn't bear to keep hearing Lucas's voice. It was too upsetting."

She shivered and I drew her to me once more.

Leonora never again lived at the house she once shared with Lucas Bennett. The week following my visit to New York, we spent mostly in bed, sometimes on the rug in front of the log fire and occasionally on the large pine kitchen table much to Tinker's disgust. I'd picked him up from the kennels earlier in the week and he seemed almost as pleased as me to see Leonora living in the house.

Early on the following Monday morning, I heard a noise downstairs. I'd been nuzzling Leonora's neck and emerged from her curtain of hair just as I heard a key turn in the lock in the front door. Jumping out of bed, I tucked a towel around my waist, and was halfway down the stairs followed by Leonora, who had the foresight to pull on a silk dressing gown, as Mrs Bates appeared from the confines of the downstairs cloakroom. The expression on her face was one of shock as she looked behind me.

"Oh! I didn't realise you were entertaining, sir. I'm sorry if I've disturbed you."

I cleared my throat. "Not at all, Mrs Bates. In fact, I'm glad that you are here. You must be the first to hear our good news. Leonora has consented to be my wife."

To be fair to Mrs Bates, she rearranged her expression very well but I could see that, quite naturally, the news had come as a great shock. "Congratulations to you both, I'm sure," she stammered, sitting down heavily on the chair in the hallway.

"Show Mrs Bates the ring, Leo, while I put something on," I urged her, my pride, at seeing her wearing the diamond ring, demanding to be shared.

Taken at the Flood

I shot up the stairs two at a time and was pulling on my jeans when I realised I had called her Leo.

Looking back now, I realise anyone who knew Leonora reacted to her with an intensity of emotion, which was difficult to explain. Evelyn's friendship with her had been intense. Mrs Bates had disliked her fervently, which was unusual in such a placid woman and Josie? Sweet, even-tempered Josie had hated her. And what about me? I felt a passion, the strength of which was frightening. She invaded my senses to the exclusion of all else often robbing me of rational thought. At those times, all I could think about was her face, her body and our lovemaking. She was an opiate inflaming my emotions and heightening my desire as effectively as any Class A drug. Henry was the only person I knew who was unaffected by her. He had no strong feelings about her either one way or the other.

Chapter 20

I believe Mrs Bates made a half-hearted attempt to like Leonora but I could see the struggle she had to keep a civil tongue in her head. I don't know exactly what drove her to act in the way she did, except I sensed she thought the two of us were unseemly in our haste to remarry, especially Leonora, as it had only been six months since Lucas died. However, we both ignored the frosty looks she gave us and accepted her hostility in the hope she would thaw out before too long.

I admit to feeling uncomfortable about not telling Henry and Josie of our good news. We were so immersed in each other we couldn't think of anyone else. It was an omission, which we had to remedy so one sunny morning, when the birds woke us early with their dawn chorus, I persuaded Leo to walk the river path with me to their house. The sun was warm, the woods to our left carpeted with bluebells the scent filling our nostrils as we walked, arms entwined, enjoying the peace and tranquillity of a beautiful May morning. When we came to the section of the path near her house, Leonora stopped, held her hand up to her face, the diamond gleaming in the sunshine and then standing on tiptoe kissed me gently on the lips. She held her hand out in front of her and twisting the ring to catch the light, said, "You're not going to like this. I'm not coming with you."

"Why not? It's not the ring is it? You don't feel embarrassed by the fact that it's so obvious? You shouldn't let Mrs Bates upset you. We should ignore her mutterings. She'll soon forget it all when some other event takes her interest."

She laughed, "No it's not Mrs Bates. I just don't see eye to eye with Josie and I know she's not going to be pleased. You go, make some excuse for me. I need to sort out a few things at home and now is as good a time as any. Pick me up on your way back. I'll wait for you." She started to walk up the lawn and I could see it was useless trying to change her mind. At the top of the steps leading to her back porch, she turned and blew me a kiss.

But the pleasure of the morning was lost to me as I dragged my feet reluctantly towards the Dangerfields' house. Henry was sitting on the back terrace, his knees covered by a red plaid rug. He was reading the morning paper. "Hello there, it's good to see you. We wondered where you had got to," he said, as I approached.

"Hullo, Henry. Is Josie about? I've something to tell you both."

"No, gone to the hairdresser's in Kings Datchet. She left me out here to have an airing as she put it. Pull up a chair and tell me all your news."

I'd hoped I could tell them together as I'd wanted to see what their joint reaction would be but I had no alternative.

"Leonora and I are getting married," I blurted out.

Henry's paper slid to the ground. He managed not to look too surprised but I could see the corner of his mouth twitching for a second or two. "Well, er, congratulations and good luck to you both. I'm so glad the two of you have found happiness again." He held out his hand and I shook it eagerly.

"Thank you, Henry. You don't think it's too soon then?"

"Nonsense. Why wait? You are both of an age to know your own minds, I should imagine. This calls for a celebration. Pop into the study, I've a good malt whiskey in the bottom drawer of my desk."

When I returned, we drank each other's health and were starting to drink a second when I heard Josie's car in the drive.

"Good Lord," she exclaimed, walking towards us. "What are you two doing drinking whiskey at eleven o'clock in the morning?"

"We're celebrating a marriage, my dear," said Henry raising his glass.

Josie looked at me with a blank expression on her face.

"Leonora and me," I explained.

Taken at the Flood

I don't know what I expected but I was not prepared for what followed. "No. No, you can't, you mustn't, tell him Henry."

Henry's glass was half way to his mouth, which had fallen open in surprise at his wife's reaction.

"I don't understand…" I began.

"Leonora Bennett is trouble. I know it and Henry knows it. I'm sorry to be so blunt but you need to hear the truth."

"I don't understand? Henry?" I looked at him imploringly.

"None of our business, old thing." Henry patted Josie's arm. She was still very agitated but was trying to control herself.

"No, of course not. I apologise," she said hurriedly. "You must excuse me, I have things to do in the kitchen."

I placed my glass on the table at Henry's side.

"Don't take too much notice of Josie. You know what women are like. She's taken a fierce dislike to Leonora, something to do with Evelyn and their friendship no doubt."

I thanked Henry for the whiskey and stood up saying, "I hope Josie will forget the past and try and make friends with Leo. You are such good friends. I wouldn't like to lose touch with you both."

Henry nodded and I could feel him watching me as I retraced my steps along the river path.

Soon afterwards, Leonora put the Bennett house up for sale. The property market was good and a young entrepreneur, who wanted to buy it as an investment, snapped it up almost immediately. Apparently, he wouldn't be living there himself but his widowed mother would be moving in as soon as the sale was completed.

Throughout the months of May and June, Mrs Bates spent less and less time at River House. Her sister seemed to require her company more frequently than in the past I observed and wondered if it was merely an excuse to get away from us.

I remember returning home one hot sunny afternoon in June to find Leo sunbathing on the back lawn. She was wearing an acid yellow bikini that barely covered her. I stood and watched her for a moment until she became aware of me. Then she stood up, took my hand and led me through the French doors into the conservatory, across the hall and up the main staircase to our bedroom. Neither of us spoke. She undressed me sensuously and slowly. And all I had to do was undo three little knots.

Later, I watched her dressing in a cool white cotton shirt and shorts. "Leo, why don't we get married abroad?"

"Where?" she said brushing her hair, her back to me.

Taken at the Flood

"Venice," I said. Her hand stopped for a second and then continued brushing vigorously.

"When?"

"As soon as possible. What do you think?"

"Fine," she replied still without looking at me. "Just give me enough time to buy some sort of wedding dress."

I spun her around to face me. "I can't wait to make you my wife," I said.

Her expression was guarded; the joy I'd hoped to see there was not in evidence. I held her at arms length. "You do want to get married?" I asked

"I was just thinking of poor Lucas," she said, burying her head in my shoulder.

I had to be satisfied with her explanation but I can't deny, it unnerved me.

Preparations for our wedding began immediately. I called in at the office, spoke with Alan Henderson about the *Andromeda* project, and my inability to make a start on it due to my wedding and what I hoped would be a prolonged honeymoon. However, I was anxious to see that my promise to Maxwell Hutton was fulfilled and so spent the following week with Chip Thornley outlining the programme, which he would be in charge of completing upon my instructions. I felt confident I could leave it in his capable hands, as I'd not been disappointed

Taken at the Flood

with his previous work and admired his ingenuity.

Later in the week, I called in at the Head Office of Thomas Cook and arranged for the ceremony as well as booking the hotel for our stay in Venice. I was so busy I hardly saw Leonora during the days that followed and found delight in the longed for evenings when we could enjoy each other anew. Her shopping trips were a closely guarded secret but I sensed her excitement and saw the twinkle in her blue eyes when I questioned her about them at the end of the day.

It was around this time she re-christened me. We'd been to see a musical in the West End and were threading our way down Shaftesbury Avenue with the rest of the theatregoers, making for a little Italian restaurant I knew in Soho. I caught her hand in mine and pulled her down a side street, much to her delight, as she was unaware where it led. Then we turned a corner bringing us into the heart of Soho. In front of us was a nightclub, trendy, bright and lit by flashing neon lights. To one side of the doorway, where a bouncer, with fists like hammers, stood suspiciously eyeing the street, was an advertising board showing the interior and a couple of exotic dancers. Someone had plastered a sticker across the rear end of one of the dancers. It was some sort of religious text and read ABe AN DON HOPE ALL WHO

Taken at the Flood

ENTER HERE. Someone with a blue felt pen had added and e to the first word. To my surprise, Leonora fell into fits of laughter, "Abe and Don Hope. That's it! From now on you will always be Abe to me."

"Oh very funny," I said, drawing her close to me as a crowd of revellers threatened to part us.

The date for our wedding day was set; it was to be the first day of July. At the end of June, we sat in the first class compartment of an Alitalia jet as Italy spread out beneath us like an animated map. It was early evening and the light was beginning to fade when we entered Venice. By the time we were sitting in a water taxi negotiating the traffic on the Grand Canal, darkness had fallen. The lights from the Hotel Cipriani shimmered on the surface of the water and as we approached, a doorman resplendent in red greatcoat and top hat trimmed with gold braid helped us alight at the hotel's jetty.

The first time I'd seen her was in Venice but Evelyn and I had been staying in a small, clean but shabby hotel in a side street. The view from our window then had been the lichen-covered walls of the building opposite and if we squeezed our heads to one side of the window frame, we were able to see the muddy brown waters of the canal, which was too narrow even for a gondola to pass through.

Taken at the Flood

I looked around me at the splendid furnishings of our suite; the crystal chandelier carved out of the finest Venetian glass gleaming above our heads, the bowl of fruit and chilled champagne waiting for us on a table in front of the window, the best that money could buy. However, the time I'd spent in a run down hotel in a back street was a memory I wouldn't forget. I must have sighed because Leo put her hands around my chest and looked up at me through eyes that put the waters of the Grand Canal to shame.

"You OK?" she asked.

"I'm fine, just amazed by this view. Where else on earth could you wake up to a view as splendid as this?"

I pointed to the Grand Canal, which was lit by the traffic passing along its length. Water taxis ferrying passengers home after a busy day at the office, sightseers relaxing in the back of gondolas, lovers, their arms entwined, oblivious of the view and families their faces aglow with the wonder of it all. We stood and watched for a moment then I filled our glasses with champagne as we toasted our forthcoming wedding with joy and thankfulness that we'd found each other.

The following day we spent sightseeing, enjoying the romance of the place, which should always be seen by lovers. Its serenity, a welcome change from the hustle and bustle of modern life, enthralled us.

"I keep forgetting," I said, as we strolled behind the Doge's Palace towards the old residential quarter with its charming bridges and park, "this is not new to you. You've seen it all before."

"No, I've never visited Venice. This is my first time; you must be mixing me up with someone else, Evelyn perhaps?"

I was shocked. Why would she lie about such a thing? After all I'd seen her with my own eyes. It made no sense, why would it matter whether she'd been to Venice or not? She was waiting for a reply.

"Yes, I expect so," I muttered taking her hand and leading her into the park.

When we were back in our hotel room dressing for dinner, I checked my mobile for messages. It was a habit I'd been unable to break. Leo was in the shower. I could hear her singing a song in Italian, her sweet voice soaring above the sound of the water jets.

The voicemail message was unexpectedly from Josie and the sound of her voice concerned me that there might be something wrong with Henry.

I'm sorry to make this voicemail call. I thought it might be less embarrassing for you under the circumstances and it does mean you'll have to listen to me without cutting me off in mid sentence. I know you're not going to like what I'm about to say but I couldn't rest until I cleared it from my mind. You know I care about you. Please listen when I say DON'T marry her. Remember, none of us knows much about Leonora Bennett. Lucas knew next to nothing and now he's dead. I'm frightened for you. Please don't think this is the raving of a disturbed woman because that's what it sounds like to me. All I can say again is please, please, be careful!

I looked at my mobile as if it were going to supply the answer and held it up to my ear once more. No, I hadn't imagined the message. I frowned and pressed the delete button but throughout the eve of my wedding, I was uneasy and it was difficult not to show it. In the event, I drank too much wine and too many brandies and fell into bed to sleep the sleep of the inebriate. If Leonora thought it unusual, she made no comment but simply passed me a glass of cool spring water and two painkillers as soon as I opened my eyes and blinked at the morning sun, which was streaming through our window.

When my head ceased pounding, I walked out on to the veranda where she was sitting reading an Italian magazine. "Sorry about last night," I said, kissing the top of her head. She just smiled and turned the pages of her magazine. I sat down beside her and slid the magazine from her hand. "You don't have any doubts about marrying me?" I asked

To my surprise, she started to cry. I went to her and cradled her in my arms. "It's not too late if you want to back out." I was beginning to feel afraid of her answer.

"I will never want to back out of our marriage. Never."

She wiped the tears away with the back of her hand. "I was worried *you* may have been having second thoughts and it was why you drank too much last night."

I sighed, holding her tightly. "I think we are a pair of fools. I love you, Mrs Hope and by the end of today I'll show you how much you being my wife means to me."

Through the heat haze, which was hanging over the Grand Canal, I heard the faint engine noise of a water taxi and the lapping of water against its sides as it sped past our hotel. I watched it pass by, comparatively empty at this early hour, and saw a couple, their arms entwined, standing in the back of the boat. The girl was wearing a straw hat, a tendril of fair hair escaping and blowing in the breeze as it fell and settled against her cheek. For a moment I drew in my breath sharply, she reminded me of Leonora when I'd first seen her. Although now I wondered if my memory had failed me, was it

Taken at the Flood

Leonora I'd seen all those years ago and if so why had she lied to me?

Chapter 21

At eleven o'clock on the morning of the first of July we stood outside the Palazzo Cavalli. The day was warming up nicely and I could feel the sun on the back of my neck and penetrating my beige linen suit. A row of gondolas bobbed up and down on the surface of the water and the traffic on the Grand Canal had increased since I'd seen the girl and the youth in the water taxi, earlier that morning.

Leonora was dressed in a simple blue dress, which matched the colour of her eyes and had piled her hair up on top of her head, soft tendrils escaping around her face as we held hands and walked towards the building. "Wait," she said, "we have to find someone to be our witnesses.

I laughed, saying, "There'll be plenty of staff willing to act for us, inside.

"No, it's more romantic to find someone in the street," she insisted, whilst looking around her.

A middle-aged woman carrying a shopping bag passed by and smiled at us. Leonora approached her and speaking in fluent Italian persuaded her to act as our witness. Then she noticed a young man with a shock of fair hair falling over his forehead.

"Ask him," Leonora urged. "He looks as if he might be English."

Taken at the Flood

He was in fact Italian but spoke excellent English and said he would be honoured to assist us.

So it was an unusual quartet that entered the Palazzo Cavalli for our civil marriage ceremony, whilst in the distance the bells from the campanile in St Mark's Square rang in our ears.

Time passed with the speed of light as we said the necessary words in front of the registrar, exchanged our rings and signed the register. I shook hands with our witnesses, thanking them for their help and for a fraction of a second, as I shook the hand of the young man, a strange feeling of déjà vu swept over me. I looked into his face and felt I'd seen him somewhere before.

The feeling passed, as Leo insisted we have a photograph taken with our witnesses before we went our separate ways. The clerk, who took the photograph for us, smiled as he returned the camera to Leonora. I watched the young man, who was our witness, disappear in the direction of the Rialto Bridge, and kissed my new wife. "Now, Mrs Hope I'm going to show you how to have a good time in Venice."

Picking her up, amid much laughter and smiles, I carried her into the waiting gondola, instructing the gondolier to take us back to the Hotel Villa Cipriani so that our honeymoon could really begin.

Taken at the Flood

The days drifted lazily by, filled with love and pleasure at being together. We had eyes for no one but each other. Although it was the height of the holiday season and there was the inevitable throng of sightseers, when Leo and I sat in St Mark's Square drinking coffee and listening to music played by a trio of musicians, there was no one else in the whole world but us.

We spent three weeks in Venice. Those were days during which we strolled through the narrow streets, drank wine in tiny bars frequented by the locals, dined in expensive restaurants and shopped in the chic boutiques and jewellery shops surrounding St Mark's Square. Shops, where if you needed to ask the price of an item, you couldn't afford it! We visited museums housing some of Italy's finest art collections and marvelled at the differing architectural styles of the buildings as we lay back in a gondola drifting down the narrow waterways, sunshine caressing our skin. It was one of the happiest times of my life.

After Venice, I hired a car and we travelled to Naples, Sorrento and the Amalfi coast, staying in hotels where and when the fancy took us. I chartered a boat and we cruised around the coast, sunbathing naked on the deck and diving into the deep blue water to cool off.

Later, I drove northwards to Florence where we visited the Uffizi Art Gallery wandering around its multitudinous rooms filled with the finest of paintings and sculptures, pausing from time to time to admire the view from windows looking down on the busy walkway below, where people hurrying by looked like worker ants.

Leo insisted on taking a photograph of me, blinking in the sunshine, in front of the bronze statue of David. The panoramic view of Florence stretched out behind her as she positioned the camera. She fell in love with that photograph, calling it Leonora's Abe, in honour of Michelangelo's David and when we returned to River House she insisted on mounting it in a small silver frame which she placed on her bedside table where, she informed me, it would be the last thing she would look at before she went to sleep.

We were travelling along a country road towards Tuscany when I suggested, as we were in the area, it might be nice to visit her aunt. It seemed an innocuous suggestion but I was unprepared for what was to follow. Her reaction was uncharacteristic. She paused, nervously plucking at the rim of her cotton jacket with her fingertips.

"Leo? What do you think?" I persisted

Biting her bottom lip, her voice almost inaudible, she said, "No, It's not a good idea, Abe."

"Oh I just thought……" I began.

"Thank you, but my aunt does not welcome visitors. She's a very private person and not at all well at the moment."

"We need not stay. I thought perhaps she'd be pleased to see us and as we're so near it seems a shame not to visit."

Her tone hardened and the sharpness in her voice took me by surprise, as she replied, "I said, no. Please leave it alone."

I did not comment further and the silence grew between us, like an impenetrable hedge. Later, when the road forked in two I took the left-hand fork towards Rome. I judged that by the distance on the signpost we would arrive in the Italian capital around teatime. We drove on in silence and I hated every moment of it but decided she would have to calm down and explain before I could trust myself to speak. As the kilometres sped away, I sensed her relaxing beside me and then felt her hand creeping along my leg until it rested on my knee.

"I'm sorry, Abe," she said, the anger in her voice having subsided. I'll explain it all to you one day, trust me. It's a long story but now is not the time nor the place."

I placed my hand on top of hers. "We'll say no more about it, darling. Let's forget this morning and look forward to spending time in Rome."

Taken at the Flood

As it turned, out our visit to Rome was destined to be shorter than planned; we had at best a few days when my mobile rang. It was Alan Henderson apologising for the call but Chip Thornley had hit a snag with *Andromeda* and he needed my advice urgently, otherwise the project would not meet our expected target date.

Leo was philosophical when I told her the news. "Never mind we've had the most marvellous time. It had to end sometime and as long as we are together, I don't mind where it is."

The end of our honeymoon made me realise why Evelyn had wanted to spend so much time with Leonora, time I'd resented, a lifetime ago. I wasn't looking forward to leaving her at River House while I travelled to the city to sort out things in the office, as I couldn't bear to be parted from her. She had a mesmeric quality that kept me wanting more. I was addicted and began to think perhaps I'd always been. But to entertain such thoughts made a sham of my marriage to Evelyn and I knew that was not the case.

Chip looked over my shoulder and exclaimed, "Of course, why didn't I see it before? I'm sorry you had to cut short your holiday. You must think I'm a prize prat."

"On the contrary," I said. " I think you've worked wonders with this. *Andromeda* was

Taken at the Flood

always a tricky concept. I should know. I spent enough time formulating it. Your work is excellent. I couldn't be more pleased that I've been able to leave you to get on with it, without my constant input. It's allowed me a certain amount of freedom at a very special time in my life and for that I'm eternally grateful."

I watched the young man's chest expand and fill with pride. My enthusiastic support, when he'd been feeling at his wits' end, had struck the right note. He bent his head towards the screen. "I'll have this finished in time for the Christmas market for certain now, Mr Hope."

Chip was as good as his word. Maxwell Hutton rang me in the New Year to congratulate me for once more 'bringing home the bacon' as he put it. Softcell's coffers were by now full to overflowing. I had a personal fortune, which at the time of my marriage to Evelyn, I could only have dreamed about. Alan Henderson bought a new house in the suburbs, where his four children could run wild, and Chip Thornley moved into an up and coming dockside apartment, solely on the strength of *Andromeda's* success.

When we'd returned from our honeymoon, I'd instructed Mrs Bates to make up the bed in the main guest bedroom for us. I didn't think Leo would relish sleeping in the room I'd shared with Evelyn but after a few days had passed she said, "Abe darling, why don't we sleep in the master bedroom? The view is much better and I think it would be nice to wake up and see the river from my bed. Lucas and I always regretted that our house faced the wood and River Road."

I could deny her nothing and so with reluctance agreed. Although the first night we spent in the large bed, with its cream silk canopy, I was haunted by dreams of Evelyn and awoke in a confused and dazed state to find Leo sleeping peacefully at my side. She looked so lovely that my breath caught in my throat and I shivered. My mother would have said someone was walking over my grave and I suppose in a way someone was.

During the following months, Leonora and I decided to look for an additional property in town. We thought it would be an investment, in addition to which, it would be a convenient place to stay when we'd been to the theatre or I was working late at the office. Unfortunately though, the property we liked in Mayfair was sold before we could make an offer and afterwards nothing seemed to quite match up to it.

One evening I arrived home, after a planning meeting with Alan, to find Mrs Bates had returned unexpectedly and in the kitchen there was an appetising aroma of beef stew, coming from the stove.

"Mrs Bates! You're back," I said, stating the obvious. "How is your sister?"

"Good, thank you, Mr Hope." She sniffed. "Mrs Hope told me to inform you she's upstairs packing."

Her tone of voice, when she referred to 'Mrs Hope', left me in no doubt as to her feelings regarding my new wife, it was something she found impossible to hide.

I raced up the wide staircase, my heart pounding in my chest. Packing? Where was Leo going? I hurried along the landing to our bedroom. She was standing in front of a suitcase folding a pair of cotton trousers lengthways with the precision I had come to expect of her.

"What's up?" I asked catching my breath. I wasn't as fit as I should be, I realised.

"I had a telephone call from my aunt's neighbour. She is unwell and has been asking to see me. I'm sorry, Abe. You do see I must go to her?"

"Of course. But why don't I come with you? Softcell can spare me; I do own the company after all."

My attempt at levity hit a blank wall.

"I wouldn't hear of it. Apart from anything else you would be so bored." She looked away and carried on packing her case.

"On the contrary," I persisted, "I'd like to meet your aunt and help you nurse her back to health. It's the least I can do."

Taken at the Flood

I couldn't see the expression on her face but I saw her back stiffen as she replied firmly, "Maybe on another occasion. I appreciate your offer but it is not the appropriate time. I know she would prefer to be well when she meets you."

"As you wish. But you know I'll miss you. Don't forget to phone me when you arrive," I replied with chagrin.

Later, as I watched the Alitalia jet rise skyward, I wondered if I would ever meet Leonora's aunt and whether Lucas had been faced with the same dilemma. I had the strong feeling he might have gone to his grave without ever having met her elusive Italian relative. Leo's ancestry was still a bit of mystery and I resolved, that on her return, I would find out more and as tactfully as I could, discover where she'd inherited her Scandinavian looks. I'd not seen many fair-haired, blue-eyed, Italians in the course of my travels and was intrigued still further by the beautiful enigma that was my wife.

Chapter 22

During the time Leo was in Italy, I viewed properties in the city in the hope that one similar to the Mayfair apartment would become available. As luck would have it, during the second week of her absence, the apartment we had originally viewed was back on the market, the sale having fallen through. I couldn't believe my good fortune and lost no time in arranging an appointment with the estate agent. I made an offer, which I knew was generous and, as I'd anticipated, it was accepted.

I felt excited at the prospect of telling Leo that we now owned the property she'd set her heart upon. However, I decided to keep the news to myself until she returned and then surprise her.

The following two weeks passed slowly and hearing her voice on the telephone at the end of the day only succeeded in lowering my spirits still further. My frustration at being unable to touch her and see her beautiful face was ruining my concentration and I paced the rooms of River House like a caged beast longing for release.

Mrs Bates fussed around me like a mother hen, concocting a variety of dishes aimed at lifting my mood, which I toyed with, much to her disgust.

Taken at the Flood

"That's your favourite, sir, go on now, try a bit more, it will do you good," she coaxed.

Since Leo's departure, Mrs Bates had reverted to her old self and couldn't do enough for me, so for her sake I dragged Tinker out to walk along the path in the opposite direction to the Dangerfields' house. I hadn't seen either Josie or Henry since our honeymoon and was in no mood to explain my eagerness to marry a woman of whom they so obviously disapproved.

The sun shone for a spell then disappeared behind badger-grey clouds threatening a downpour. Tinker seemed happy enough but clung to my heels like a strip of cellotape.

"Go on boy, fetch," I said, throwing a stick into a thicket. Reluctantly, Tinker disappeared into the undergrowth as the whirring of a motorised disability scooter filled the air.

Henry was alone. He was wearing a green jacket and I noticed a large golfing umbrella resting at his side. I felt a twinge of embarrassment, which dispersed as soon as he opened his mouth. "Looks like rain," he said. "Josie insisted I bring this." He tapped the umbrella. "Damn nuisance. Women bless 'em."

"How are you, Henry?" I asked falling into step alongside him.

"Fine. More to the point, old thing, how's life suiting you?"

I noticed his choice of words; there was no mention of my recent marriage. I began to feel annoyed but knew it was foolish to feel so. Nevertheless, I stomped off like a spoilt child.

"Nice to see you, Henry. Got to go. See you around." I said, turning back towards River house. "Tinker!"

The dog fell out of the undergrowth, rushed towards Henry who patted him, then bounded after me. My anger had cooled by the time I walked up the lawn towards the back porch but I realised that from the minute Leonora and I had said our vows, the relationship between Henry, Josie and myself had shifted to an uncomfortable impasse.

That night I dreamed I was in Venice again, sitting, as before, at a table in a restaurant near the Rialto Bridge. I was near enough to see the gondolas on the Grand Canal and saw a young girl with a cream hat and blue dress sitting in the back of one of them as she drifted towards me. I waited with baited breath to catch sight of her face and as she came nearer, she removed her hat and turned towards me. It was Evelyn. Her cute smile and dark curls framing her face were almost too sad to bear. I awoke to feel my cheeks wet with tears.

The day Leonora was due to return from Italy, I woke early. I was to pick her up from Heathrow at 11.30 and could not settle, excitement at the prospect of seeing her again rose up inside me like champagne bubbles repressed too long by a well fitting cork. When the telephone rang, I rushed to answer it but was not as quick as Mrs Bates, who was in the hallway. Lifting the receiver, I heard her say. "I'll see if I can find him."

"Thank you, Mrs Bates, I'll take the call on the extension," I said, into the mouthpiece.

It was Leo.

"Abe it's me. Would you mind awfully if I stayed here for another week? My aunt is very frail and I hate to leave her. I'll be home on the same flight next week, I promise."

The day slid downhill from that moment on. Alan Henderson called, there was a problem in the office and did I mind calling in. I picked up my laptop and with a heavy heart told Mrs Bates to leave something in the oven for me. "Just for one, is it, sir?" Mrs Bates asked, confirming a fact I'd long since suspected that she was not averse to listening in on the extension.

"That's right, Mrs Bates. How clever of you to know," I answered, the irony of my tone escaping her.

The problem in the office was minor, a document requiring my signature. I stopped short of pointing out he could have easily e-mailed it to me for my ratification, as I understood the reason behind his phone call. It was obvious he thought I needed some company, especially as during the conversation I'd explained that Leo had been delayed.

Taken at the Flood

The day passed in a flash and I realised I'd almost forgotten the feeling of being needed in the work environment, as I'd already relinquished most of the administration to Alan. It was a refreshing change and I even contemplated working from the office more frequently. Of course I was forgetting that, once Leo returned, I'd be obsessed with her and the office would take second place.

That evening I stayed in the wine bar with Chip, drinking far more than I'd intended. However, I enjoyed chatting to him about future projects and concepts that were floating around in my mind like debris on the tide. I decided to give the Dorchester a ring and booked a room for a few days so that I could spend some time working at my office. It might help me to forget the emptiness of River House and meant I could have an early start in the morning, a perfect opportunity to work on a new project, without Leo my main distraction.

After making a few phone calls, I turned to Chip. "Are you in a hurry or shall I get us another bottle?"

"I'm not going anywhere, Boss. In fact I'm glad you're not rushing off as it will give me an opportunity to talk over a few things with you."

Since Alan and I had taken Chip on board I'd grown fond of the eager young man whose ambition was his driving force and who seemed unaware of his ability to get straight to the problem without preamble. We talked for a while about work related topics and as the wine flowed, I discussed the outline of the new software I'd named *Orion,* which I hoped would be an even bigger seller than *Andromeda.* For the first time in ages, I was excited at the prospect of working on a revolutionary concept, which would stretch my atrophied brain cells.

The more we talked I felt the old feeling of adrenaline rushing through my veins and although alcohol aided its passage, I welcomed the sensation.

"I'm going to make a start over the next few days," I said, trying to keep the excitement out of my voice." I'll be in my office first thing in the morning. If Alan has nothing lined up for you why don't you drop in and see how it's progressing? You never know, I might be glad of your input."

His face reddened, and I suspected not merely from the effects of the wine. I smiled, had I ever been as young and naïve as he? I decided that perhaps I had, which was why I recognised a little of my youthful self in Chip.

The initial stages of *Orion* progressed well and by the end of the week, I was sure the basis for production was in place. Admittedly I worked well into the night and Chip and I spent long hours mulling over production details and ironing out minor flaws in the programme.

Taken at the Flood

Lying in my hotel bedroom on Saturday morning, I felt pleased with the results of my week's work. Although most of the structure of Orion had been developed years before, whilst I was married to Evelyn, it was still immensely satisfying to bring the idea to fruition.

I hadn't heard from Leonora for two days. As a rule I'd have rung her mobile but I'd been so absorbed in the complexities of work that by the time I tried to phone her, I realised it was far too late. I decided to take a shower and then ring Leonora the following morning. But as it turned out, before I could make the call, my mobile rang. It was the Estate Agent letting me know me know I could pick up the keys to the apartment. He said the paper work was just a formality and if I wanted to show my wife around next week there would be no problem.

This time Leo arrived on schedule and I felt that stomach churning pleasure as I saw her walking towards me through the arrivals lounge. She rushed into my arms and flung hers around my neck. The smell of her hair and the lingering perfume, I'd missed so much, drifted in the air and I took a deep breath before kissing her with a hunger that was simultaneously a pleasure and an embarrassment to us both.

"Let's get home," I said, tucking her hand into the crook of my arm as I pushed the trolley containing her luggage, which seemed to have

Taken at the Flood

grown in the space of the three weeks she'd been away.

Having Leo home once more was like renewing the excitement of our honeymoon. We acted like children enjoying a new toy. Laughter filled the house and once more and we had eyes for no one but ourselves. Mrs Bates was not impressed and after a few days took her leave by inventing yet another excuse to visit her sister.

I'm afraid we neglected Tinker shamefully; he was left to roam in the grounds for his daily exercise, as we were too preoccupied to take him for walks through the woods.

I realised also that my neglect of Henry and Josie was only partly due to my absorption with Leonora. The real reason I steered clear of them both lay with Josie's antagonistic attitude towards Leo. Captivated by her, I failed to understand why anyone could feel such enmity where she was concerned.

During the following week when we were shopping in the city, I placed the carrier bags in the back of the car and instead of driving towards the motorway, turned in the direction of Mayfair.

"Why are we going this way?" Leo asked, looking up from a magazine, she was reading.

Taken at the Flood

"I thought we could look at that apartment you fancied. You never know it might be on the market again."

"I doubt it somehow," she commented, picking up the magazine and continuing to read an article about older women and toy boys. She hardly noticed when I slowed the car down to a halt and drove down into the underground car park.

"Abe? Where are we going?"

"You'll soon see," I said, closing the car door and steering her towards a stainless steel lift against which stood a row of buttons each with a nameplate alongside them. Without commenting further, I pressed the top button and the lift took us to the penthouse apartment. Then removing the key from my pocket, I let us into the hallway.

The place was fully and expensively furnished which had bumped up the price still further. To my mind it was an added attraction. I didn't have the time to start looking at furniture or the inclination to employ an interior designer. I'd hoped Leo would like it as it was and I was not disappointed by her reaction. She was enthralled, delighted and happy beyond anything I could have imagined. Reaching up she brought my head forward and kissed me repeatedly until I begged for release, in order to breathe. You're the best husband in the world.

We will make love in every room. I cannot wait to move in."

I hesitated, wondering if she thought we were moving out of River House.

"You do know we are keeping River House? I thought this might be useful when we are in town."

If she had thought otherwise, she managed to hide it. Turning to look out of the French doors at the roof garden she said, "Yes of course, where else would Tinker have such splendid walks? We'll have plenty of time to spend in both our properties." She laughed and spun around like a ballerina in a music box. "I never thought I'd be wealthy enough to say that."

She was like a little girl, innocence and enthusiasm seeping out of every pore.

The Mayfair apartment became a magical retreat for us. I was aware it should have been the other way around but also mindful of the fact that River House had been the home I'd shared with Evelyn and that the house she shared with Lucas was but a stone's throw away. The apartment was ours and no ghosts lingered within its walls.

The summer months passed in a flash and winter followed damp and dark. We spent more and more time in London and Mrs Bates spent more and more time in River House, her excuse being it was better for Tinker as he hated the kennels. It was an arrangement, which was mutually beneficial to us both.

We celebrated our second wedding anniversary by dining at The Ivy, surrounded by minor celebrities and a few of our friends. Josie and Henry were not invited. I still walked over to see them on the odd occasion whilst we were staying in River House but Leo always seemed to have some task or other that prevented her from joining me. I never encouraged her to visit them and they never asked about her.

The years passed with no sign of a family. Neither of us attempted to find out if there was a reason for our childless state and I suspect that in reality neither of us was too bothered. Our joy in each other's company was enough.

Softcell still managed to compete quite comfortably on the open market. Orion had been a blockbuster but other companies were expanding their horizons and I knew I would have to come up with something revolutionary if we were not to stagnate. I'd neglected my work in favour of my marriage. We were financially secure but Softcell was important enough in my life that I couldn't bear to see it going downhill. There was no reason why I shouldn't work at both, I decided, and with this in mind, I planned to spend the summer months in River House during which time I would focus on a successor to *Orion*.

Taken at the Flood

Every morning I sat at my computer formulating and re-formulating data, until I came up with a format I knew was leading me into uncharted territory. Adapting the protocols and concepts, which had formed the basis of both *Andromeda* and *Orion* to achieve the highest standard of consumer continuity and comprehension, I worked with an intensity and pleasure that had been lacking in recent years. Finally, I was able to transform the new package, whilst lifting it to a higher level.

Nano technology had advanced considerably since *Andromeda* and I was thrilled with the prospect of unfolding a new series of programmes using the new techniques. However, Leonora, eager to prevent me from over working, insisted I set aside some time each day to either walk the river path with her and Tinker or relax in the garden. When she was satisfied my period of exercise was acceptable, she was content to let me lock myself away in my study during the evening without comment.

One afternoon when we returned from our walk, she followed me into my study. "How are things progressing? I sense you are excited. Something new has happened?"

"I see I can't hide anything from you, my love." I said, relishing the prospect of showing off. "Sit down and I'll explain it to you."

Evelyn had been right when she'd described Leonora as being intelligent and quick-witted. I

Taken at the Flood

was astonished at how quickly she understood the basics of the new software. So much so that the following afternoon I agreed to show her the intricacies of the programme, which would be responsible for elevating it above the packages already available, to the product I knew would revolutionise personal computer use for the foreseeable future. With the right marketing, we would make our competitors look like novices.

Leonora sat at my side and watched as I backed up data and transferred it to a miniature portable storage device, which I then placed in the top pocket of my shirt. Then I made compact disc copies from my hard drive and stored them in the wall safe.

"I'm intrigued why you keep that in your pocket," Leo said

"Until this is on the open market this stays with me at all times. There is no way I'm letting it out of my sight. The back-up copies are secure." I inclined my head in the direction of the safe and no one knows this even exists, except the people I trust." I kissed her forehead, adding, "Why don't I let you name this one.

"No, I couldn't" she smiled.

"Why ever not?"

She thought for a moment then smiled.

"Gemini," she said.

And Gemini it became. How could I know that at its inception I was destined to share the

Taken at the Flood

fate of Castor and Pollux and that the angel of death would circle River House once more.

Chapter 23

Eager to run over the details of *Gemini* with Chip Thornley and Alan Henderson, and carrying my PSD in my breast pocket where I could feel it against the beating of my heart, I left River House. I don't remember the drive to the office, all I could feel was excitement at the prospect of sharing Gemini with Alan and Chip.

As I'd anticipated, their elation matched my own, Alan's enthusiasm at the prospect showing in his voice, "This is the breakthrough we need and as far as I'm concerned it couldn't come at a better time." He walked towards the window. "Have you thought much about security? If details of this one get out we're set to lose big time."

I removed the storage device from the USB port and replaced in my breast pocket. "When we're ready to go into production, I'll bring a back-up copy to the office and store it in the safe. With the security measures we have in place, I don't see I can do much more to protect it. At the moment nothing will be stored on our office computers. I will of course discuss refinements with you and Chip but only when the three of us are present and only when this little beauty is in place." I tapped my pocket. "If you two can think of anything I've missed, get in touch immediately, other than that I'll start putting it together in a workable format."

Taken at the Flood

Chip listened in silence but I could see beads of sweat glistening on his forehead.

"Chip? Anything to add?"

"Nothing, Boss. I'm still trying to picture what this will mean."

I smiled, and thought 'the innocence of youth' although, he'd soon find out exactly what *Gemini* would mean. But as it turned out, none of us could have contemplated the outcome awaiting us.

I saw little of Leonora during the following weeks. She understood I needed peace and quiet in which to work and spent her time gardening or shopping in town. When evening came, she insisted we eat together and, over our meal, I caught up with her news. It was a welcome distraction after hours spent refining protocols and concentrating on data analysis.

One night at dinner, she said, "I met Josie in town today."

I looked up.

"I think she would have liked to pretend she hadn't seen me but she had no choice but to speak."

I waited to hear the rest without commenting.

"She asked how you were and when I said you were fine, although working too hard, she said a most peculiar thing."

"Oh? What exactly?"

"She said, the last time you and she met you looked in perfect health and she and Henry would be very concerned if that condition were to deteriorate. Her manner was most peculiar; it was almost as if she were making some sort of threat." She looked up at my as she toyed with her meal. "I wasn't sure how to answer so I muttered something about having to rush and left. I've always known Josie doesn't like me but I really don't understand why. When Evelyn was alive I thought perhaps she was jealous of our relationship but why now?"

She looked so despondent I took her hand in mine and kissed it. "Some women are jealous of beauty, my darling."

She smiled up at me then. "I wish," she said.

That was when I realised my lovely wife had no idea how beautiful she really was and her inability to understand why Josie should dislike her somehow made that vulnerability urgently appealing. *Gemini* would have to wait until morning; I had a more pressing engagement.

The official launch was set for November. During the first week of September, I carried the disc copy of *Gemini* to my office, feeling some trepidation at the prospect of releasing my baby into the care of others. Although I knew Alan and Chip were exemplary caretakers, the feeling persisted as I took the lift up to the fifth floor.

Taken at the Flood

They'd organised the equipment ready for my arrival. The expectant hum of black sightless screens devoid of savers, with cursors flickering, greeted me as I opened the door. Alan was pacing the floor, his usual habit when nervously awaiting an event and Chip sat at a desk in front of the only active computer screen. He was completing a game of Solitaire.

"Right," I said, not wishing to prolong their agony further. "Let's get down to business.

We worked through lunch whilst drinking copious amounts of coffee. Alan formulated the marketing structure, which was merely a formality, as we were certain *Gemini* would sell itself, once the launch was over. I knew Maxwell Hutton would be interested and anticipated he might be its highest bidder, although Macrosoft, a relatively new company, had substantial backing and could possibly be a contender.

Our commitments to Megacells had been fulfilled, therefore we were at liberty to hold out for the highest offer but loyalty had always played a big part in my life and I wasn't about to see Maxwell Hutton lose *Gemini* if it was at all possible.

Chip worked on refining the protocols that would make the package idiot proof, which meant that however young and immature the user, there would be neither a possibility of compromising its basic structure nor that of other software components already in place.

We ordered take-away food from the Italian restaurant on the corner and at midnight we put Gemini to bed and opened the bottle of champagne waiting in my desk drawer for an opportunity such as this.

I spent the night in our Mayfair apartment. I'd been too engrossed with work to ring Leo earlier and realised it was now too late. My brain was still working overtime and I knew sleep was not about to make an appearance.

In the kitchen, I opened the fridge forgetting it was unlikely to be stocked, as it was a while since we'd used the place. An unopened carton of orange juice, still within its use by date, looked back at me forlornly. I was in a mood to celebrate and missed talking to Leo so I opened a more modest bottle of champagne than the one we'd drunk earlier and, with the addition of the orange juice, drank myself into a pleasant stupor.

When I awoke, the sun was slicing through the half closed blinds and cutting across my eyelids with the intensity of a laser beam. My head was pounding like a jackhammer and my neck ached. I'd fallen asleep on the couch. Screwing my eyes into slits, I peered at my watch. It was nearly noon and my mobile was ringing.

Chapter 24

She sounded as if she was worried but trying hard not to show it. "I thought you might have decided to stay in town. Did everything go well?"

The pounding in my head was turning into a dull ache behind my temples. "I'm sorry I didn't ring, darling. We worked until midnight and yes, everything went well. There are a few loose ends to tie up today but I should be home this evening. Don't bother to make a meal; we'll dine at Georgio's. I love you."

"I love you too, Abe but then you know that already," she said.

Later, after showering and taking two painkillers, I felt ready to face the world. Alan and Chip both looked the worse for wear as I joined them at the coffee machine.

"How long?" I asked.

"About a month, three weeks at a push, if we offer an incentive. What d'you think?" Alan asked.

"Double time if completion is within three weeks."

"That should do it. Gemini's launch date should coincide with Bonfire night then. Appropriate in view of the fireworks it will set off in the boardrooms of more than a few of our competitors."

Taken at the Flood

I nodded. "Right, I can leave it in your capable hands.

I left my office at half past four after making certain the usual security measures were in place. Alan was the only one who had access to the safe and although during the initial formulisation processes my trusted workforce would see parts of the software, the key to the final product was on the hard disc in the safe and would not be removed until the day before the launch.

During the drive to River House, I felt that familiar longing to see Leo. Every minute we were separated felt like a lifetime. I could smell her hair in the clear air filtering through the vents and feel her skin in the sunlight burning through my windscreen. She was waiting in the front porch as I drew up. The late afternoon sun was turning her hair to silver, the cream dress she was wearing clinging to her figure like a second skin. Once more, I marvelled at her ethereal beauty and once again thanked fate for giving her to me.

At the end of October, I received a frantic telephone call from Alan asking me to come into the office. Luckily, we were spending some time in our Mayfair apartment, as Leo wanted to do some shopping for winter clothes, so it was simply a matter of a short drive away from my office.

Taken at the Flood

I parked the Mercedes in the Chief Managing Director's space and took the lift from the basement to my office on the top floor. Alan was pacing the floor in the corridor outside my office his mobile glued to his ear. I could see beads of sweat glistening on his forehead as he stared incredulously out of the window.

"What's up?" I asked, when he had finished speaking.

"Your office," he said, following behind me. He closed the door and leaned against it. "I don't know how to tell you this, Boss." He walked over to my desk and bent forward. "It's *Gemini,* it's been copied. It's on the open market now. Megacells have bought it so have Microbites."

I sank into my chair. "I don't understand. How?"

"That's the six million dollar question. It's not just a programme that has some similarities to ours. It's exactly the same. It's been copied and sold to Magnum International for distribution."

Gradually my brain began to work as realisation sunk in. I shrugged. "Our legal department will deal with it, Alan. Remember there's such a thing as copyright and ours was registered as soon as I'd completed."

"I'm afraid it's not as simple as that. We're the ones likely to fall foul of the copyright laws if we try to argue that *Gemini* is our product.

I've made preliminary investigations before contacting you but they're insisting *Gemini* is their product as copyright was taken out just one week before our own."

"I don't see how. Surely, that can't be true. We would have come up against it with the name alone, when we registered copyright ourselves."

"That's just it. They re-named the software."

"I see and what did they decide to call this programme?"

I was beginning to feel furious. Someone was going to have to pay for this. All my months of work down the pan.

Alan Henderson shifted from one foot to the other and ran his fingers through his hair. He didn't look at me as he replied, "*Leo.*"

"What did you say?"

"It's the name Magnum used to register copyright on *Gemini*. They've named it *Leo.*"

I brought my fist down hard on the desktop. My anger and frustration making me raise my voice, as I said, "I want to know where this leak has come from. Ring security and have them meet me here in half an hour. We must keep this between ourselves for the time being. Don't mention it to anyone, until we find out exactly what has been going on."

Alan nodded then ran his hand over his chin. He was as agitated as I was, his anger just as difficult to keep under control.

Alone, I mulled over the facts. On completion of *Gemini* I had, as usual when a project was finished, copied my file on to two discs. One lay in my safe at home and the other in our safe in the office; both were controlled by an electronic keypad, which required a pass code to open them. In addition, the office safe also required a key. Alan had one and I the other. I trusted Alan implicitly, there was no way he would jeopardise his position. He was committed to the company, which had supplied him with a very comfortable lifestyle. I was certain of his loyalty. He would have been shooting himself in the foot to attempt to sabotage our future. Besides, he'd be the first person to come under suspicion, as he and I were the sole key holders.

I was purposely not dwelling on the alternative, which was too distressing to contemplate. However, my mind would not rest. Leonora could have discovered how to open the safe in my study at River House if she'd been devious enough but again, why would she? It was in her interest that I should make a success of *Gemini* and she'd given me no reason to doubt her love for me.

This last thought lingered in my mind rather longer than it should have. I was perplexed as to why she'd thought it necessary to lie to me about inconsequential details in the past; her supposed allergy to dogs for instance. Either

Taken at the Flood

she'd been lying to Evelyn in order to avoid having to take on Tinker, or she'd been lying to me. However, the latter seemed not to be the case, as I'd seen no evidence that she was allergic to Tinker, whom she'd fondled at every opportunity without any ill effects. Then there was Venice. I'd seen her with my own eyes; her looks were so striking it was impossible to mistake her for someone else, so why had she found it necessary to lie to me? I preferred not to dwell on the existence of her mysterious aunt, the one I was not allowed to visit.

This was ridiculous, I thought, I was letting my mind run into a quagmire of doubt and if I were not careful it would drag me under. Although it was understandable in view of the fact that Magnum International had registered *Gemini* under the same name as my pet name for my wife. It was a shock but coincidence, surely? After all, I'd already decided that follow up software packages would be named *Libra* and *Taurus* adhering to the of the Zodiac as a theme. Therefore, I could see it was not a massive leap of the imagination for someone to do the same and re-title the copied software *Leo*.

I was still trying to make sense of it all when Alan Henderson, followed by Tom Edwards, Softcell's Head of Security, entered my office. "Sit down, gentlemen. We have a problem…" I began.

Taken at the Flood

We spent the best part of the afternoon discussing how we should go about discovering who was behind the *Gemini* leak, without arousing suspicion and as the sun sank lower in the sky, we agreed upon a strategy.

The weeks passed and I was careful not to mention *Gemini* 's sabotage to anyone, not even Leo. When she innocently enquired how things were going with the programme, which she had named, I skirted around the subject in a non-committal manner and she seemed to accept it without question.
During the following months, I worked on *Taurus* and *Libra* both of which were linked to *Gemini* but in such a way that it would be impossible to make the connection. Although the saboteur had stolen the basis for the programme, *Gemini* was only a beginning and I was the only one who knew how it would develop. The clues were in its structure but the key was in my brain. This time I was convinced I'd be able to ensure that there'd be no breach of the copyright law. I was the only person who knew the intricate workings of the original package and as such would be able to unlock the properties, which I'd taken care to protect during the months of its inception. I was determined not to trust anyone.
The months flew by, the work easier this time. All I had to do was to make sure there was

no chance that *Taurus* and *Libra* would produce a charge of plagiarism aimed in my direction. A name change was vital I discarded several before finally favouring *Venus* and *Jupiter*.

Just as before, I copied the compact discs from my hard drive, placing one in my safe at River House alongside my PSD and one in the safe in my office but unlike previously, I made sure that I registered copyright in the morning before placing the copied disc in the office safe. Then I contacted Maxwell Hutton and arranged for Alan to go to New York with the new packages.

I was relaxing in our Mayfair apartment, confident that although we'd not yet discovered the breach in security, our new packages would soon make up for our losses, when Leo called me. "Abe darling, it's Alan for you. The line is not good. There seems to be some interference. I can't quite make out what he is saying." She handed me the phone.

The mobile signal cleared but Alan's voice, distorted by anger, made his words almost unintelligible. "You are not going to believe this!" he began. "Megacell doesn't want the new packages. Maxwell Hutton said he's been offered similar two days ago and he'd bought them at a very competitive price."

I sat bolt upright. "I don't understand."

"It's happened again. Pirated copies have already been sold."

Taken at the Flood

The colour must have drained from my face for, as I replaced the receiver, Leo rushed over to me. "Abe? What is it?"

I shook my head in disbelief. "Just some bad news from the States. Hutton has refused *Venus* and *Jupiter.*"

"I'm sorry," she said, turning towards the drinks cabinet. "Here take this." She handed me a brandy and I took a gulp and felt the colour rush to my cheeks. The news from the States was serious. We had a massive problem on our hands. I thought it best not to go into details with Leo as I didn't want to worry her but I was fast coming to the conclusion that Softcell would be in big trouble if we couldn't sort out this problem ASAP. There was a major breach in security and I was at a loss to know where to look for the answer.

When Alan arrived back from New York, we arranged another meeting with Tom Edwards, who assured us his team had been working flat out. There were no obvious security problems, everything seemed to be in order. He promised to expand his search to see if he'd missed something but I could see he didn't hold out much hope. There had been limited access to the software and it was a mystery how it had been copied so quickly.

The week following Alan's return from New York, I had a telephone call from Maxwell

Hutton. "I thought I should call you. Are you alone?" he asked.

I assured him I was and became intrigued by his hesitancy. Hutton was a larger than life character who called a spade a spade. It was unlike him not to tell me straight away what was on his mind. But I sensed his embarrassment as he talked about inconsequential trivia, skirting around the main reason for his telephone call.

"Maxwell, I appreciate your call. I understand why you couldn't do business with us, although I've yet to find out who is responsible for sabotaging our software," I said.

Suddenly I heard him take a deep breath as if he had come to an unpalatable decision. "You haven't heard this from me remember," he said. "But I suggest you look closer to home."

"What? I don't understand. Do you know who is behind this?" I asked incredulously.

"I can't say anymore. Just take my advice, there's a good man."

The line went dead. I stood holding the phone in my hand wondering if I had just dreamt the last five minutes.

Chapter 25

Replacing the phone, I frowned. Hutton's comment was not like him at all. He was usually forthright and to the point. What did he know or suspect? It was obvious he thought he was doing me a favour but one, which left me with a bad taste in my mouth. Once again, the face I loved most in the world swam before me in a miasma of doubt and mistrust.

I closed my eyes. Was I blind? This latest bit of information, suggesting I look nearer to home for the answer to my problems had shaken me. Leo was the only person, other than Alan, and myself, who could have had access to all three discs. Josie's voicemail when I was on honeymoon came back to haunt me. 'What do we know about her? What did Lucas know and now he is dead.' I shivered, not Leo, it couldn't be her.

I'd left her in town shopping as she was planning to spend an afternoon at the beauty parlour. I had the afternoon free. I looked at the time and rang Leo on her mobile. "I've decided to go down to River House this afternoon. I think I need to get away from the city for a few days."

"Fine, I'll pick up a few things and see you there around seven tonight," she said.

Taken at the Flood

Then I rang the Dangerfields' number. Josie answered. "Could I come over and see you later this afternoon?"

If she was surprised at hearing from me, Josie didn't show it. "Wonderful, I'll be on my own actually. Henry has an appointment with his physio, in town. He usually takes most afternoons off and I know he likes to pop into the library at Kings Datchet on his way home. I'll be waiting for you."

When I reached River House, Mrs Bates eyed me with suspicion. "Mrs Hope not with you then, sir?"

"Leo will be driving down later," I replied, following her into the kitchen where Tinker leapt on me, licking my hand with undisguised joy. I broke away from his attentions and turned to Mrs Bates. "Mrs Bates, could I ask you why you dislike Leonora so much?"

"What makes you say that, sir?" she had the grace to blush and look uncomfortable at my forthright question.

"You don't manage to hide your feelings as well as you might think."

She put a flour-speckled hand to her forehead. "It's difficult for me to put into words, sir. You see, I was very fond of Mrs Hope, I mean the first Mrs Hope. She and I spent hours chatting away about one thing and another. We often talked about her friendship with Mrs Bennett."

Taken at the Flood

Mrs Bates sat down on the kitchen chair and I sat opposite her as she started to explain. "She used to tell me all about their shopping trips and the funny stories Mrs Bennett told her. She also told me Mrs Bennett had married for money and not for love. I remember her saying, 'Leo said Lucas had saved her life. If it hadn't been for his money she would have been in a sorry state.'"

"Evelyn used those exact words?" I prompted.

"Yes, I remember it well. You were about to go to New York and Mrs Bennett was going to come and stay for a few days. I soon made myself scarce I can tell you. I could see through her. The more stories Mrs Hope told me the more they confirmed my opinion." She hesitated looking at me as if to gauge my reaction then decided to carry on. "I knew as sure as eggs is eggs that Mrs Leonora Bennett was a man eating gold digger and when you announced to me you were going to marry her, I nearly had a blue fit!"

She sighed, the relief of having got her feelings off her chest was plain to see. I said nothing and as the silence lengthened, she said, "I'm sorry for speaking my mind but you did ask."

"I shouldn't have put you in such an awkward position, Mrs Bates. I value your directness and can only say I hope time will prove you wrong."

Taken at the Flood

After calling to Tinker, I said, "I'm off to the Dangerfields' house. We'll eat at half seven, please."

"Righty O, Mr Hope," she replied and with business-like efficiency returned to rolling out the pastry on the board whilst humming softly to herself.

My housekeeper's relief at having voiced her misgivings had done nothing more than transfer her concerns to me. I couldn't believe Leo had married me simply for my money. It didn't make sense. She'd inherited a respectable sum of money from Lucas and with the sale of their house had become independent financially. Mrs Bates must be mistaken. I could understand she didn't wish to see me replace Evelyn in my affections quite so readily, although I could never explain to her that Leo and Evelyn each held a different part of me within their grasp.

Tinker sensed the downturn in my mood and stayed at my heels rubbing his head comfortingly against my leg, as I walked along the river path. My mind was in turmoil. I had to talk to Josie and yet in doing so felt I was betraying Leonora.

Their garden was a riot of colour, purple-headed daisies rose from a bed of red begonias and Busy Lizzies tumbled over the top of terracotta pots lining the path leading to the French doors. There wasn't a weed in sight. Everything about Josie was neat and orderly. It was the first thing I'd noticed about her, all those years ago.

As I approached the house, my despondent mood lifted. I was looking forward to seeing her. But would she have changed towards me? I needn't have worried. Josie welcomed me warmly, insisting I sit on the terrace while she put on the coffee. She was the one constant in my life, I realised. Josie would never change; I could rely upon it.

"I can't wait to hear your news. Henry and I were only saying the other day that it would be nice to see you again." She handed me a mug and as our fingers touched, she said, "We're always here if you need us you know."

I smiled and patted her hand but it was a while before I felt able to bring up the topic that was uppermost in my mind. In the meantime we chatted about old times and Josie filled me in on what had been happening to them both since I'd last seen them.

There was a gap in the conversation. We were sitting side by side enjoying the view down to the river when I found the words I'd been avoiding, "Why did you try to warn me about Leo, Josie?"

Unlike Mrs Bates, Josie's was unconcerned and straightforward. "You know how friendly Evelyn and I'd been before Leo came along, so I expect you think my antagonism stemmed from some sort of jealousy. Well you would be quite wrong. I'd met Leonora and Lucas some time before I met up with Evelyn again. We'd invited them over for dinner when they first moved in and I had the distinct impression from Lucas that Leonora had engineered their marriage. As I got to know them that impression deepened into a certainty that she'd married Lucas for money and money alone."

"Did Lucas say that?"

Josie pondered the question for a moment.

"Not in so many words but he was no fool," she answered thoughtfully. "After Evelyn came on the scene, Leonora and she became thick as thieves. At the beginning, Evelyn used to telephone me on the odd occasion and relate some of the conversations between herself and Leonora. Then I began to feel she was being manipulated, especially when Evelyn became pregnant. I noticed she seemed to rely on her for everything. If she needed a prescription collected, Leonora fetched it. You could argue it was out of the kindness of her heart but I'm afraid I had some uncharitable thoughts, especially at the time of Evelyn's miscarriage."

"What do you mean by uncharitable?" I asked, turning my chair to look directly at her.

"Look, don't take this too much to heart. After all, I have no proof and I feel it's the wrong thing to say to you, now you're married to her."

"Spit it out, Josie. I can take it!"

"Henry said I was paranoid when I told him what I'd been thinking. You see, I began to think that maybe Leonora had something to do with Evelyn's miscarriage and maybe even her death."

I gasped and she turned away from me.

"I'm sorry. You must think I'm a mad woman to think such a thing and maybe I am. However, there remains the fact that Evelyn's accident did come at a very convenient moment for Leonora especially as within the year she was burying Lucas."

"What are you saying?"

"Just that the way was clear for her to marry you."

My mouth dropped open. "Josie, you must know that's nonsense," I said.

"Sorry, it was just me being stupid again. I shouldn't have said that. Henry would kill me if he knew I had told you. Please, forget what I said."

"I'm shocked. I can't believe you could think such a thing. Why would she want to be so desperate to marry me?"

To my surprise Josie laughed. "My dear friend. You were as HI LIFE magazine pointed out, exceedingly eligible and most definitely unattached. Why wouldn't she?"

It was true Leo had suddenly appeared after the magazine article had been published but I was sure it was purely coincidental. I felt disloyal having such thoughts and angry with Josie for voicing hers.

"You must hate Leo very much." I started to get up but Josie put a restraining hand on my arm.

"There's something I must tell you," she said. "I don't want you to run away with the idea that this is something I've made up out of a fierce dislike of Leonora but I can't have you leaving like this without trying to explain."

With a sizable degree of reluctance, I sat down as she continued, "The day before Evelyn's miscarriage, I bumped into her in town, Leonora had been delayed at the hairdresser's and Evelyn was waiting in the coffee shop in Harvey Nicks. I asked if she'd mind if I joined her whilst she was waiting. She looked uncomfortable but eventually agreed. In front of her on the table was a small pill bottle. Two pills sat at the side of her cup. I think I must have glanced at the bottle because she mumbled something about vitamins and slid it into her handbag. During the conversation, she told me Leo had been kind enough to pick up her prescription for vitamins the previous day as she had run out."

"What's suspicious about that?" I asked, beginning to feel my anger threatening to erupt.

"When I was younger I had what was known as a photographic memory. You know the kind of thing; if I subconsciously notice something,

I'm able to bring it back precisely word for word. It used to be very useful during my schooldays when I had to study for my exams but I don't often have call to use it these days.

"However, after Evelyn lost the baby, I began to recall the tablets I'd seen her taking the day prior to her miscarriage. I clearly recalled the label on the bottle and the word **Cervotab**. The more I thought about it the more worried I became, so I rang an old school friend who is a G.P. over in Kings Bentham. Somehow, I brought the conversation around to the fact that a friend of mine had been prescribed some tablets and was worried about side effects. I repeated the name I'd seen on Evelyn's tablets and she told me they were safe as long as used for the purpose for which they were prescribed."

"Well there you are then," I said unable to see what she was making such a fuss over.

"But that's just it! The tablets Evelyn was taking, thinking they were some sort of multivitamins, were in fact to be taken for the purpose of inducing an abortion. They were only to be prescribed for that purpose alone."

Chapter 26

I returned to River House like an automaton, my legs moving, my eyes focusing and the sun burning my face but I was oblivious to all sensations, my brain desperately trying to make sense of Josie's words. There had to be a reasonable explanation for Evelyn taking those tablets but for the life of me, I couldn't see what it could be. The possibility that Leo had been responsible for replacing her vitamin tablets in such a way was too horrible to contemplate. My beautiful trusting Leo - her gentle nature, which I'd hoped was obvious to everyone, it seemed, was only as far as I was concerned. Josie had to be mistaken.

As the house came in sight, I heard Evelyn's words, 'Leo is so clever, she knows so much about Lucas's work, knows the names of medical conditions and what drugs should be taken for them.'

I pushed open the back door and reached my study dazed and uncomprehending. The drone of the vacuum cleaner sounded from somewhere above my head as Mrs Bates set about cleaning the bedrooms but I sat staring out of the window trying to make sense of it all.

At some stage, there was a knock on my study door. I heard Mrs Bates speaking and struggled to return to the present. "I'm off to visit Emily for the evening, Mr Hope. There's a chicken casserole in the oven for you both and I've laid the table in the dining room."

Emily was the old lady who was now living in Leo's old house and she and Mrs Bates had become friends. I think I answered her but she was out of the door and down the river path before I'd registered the fact that she'd spoken.

I remained staring out of the window until I heard Leo's car draw up outside. I watched as she unloaded carrier bags from the boot, her blonde hair rippling in the breeze. I sighed with regret, that slurs and innuendos should have tainted my love, all of which would be impossible to prove one way or the other; it was unbelievable. I had to try and ignore it. But it was easier said than done.

"Abe I'm home," she called from the hallway. I went to meet her having decided if I was to get at the truth then I must appear as if nothing had happened that afternoon.

Throughout the evening, I behaved as if I'd never heard Josie's accusations. Leo appeared not to notice anything was wrong, although what did I know of my second wife? Was she merely biding her time, waiting to move on to pastures new when the time was right? Thoughts, which would never have crossed my mind, flitted like fireflies dancing in the night, just out of reach but managing to leave an impression.

Taken at the Flood

However, the day's events left me with little appetite for lovemaking, even after feeling her naked body cuddling up to mine seductively and the caress of her sweet breath on my neck. It was fortunate that Leonora put my lack of interest down to the fact I was worrying about my business problems and slipping her hand into mine, whispered, "Try not to worry, darling; I'm sure you'll find the culprit soon. Relax: things always look better in the morning."

Leonora's comforting words did little to reassure me, as 'things' did not look better in the morning. I slept fitfully and when I did manage to fall asleep, it was to dream of Evelyn. She was trying to tell me something, her mouth opening and closing as I tried in vain to understand what she was saying. When I awoke, it was to the sound of Mrs Bates calling after Leo as she started out on an early morning walk with Tinker. "Mrs Hope, here's the stale bread you wanted to feed the ducks."

She was trying to make amends for her dislike of Leo but the tone of her voice spoke volumes.

I stood under the shower, wishing the water could wash away yesterday and erase it from my mind. I wanted Leo to be innocent; I wanted them to see her through my eyes. To me she was clever, bright, intelligent, funny Leo, the woman who had enthralled and filled me with curiosity

Taken at the Flood

from the first moment I saw her all those years ago. But even that memory was sullied. Once again the question of why she'd denied ever visiting Venice raised its head.

There was nothing for it, as the jets of water hit my body I concluded I would hire a private detective. I had to find out what my wife was up to and if she was as innocent as I'd hoped.

To begin with I resolved that the next time Leo decided to visit her aunt in Tuscany then I would not suggest I join her, as I had done previously. But this time I would employ a professional to do the job for me. If her visit turned out to be entirely innocent then I could put the rest of my fears into perspective and deal with them one by one. In view of my suspicions regarding the sabotage of my company's products, I had no alternative. She had to be above reproach and that meant I required proof she wasn't lying to me. I would not mention what I proposed to anyone, including Alan Henderson.

The offices of Brockwell and Hansen were in a side street off Russell Square. A brass plaque on the wall to one side of a red-painted wooden door, read 'Brockwell and Hansen Investigators'. I pressed the button on the intercom, introduced myself and heard the click of the door release. A glass-panelled door, leading off a hallway, the floor of which was

Taken at the Flood

covered by large black and white marble floor tiles, opened into a reception area and sitting behind a desk was a small middle-aged woman. She wore her grey hair in a French pleat, tendrils escaping and curling around her face like wire wool. She smiled encouragingly as I approached the desk. "Go right in, Mr Hope, they are expecting you."

Pointing to a door behind her with the end of a ballpoint pen she turned quickly, as the telephone on her desk began to ring insistently.

Messrs Brockwell and Hansen were, at first sight, as alike as the proverbial two peas. Both wore navy pinstriped suits, metal-framed glasses and sat behind identical leather topped desks. I could have been forgiven for imagining I was in the offices of a well-respected firm of solicitors or accountants so business-like were they.

"Mr Hope, do sit down."

They spoke the words simultaneously, reminiscent of Tweedle Dum and Tweedle Dee. The fantasy didn't stop there. I began to feel as if I was entering a dream. What was I doing here in the first place? The temptation to turn and run hovered at the edge of my consciousness. If I lingered, spilling my doubts like scattering birdseed, I would give voice to my fear and somehow make it a reality.

Tweedle Dum cleared his throat. "Take your time, Mr Hope. We often find our clients are reticent at this first juncture. Maybe you would like to collect your thoughts over a cup of coffee?" His hand strayed towards the telephone.

"No, thank you. I won't delay you further. I'm ready," I replied

Without preamble I explained the reason for my visit succinctly and when I'd finished opened my briefcase and removed the photograph of my wife. It was a close-up, the blue eyes and pale blonde hair clearly visible as she smiled into the camera.

My confidence began to ebb. They passed the photograph between them, inspecting it in detail. Martin Brockwell whistled softly through his teeth and I found myself waiting for Ian Hansen's response as if they were unable to operate independently of each other. It was obvious, that after looking at the photograph, they concluded I was a jealous husband intent on catching out an errant wife. So be it, I thought, it suited my purpose admirably.

Finally, I told them about Leonora's visits to Italy. "When the situation arises, I'll let you know the departure time of my wife's flight and wait to hear from you when you have news," I said, closing my briefcase.

We reached an agreement as to the cost of their services and they both rose to shake my hand, the movement synchronised to the second. However, it was when they stood up that I received the first of the many shocks that they would produce during the time they were employed by me.

Martin Brockwell was tall, he towered over me and I am six foot two. His partner by contrast was a much smaller man barely five foot five inches tall. I tried unsuccessfully to disguise my humour at the disparity in their heights, which had not been discernible whilst they were seated.

"Eileen, see Mr Hope out will you, dear?" they chorused behind me as I turned towards the door the corners of my mouth twitching uncontrollably.

It was during the first week of September when Leo announced she was to visit her aunt again. I agreed but did not suggest I go with her this time. She looked a little disconcerted by my lack of interest but didn't comment, assuring me she would miss me every moment she was away and promising not to stay longer than the proposed two week visit this time.

Later, watching her disappear through the door of the departure lounge at Heathrow, I felt my insides churn. My disloyalty did not sit easily on my shoulders, even though Messrs Brockwell and Hansen had assured me of their discretion. I felt uncomfortable with my duplicity.

I walked back towards a bookstall and bought a newspaper as a short man wearing corduroy trousers and a cream linen jacket hurried past me in the direction of the departure lounge clutching an artist's easel folded under one arm and a leather flight bag under the other. I doubt if I would have recognised the figure of Ian Hansen, if it had not been for his diminutive stature and the purposeful glint in eyes, magnified behind metal-framed glasses.

At the end of the first week of Leo's visit to her aunt, I received a message from Martin Brockwell. He said he had some paperwork at the office that he would like me to see.

I drove through the lunch hour traffic and parked in a side street a block away from his office. My heart was pounding uncomfortably against my ribs as I anticipated the result of his investigation. Part of me wanted to return to my car and forget I'd ever doubted my wife but somehow my feet propelled me towards the red painted front door and deposited me in Martin Brockwell's office.

The paperwork turned out to be a photo-fax from his colleague in Tuscany. The grainy print was clear enough for me to recognise Leo wrapped in the arms of another man. I desperately tried to appear calm, thanked Mr Brockwell for contacting me and asked him to let me know if there were further developments. It was all in a day's work to the investigator. He'd seen it all a hundred or more times;

Taken at the Flood

beautiful, unfaithful wife cheating on wealthy older husband with a much younger man.

Outside, the rain chilled my cheeks and dampened my spirits. By the time I'd reached my car my cheeks were wet with tears of anger mingling with the raindrops sliding down the collar of my shirt and dripping towards my heart. I drove through the city streets oblivious of my surroundings and let myself into our apartment with a sinking feeling of despair. After pouring a stiff measure of whiskey into a glass, I stood at the window and watched the rain turn from a shower into a torrent. I felt wretched and foolish. It was a sobering fact to think that my neighbour and my housekeeper had been able to see what I could not. My beautiful Leo was a liar and a cheat at the best and at worst had more than likely hastened Lucas's premature death. The rest I could not bear to think about.

Removing the grainy fax from my jacket pocket, I took a closer look. It was bad enough to look at my wife standing on tiptoe to kiss the cheek of another man, his arm resting about her shoulders. It was quite another thing to realise I recognised the man the in the picture.

Tomorrow, I decided. I would go down to River House and compare the fax with the photograph standing in a silver frame on my desk. I was apprehensive about confirming my fears, as I feared what that would mean.

Chapter 27

The following day dawned bright and clear but as I drove towards River House rain clouds hung ominously on the horizon and by the time I'd reached Kings Datchet it was raining heavily.

Mrs Bates was out when I arrived. In the kitchen, Tinker lay asleep in his basket in front of the Aga. He opened one eye as I entered the room only to close it moments later, followed by a grunt and a snore. Searching in the fridge, I removed a can of beer, which I attacked with the urgency of a man stranded in the desert. My arid wilderness was of my own making and I had no one to blame but myself for the way things had turned out. If I'd not spent so much time on Softcell I might have been more attuned to events that were playing out in front of me and could have given Evelyn the support she needed. If I'd not been so blinded by Leonora's beauty then maybe I would have seen through her earlier. 'If only's' mounted up like bricks in a wall. I wanted them to come crashing down into a pile of useless rubble but with each thought, the wall became firmer and more impenetrable.

Whilst I was driving down from the city, the urgency to see the photograph in my study to confirm my suspicions was uppermost in my mind, but once I was within feet of my destination, I wanted to delay the inevitable.

Edging my way around Tinker's basket, I opened the back door. The earlier rain had eased and the bushes in the shrubbery were coated with a fine layer of drizzle. Cobwebs clung to branches like a bride's veil, gossamer threads of raindrops gleaming in the afternoon air.

I walked towards the river. The level of the water was low, a summer of minimal rainfall having had its effect. I remembered the time Evelyn and I had first seen the house; it was springtime and the river had been high enough for us to dangle our toes beneath its surface. An image of Evelyn laughing up at me as she dried her feet on the grass made me gasp. What was I waiting for? I strode up the garden and entered the kitchen, determination in every stride. This time Tinker raised his head and sniffed the air. He sensed something of the emotion I was feeling, padded out of his basket, and rubbed against my legs in sympathy. I patted his head. "Don't worry boy, go back to sleep," I murmured then took the stairs two at a time.

The room smelled of furniture polish and disuse. I opened the blinds and saw the dappled surface of the river winding its way along the bottom of the garden. Turning to face my fate, I walked to Leo's side of the bed and picked up the photograph. There was no mistake.

Taken at the Flood

I felt the twin emotions of anger and sadness sweep over me by turns as I looked at the image of Leo and I standing with our witnesses inside the register office on the Palazzo Cavalli. The registrar's clerk had taken the photo; Leo thought it would make a nice picture, the four of us, a constant memory. Anger surfaced as I remembered her suggesting that I ask the young man with the shock of fair hair, falling over his forehead, if he would be our witness. My anger dissolved and was replaced by sadness as I realised the fax I held in my hand was the catalyst that would end our marriage.

Downstairs in my study, I opened my desk drawer and removed a brandy bottle. I hadn't touched it for months but I was in need of more than the means to see me through the night, I needed something to see me through the rest of my life, a panacea for all ills.

I had to find out more about the woman who had so effectively conned her way into my life. How could I have been such a fool? She'd mesmerised me with her eyes and, besotted idiot that I was, I'd fallen completely under her spell.

I filled my glass once more and knew the time had come to open up some old wounds. Perhaps Evelyn's death would lead me into the future. Crossing the hallway as quietly as I could, without disturbing Tinker, I opened the door to the basement. The steps leading down were carpeted. It was one of the things that had reduced Evelyn to a fit of the giggles, when we'd first moved in. 'Who in their right mind would put carpet on basement steps?' she'd asked. But I had to admit there was something comforting in feeling the softness underfoot, especially as the effects of drinking on an empty stomach had made my feet unsteady.

The room was warm, central heating pipes above my head giving enough heat to make the atmosphere comfortable. I switched on the light and the neon strip illuminated the shelves packed with containers. On the bottom shelf stood the plastic storage box containing Evelyn's handbag and personal belongings. I'd been unable to face opening her handbag at the time of her death and had placed it in the container together with her diary, watch and jewellery.

I opened the lid and carried the box over to a table in the corner of the room then removed the leather handbag tipping the contents out on to the table. A long forgotten scent of Evelyn seeped into my nostrils and I closed my eyes conjuring up her image as if she were in the room with me. When I had the courage to open them, I saw a leather purse, containing some coins and a few notes, on the table. There was also a credit card wallet in the same brown leather, a lipstick, mobile phone and a small bottle containing tablets with the name **Cervotab** written in bold print on the chemist's

Taken at the Flood

label. I picked up the bottle and saw in faded typewritten print Mrs E Hope. Closing my fist tightly around the bottle, I felt a shaft of pain shoot down my left arm and a heavy feeling in the middle of my chest. I gasped, the pain was so intense; I struggled to catch my breath and felt air entering my lungs and the pain gradually fading. Slipping the bottle into my jacket pocket, I picked up Evelyn's diary, replaced the handbag and its contents in the storage box and left the room. As I climbed the basement stairs, I felt a twinge of pain in my arm that radiated towards the centre of my chest.

Carrying the diary into my study, I put my feet up on the couch and opened the yellowed pages. Evelyn's perfume lingered on the paper and again I felt her presence as if she were standing in the room alongside me. Turning the pages, I stopped at the day when Leo had first come into our lives, the day of the Dangerfield's party and started to read.

Chapter 28

We met the most amazing person today; her name is Leonora Bennett. She is beautiful and witty, I know my darling husband could not take his eyes off her and I noticed Henry had fallen under her spell too; the only person who was not impressed was Josie!

I heard Mrs Bates open the back door and Tinker's welcoming bark so closed the diary, slipping it into my desk drawer beneath some papers, there would be time enough to continue with my search through Evelyn's journal later, when I was alone.

"I'm taking a walk, Mrs Bates; I'll be back in an hour or two," I called to her from the hallway.

"Right, Mr Hope, see you later," she replied, pushing Tinker away with her foot.

Josie was clearing debris from the bottom of the garden as I approached. She raised her hand in greeting. "I've been so worried about you. I haven't seen you since I told you about Evelyn's pills. I think it was quite wrong of me. I haven't been able to tell Henry yet. I'm still waiting to pluck up the courage. I know he would, most definitely, not approve."

I put my hand on her arm and patted it gently saying, "Don't worry. It would seem you've done me a favour. I think your dislike of Leo may be well founded."

She frowned as I took the photo-fax from my pocket and held it up in front of her. "I think she's having an affair," I said, "but I'd be grateful if we could keep this news just between ourselves, until I have a chance to confront her."

She pushed a strand of hair away from her face and slipping her hand through the crook of my arm said, "Come on up to the house. I think we both need a stiff drink and as far as Henry's concerned or anyone else for that matter, you don't need to worry, I know nothing!"

I sighed and felt a twinge of pain across my chest.

"What is it?" she asked, her face full of concern.

"Nothing, just a twinge. I've had a few lately, perhaps I should see someone."

"Absolutely, promise me now, you will ring for an appointment tomorrow?"

The next day, at Josie's insistence, I telephoned an old friend of mine, who had a practice in Harley Street and to my surprise, he told me to come along to his consulting rooms at four o'clock that day. Adam Broadbent, consultant physician, and I had been in school together and had met socially a few times over the intervening years: I knew he was on our Christmas card list and that was as far as it went. I was therefore somewhat taken aback that the intervening years had turned the, once athletic dark haired, Adam, into the balding overweight man who was shaking my hand.

"Good to see you after all these years. I heard you had remarried, quite a looker, I gather," he said, removing his stethoscope from the top drawer of his desk and warming it between the palms of his hands.

I nodded unwilling to discuss my marriage in even a perfunctory manner, as the wounds were still raw. After exchanging pleasantries, I briefly explained my symptoms, adding, "I expect it's indigestion, but a friend of mine insisted I check it out."

He smiled and indicated I should lie on the couch in order to examine me.

After a while, he removed his stethoscope from my chest and frowned. "I don't think it's as simple as indigestion. In fact I'd like a cardiologist colleague of mine to take a look at you." He was writing on a pad, not looking up. "I'll give him a ring."

The moments passed in a daze, as I waited whilst he spoke with his colleague using the phone in the outer office. "That's fixed then," he said, as he sat behind his desk. "You have an appointment for ten o'clock in the morning. Here's his card. You'll see directions to the clinic on the reverse."

I thanked him and we promised to meet up again in the not too distant future.

When I reached my car, I looked at my reflection in the rear view mirror. There were dark rings around my eyes, the strain of the past few months clearly visible. I had to admit I was shocked by Adam Broadbent's haste in arranging my appointment with the cardiologist and began to wonder if there might be something seriously wrong. Shrugging my shoulders, I put the thought to the back of my mind. I'd far more pressing things to worry about than what I was sure would turn out to be nothing.

I decided to stay in town that night in order to drive out to the private clinic, which was near Hampstead Heath, first thing in the morning. I spent a restless night, dreams, of Evelyn and Leonora merging into a faceless creature that held my future within its grasp, were interspersed with wakeful periods, until dawn slid between the gaps in the blinds and released me from the horrors of the night.

It was raining when I arrived at the clinic so I walked quickly, dodging the puddles, towards a sign, which read Cardiology Out Patients. A nurse in a pink and white striped uniform showed me into Mr Edward Bentley's surgery. The room comprised an examination area with a corridor leading off it above which was a sign with the words Lung Function Laboratory and

Taken at the Flood

ECG department written in large blue letters. I realised my friendship with Adam had probably prompted such a speedy appointment - at least I hoped that was all it was.

Edward Bentley introduced himself, took a few preliminary notes and then examined my chest, saying, "We need to complete a series of tests this morning, which will take some time and when we have the results, I'll see you again to discuss how we should proceed. The preliminary test results should be ready later, probably after lunch. But we have a fine restaurant which I'm sure will help to make the waiting more bearable."

His well-practised bedside manner carried out to perfection, he stood up, shook my hand and left me to follow the nurse down the corridor.

The tests seemed interminable and to my mind, completely unnecessary. First I had to blow into a tube several times then run on a treadmill whilst electrodes recorded my heart rate and finally I was attached to an electrocardiograph machine and watched as a needle recorded the activity of my heart by means of peaks and troughs on a ribbon of graph paper. However, no machine could ever record the level of despair that had gripped my heart since I'd learned of Leo's treachery. The tests completed, I walked to the restaurant where the food on offer was of the nutritional

Taken at the Flood

kind but found I'd little appetite and picked at my meal disconsolately.

Later that afternoon, I sat in front of Edward Bentley and listened as he explained his diagnosis. I was suffering from acute angina, a condition, which should not be treated lightly. He said it was a warning and I must slow down, worry less, eat more healthily, cut down on alcohol, the list of forbidden pleasures seemed endless.

"I have written out a prescription for you, Mr Hope. If you take it to our pharmacy department, they'll have it made up for you. When you experience a return of the symptoms, slip one of these under your tongue and it will relieve the pain during an attack. However, I will want to see you in one month's time and then I'd like to arrange another chest X-ray and run some further tests."

After thanking him, and picking up my prescription, I headed for the car park through the downpour, which had continued since early that morning.

When I reached River House, I smelt the rich aroma of steak and kidney pudding wafting through the house. I felt my appetite resurface as I removed my coat and walked towards the kitchen.

"You're just in time, Mr Hope. I've laid a place for you at the kitchen table then I'm off to Emily's for the evening. There is a fresh cream trifle on the top shelf in the fridge." Mrs Bates was hanging her apron up on the hook near the back door as I entered the kitchen.

I thanked her and made a mental note to tell her about my radical change of diet but decided that tomorrow would be soon enough. The condemned man ate a hearty meal, I thought wryly

Later, having the house to myself, I removed Evelyn's diary from my desk drawer and read on.

Met L.B. today in town; I was with Josie and she didn't bother to disguise her feelings I felt most uncomfortable I don't know what is wrong with Josie. It's not like her at all.

I could imagine Josie's face registering her disapproval; she had no guile, no mendacity; her honesty showed for all to see. I turned the pages, mundane notes about shopping trips, dental and hairdressing appointments and increasingly references to meeting L.B. I also noticed that Josie was no longer mentioned and L.B. was also occasionally referred to as Leo.

Had lunch with Leo today; it was such fun we laughed and laughed .I hope Josie doesn't find out, she wouldn't be too pleased.

Anyway, what do I care? I feel alive and full of life when Leo and I are together. Who would have thought we would get on so well together? I can't wait for our next shopping trip!!!

I skipped a few pages and read,

Taken at the Flood

I'm starting to show. I don't think Leo likes it. I have to take iron tablets and vitamins and L.B. said she'd like to help. It would be easy for her to pick up repeat prescriptions from Lucas, she said, and it would be no trouble to collect them from the chemists in Kings Datchet. It was practically on her way to River House, she said. I think that is a slight exaggeration but it does mean Leo and I can spend more time together. Although, it is a bit of a nuisance to drive over to Kings Datchet, when we are having lunch in town.

I stared at the page, felt a twinge of pain and removing the tablets from my inside pocket, slipped one under my tongue. The pain subsided. It was beginning to look even more as if Leo was responsible for substituting Evelyn's tablets, in order to induce a miscarriage. How could anyone could be that evil, especially my Leo? I read on, afraid of what lingered inside the pages but unable to stop.

Leo has made things plain at last. An abortion would mean we would be able to enjoy ourselves without the hindrance of a baby, which would naturally take up most of my time. I was shocked. At first it was something I refused to contemplate, saying it wouldn't make that much difference to us. But there are pills apparently, so Leo said. It would be easy, no fuss, no one knowing except us.

Taken at the Flood

L.B. has been so kind. I think I might be wrong; she is trying to help me all she can. I had started to believe that she might not be such a good friend after all but now she cannot do enough for me. I was so tired today and she picked up my prescription..........

The following pages were blank and the date showed it was the day before the miscarriage. There was no doubt in my mind Leo had been responsible, it could not be more obvious. I turned the pages until I saw three pages completed the day before Evelyn's accident.

Met Leo, who is happy at last; we had a wonderful day together. I was able to forget the past few weeks and concentrate on enjoying Leo's company. I don't think I have laughed so much in all my life. Leo was right about the baby.....

There was another gap and then I read about the night Josie and Henry came to dinner.

Leo came to the house; my darling husband likes Leo I know. I can tell. It makes things a lot easier. I have taken antidepressants today. I'd forgotten how good they make you feel especially if you have had a drink. I don't think my darling husband approved and he didn't like L.B's dress either, well not on me. Anyway, I thought it was great and after all Leo likes it, so what does it matter what he thinks!!!!!

I began to wonder if Leo had altered Evelyn's antidepressant tablets as well. It would

Taken at the Flood

explain her unusual behaviour on that evening. The more I read the angrier I became, to think she had been responsible for robbing me of my baby and I was beginning to dread what else she had done.

I put the diary down on the side table and paced the floor. It couldn't be, my thoughts were running away with me. I refused to believe she had been responsible for Evelyn's death. It must have been an accident. I picked up the diary again and read the last page.

Meeting L.B. in town tomorrow. We have appointments at the hairdressers. I am going to go back to my natural colour. My darling husband wants me to and so does Leo so I don't see why not. I'm fed up with it anyway. L.B gave me an empty box of mints today because I liked the picture on the front. It was a picture of a clock with the words ANYTIME MINTS on the front. It made me laugh and she said why didn't I keep it

Throwing the diary down on the chair my face suffused with rage, I crossed the hall. The basement door was locked. I turned the key with shaking hands, rushed down the stairs two at a time and dragged the storage box from the bottom shelf with such force that the lid slid open spilling part of its contents on the concrete floor at my feet. The sealed plastic bag, the police had given me after the inquest, still contained a square package in a Harrods carrier bag. Inside was an oblong box containing a silk tie. It had been opened by the police and loosely re-packaged. I fingered the navy silk feeling it slip sensuously through my fingers. It was the last present Evelyn had bought for me and I had to swallow the lump that had risen in my throat, as I'd never been able to thank her.

At the bottom of the plastic bag lay the tin I'd forgotten was there. Inside its buckled lid, lay the dried remains of a large spider with two of its legs missing. I sat down heavily on the basement floor, resting my head in my hands. Now I knew what had happened to my wife on that icy road, as clearly as if I'd been sitting alongside her at the time. It had been no accident, no freak of nature that had made her skid on black ice. Leonora was well aware of Evelyn's fear of spiders. What could be simpler than to slip a handful of the creatures into the tin she had given her the day before and which no doubt was still in the car? When Evelyn dropped her off at the Bennetts' place, all Leo needed to do was to slide the lid open and let nature take its course. In my mind's eye, I could see it all: Evelyn driving along the road, catching sight of the spiders, there had to be more than one. I could see the panic in her eyes as she swerved and skidded on the ice. Glancing once more at the charred remains of the large spider, I imagined her horror as the creatures had crawled towards her.

Taken at the Flood

There was now no more doubt left in my mind. Leonora had killed her first husband, my child and my wife. I was waiting to welcome a murderer back into my bed at the end of her romantic holiday with her Italian lover.

I climbed the basement stairs, my steps heavy with despair, gaining no comfort from the softness underfoot. When I reached the cloakroom vomit rose up to my throat, hatred for the woman I'd married and what I'd inadvertently become rose in my throat as bitter as the bile trickling from my lips.

She was a stranger, who had wormed her way into my life like a poisonous snake ready for the kill. She was due to return from Italy the day after tomorrow. I would make sure I was waiting for her. I knew with certainty I had to avenge the past, if not for myself, for Lucas, Evelyn and the sake of my unborn baby.

Chapter 29

The Alitalia jet touched down on the runway, the roar from its engines ceasing as it taxied towards the landing gate. I watched it gradually cruise to a halt and link up with the terminal entrance then walked towards the arrivals lounge. She was the first to arrive. She was pushing a trolley packed with luggage and bulging carrier bags as she steered it towards me. I tried to smile but felt my facial muscles contract into a grimace. She ran to me, throwing her arms around my neck and kissing me full on the lips and I tried so hard not to push her away, tried hard not to feel the old familiar thrill as her body touched mine but was unsuccessful on both counts.

"Abe, are you all right?" she asked taking a step backwards and anxiously looking up at me, whilst scanning my face with her incredible eyes.

"Of course, darling." Desperate now to appear normal, I said, "Missed you, that's all." I turned towards the trolley and began to push it towards the exit.

"Oh, you had me worried for a moment. Let's hurry home and then I can tell you all about my trip."

Would she leave out the bit where she'd kissed another man, where she felt the pressure of his hands on her shoulders? I tried to keep calm, to at least look like it, 'If you torture yourself like this, she will notice,' I thought. It would be so easy to forget about it all, to love her unreservedly and forget about the past.

The drive to River House seemed endless. Leo chatted and I answered her, although what the conversation was about I cannot now recall.

Mrs Bates was spending time with her sister again. She'd suddenly remembered she had to leave, when I told her my wife would be returning and this time I couldn't blame her.

"It's so good to be home again. The weather in Italy was beautiful but it was very hot. I never thought I'd miss River House and the rain so much."

We were standing in the hall, her cases at the foot of the stairs. She stood on tiptoe in front of me waiting to be kissed. I swallowed hard, bent my head and our lips met. I inhaled her perfume, felt the silky curtain of hair against my neck and tasted her mouth. Even as I broke away with a lame excuse about having to carry the cases upstairs, I was desperate to return to the moment our lips first met and the rest of it was still in the future. She seemed satisfied and had not detected the coldness in my kiss nor the ice in my heart. I had passed the first test, it seemed.

"I can't wait to get into the shower and wash the grime of travelling away from my body. Why don't you join me?" she asked

Her eyes met mine and once more, I felt my resolve weaken. She was so beautiful. It would be easy to forget the past few weeks, to relent and enjoy the pleasure of being with her but Evelyn's face swam before my eyes and wiped away my hesitancy.

"You go on up. I've a few things to do in my study first."

Leonora did not change for dinner. After her shower, she floated around the house in a flimsy housecoat that barely covered her thighs and was tantalisingly transparent. Throughout dinner, she chatted about her trip and encouraged me to tell her what I'd been doing whilst she was away. My powers of invention were stretched to the limit as I tried to entertain her. The evening wore on interminably, as I tried to postpone the inevitable moment when I'd have to take her upstairs and make love to her, but to my surprise when I suggested we go to bed she said, "You go first, darling and I'll come up in a minute."

By this time I was suspicious of her every move and so making sure she saw me climbing the stairs, I waited out of sight until I heard her in the cloakroom. When she emerged I watched as she floated across the hallway, silent in her bare feet, towards my study. She took care not to make a sound as she opened the door.

I crept down the stairs and looked through the gap between the open door and the

Taken at the Flood

architrave. She was standing in front of the wall safe, which was open. Her hands were thrust deep into the body of the safe and a smile lingered at the corner of her mouth.

I'd seen enough and was in the bedroom by the time she crossed the hall. She had given me the knowledge I was seeking. It *was* Leo who was trying to ruin me financially. She'd obviously memorised the combination of my safe and in doing so had access to the computer discs and memory stick, which had been stored there. It had all been so deceptively simple; she had smiled at me, loved me and betrayed me and I had not suspected a thing.

After undressing, I slid beneath the sheets, my fists balled in uncontrollable anger. When she entered the bedroom, she slipped the robe she was wearing to the floor and joined me, her firm body spooned into mine.

She was tired. I felt her relax and her breathing deepen. My anger increased, I could not look at her without thinking about what she'd done to my life. If we had never met, Evelyn and I could have continued to live at River House, our child playing contentedly in the garden. My business would have prospered beyond my wildest dreams, devoid of a saboteur whose venomous body writhed in sleep at my side.

It's easy to say now that I should have left her, reported my suspicions to the police, or at least given her a chance to explain but rationality wasn't an option. Images crowded inside my head one after another, dreadful, heart-breaking pictures of the lives I'd lost. At that moment, my brain could take no more, something snapped. I unclenched my fists and wrapped my fingers tightly around her throat. Her ice blue eyes flew open, terror and confusion contorting her beautiful features. She struggled to breathe and as she struggled, I tightened my grip until every breath left her body and she lay motionless at my side.

Afterwards, I sat at the bottom of the bed, relief that I'd been able to go through with it, flooding my body. Sensation returned and with it clarity of mind. I dressed in an old pair of blue jeans and a black hooded parka, removed an oversized plastic cover from one of Leo's ball gowns and slid her body inside, zipping up the opening so she was completely encased in the cool silver-grey plastic. I refused to think of the pale lifeless form inside as my beautiful wife. The odd part of it was I didn't feel as if I'd lost my mind - I felt completely sane. She'd taken the life of my wife and child - I felt no guilt - a life for a life.

Somehow, I managed to carry her down to the utility room at the back of the kitchen. A surge of adrenaline had given my body the strength it lacked. She was a light as a goose down quilt. Nevertheless, I felt my heart pounding and the blood rushing to my face as I laid her on the concrete floor. I'd taken the precaution of putting Tinker in the kennels for a while. He missed Mrs Bates and I wanted to be free from the responsibility of caring from him.

There was a light breeze blowing up from the river as I removed the spade from the potting shed and walked towards the woods bordering the river path. It was dark – there was no moonlight that night and I had to rely on the beam from my torch to guide me. The ground was soft but even so it took me the best part of two hours to dig a hole deep enough to cover the body; I no longer thought of it as Leonora.

When I was satisfied, I carried the grey plastic cover and its contents across the lawn and into the woods. To my right I heard the gentle lapping of the river against its banks and an owl hooted high above my head. Taking care not to disturb the earth on either side, I lowered the body into the hole and covered it with earth, twigs and leaves, until I was sure no one would notice the ground had been newly dug. But I decided I would plant saplings there at the earliest opportunity just to make sure.

When I'd finished, I removed my clothes and placed them in the washing machine/dryer knowing that by morning all trace of my night's activity would be gone. Then I showered and went through Leo's suitcase removing her clothes one by one. The items she'd taken with

Taken at the Flood

her to Italy, together with the new clothes she'd bought there, I placed in the central heating furnace in the basement. Next, I removed the luggage labels from her cases, put them in the loft space with the rest of our luggage, and then went into my study to write the letter. It took me about an hour and a half to copy Leo's handwriting successfully. Dawn was breaking as I signed her name.

I couldn't eat but had to force down a cup of hot sweet tea and a biscuit whilst I waited for the hands of the clock to reach ten o'clock when I thought it would be reasonable to visit Henry and Josie.

At the bottom of the garden, I joined the river path and kept my eyes on the river. I couldn't look into the woods to my left for fear of losing the remaining contents of my stomach. The events of the previous night seemed more real in the first light of day as I struggled to wipe them from my mind.

My feet slowed when I saw the house. I wanted to run; anything to put off the task I knew I must perform. Taking a deep breath and ruffling my hair into an untidy mop, I rushed up the garden towards the conservatory where Henry was reading the morning paper.

"Good Lord, what on earth's the matter? You look as if you've just seen a ghost." Henry's paper slid from his lap as Josie arrived carrying a pot of coffee. She took one look at my face, placed the coffee pot on the table in front of Henry and took my arm. She guided me like a blind man towards a chair and waited until I felt I could speak.

I wasn't acting. I had genuinely lost my voice. My heart wanted my lips to blurt out, I've killed her, I've killed my beautiful Leonora, but thankfully my brain ignored it as I mumbled, "She's left me." I held out the letter. "I found this when I awoke. It came in this morning's post."

Josie and Henry looked at me aghast, their faces full of sympathy and understanding. Then Josie read the letter I handed to her,

My dear Abe,

I'm sorry I have to let you know by letter but haven't got the strength to tell you in person. I'm leaving you. I wish things could have been different and I did try to make a go of our marriage. The truth is, on one of my Italian visits, I met an old friend and we became lovers. I realise there is no way I could make a sham out of our marriage. It wouldn't be fair to you. I hope you'll try to forgive me. Please don't try to find me. I'll not be coming back to River House. Do as you wish with my clothes and jewellery. I'm sure there are some worthwhile charities that could benefit. I took all I needed with me on my last visit.

Leonora

Henry coughed and muttered something about, if there was anything he could do to help I only had to ask, and Josie took me in her arms and patted my back like a baby.

"Where is she now? The letter doesn't say?" Henry asked.

"I don't know, the envelope was posted in Rome but I couldn't bring her back, even if I tried. You can see that. She doesn't want to be found. Well not by me anyway."

I shivered and Henry coughed.

Then, I said I was devastated and would like to spend some time alone for a while. I told them I'd be speaking to Mrs Bates and asking her not to return to River House until I contacted her again. They nodded, their sympathy plain to see, and, as I walked back along the river path, I could feel their compassion flowing behind me like an unstoppable tide.

The day after I buried Leonora, I rang the offices of Brockwell and Hansen, spoke to their secretary and arranged an appointment for two o'clock that afternoon.

Taken at the Flood

The reception area was deserted when I arrived so I waited until the door to the inner office opened and Martin Brockwell emerged carrying a thick manila folder under his arm, followed by the redoubtable Eileen. "Ah, do go in, sir," she said, sliding past me to her seat behind her desk.

The room was as it had been before, except that the blinds covering the windows were open this time, and I could see into Russell Square. Ian Hansen was speaking on the telephone and indicated a chair in front of him. I sat down and waited. When he'd finished, he replaced the receiver, a frown creasing his forehead. "Sorry to keep you, Mr Hope, tricky problem to deal with, I'm afraid."

"Hazards of your profession I should think, Mr Hansen," I said, taking a seat. He nodded absentmindedly, opened a ring file, which lay on the desk in front of him and removed a large brown envelope.

"Here are the photographs I took during my stay in Tuscany," he said, sliding the envelope across the desk towards me. "I must say I was surprised when my colleague instructed me that surveillance was to be terminated after only seven days. I'd planned to make further enquiries on your behalf during the second week of you wife's stay. You see I have very little to show you except these."

Taken at the Flood

I glanced briefly at the photographs. Leo walking through cobbled streets, a large tower in the background, her arm linked with that of the witness at our wedding, Leo, laughing with him as they drank wine at a kerbside table. Another in a café drinking frothy coffees from large mugs, their heads together, lost in deep conversation. I'd seen enough.

"There was no need to delay your stay further Mr Hansen, the evidence was clear enough when you forwarded the photo-fax of them together, at the beginning of the week. I recognised the man in the photograph immediately. The same sad sordid story, no doubt, you've heard a thousand times before."

He sighed as I handed him the brown envelope. "Destroy these if you will, please." I reached into my inside pocket and removed the letter. "I received this from my wife yesterday." I reached across and handed him the letter I'd written.

He read it through to the end and sighed again, "I see, well that is rather what we expected, did we not? I'll carry out your instructions to the letter, sir and as it appears our business is terminated, I'll direct Eileen to make out an invoice immediately."

I waited in the outer office while Eileen typed furiously on an electronic keypad, settled the account in full, turned to Mr Hansen, who'd come into the outer office to shake my hand and

Taken at the Flood

said, "Thank you. Your discretion in this matter is appreciated."

"Our watchword is discretion, Mr Hope. Discretion in all things!" he replied tapping the side of his nose with his finger as he showed me to the door.

That night I began writing this journal. As usual, I lay awake waiting for sleep to come. At four o'clock, I sat up and walked downstairs to my study. In the top drawer of my desk, I found what I was looking for. A loose-leaf notebook secured by a circular ring binder. Taking a pen from the stack on my desk, I carried the notebook and pen back to my bedroom and began to write it all down until sleep at last overcame me.

At the end of the month, I visited the clinic for my appointment with Mr Edward Bentley. I sat in the consulting room and felt an uneasy stirring in the pit of my stomach as I waited for the cardiologist's opinion.

"I've evaluated the results of your tests, including today's X Ray's, Mr Hope. The news is not quite as bad as I had, at first, feared. None of the coronary arteries appear to be blocked, which means that for the moment by-pass surgery is not an option. However, your arteries are in a poor state for a man of your age. There is a degree of narrowing, usually associated with someone in his sixties, so it is therefore

Taken at the Flood

imperative you change your lifestyle and change it drastically if you are to avoid surgery in the future."

The clock on the wall ticked loudly as I listened to his voice telling me if I continued to work at a pace which caused stress to build up, I would experience repeated angina attacks and I must avoid placing myself in stressful situations, as often as possible. I wondered if burying your wife in the shrubbery came into that category and felt hysterical laughter bubbling inside like a geyser about to erupt.

When he'd finished, he showed me to an office at the end of a corridor, where he said a dietician would provide me with a healthy eating plan and shook my hand as he emphasised, "Angina is a warning, Mr Hope and one which you would be foolish to ignore."

I left the clinic clutching a repeat prescription and diet sheet, determined I would take a break from work, forget the past week, and relax.

The following week, I drank to find oblivion. The second week Mrs Bates returned, released Tinker from the kennels, admonished me for getting into a state about 'that trollope' as she had taken to calling Leonora and set about baking enough food to feed the five thousand. Leaving the whiskey untouched, I ate enough to keep Mrs Bates happy and read a stack of trashy novels I'd never had time to complete.

Taken at the Flood

The lawn at River House was white with frost. The sun's weak rays filtering through grey clouds turning the woodland, where Leonora lay, into a wonderland. Cobwebs glittered as they clung to bare branches and twigs swayed in the breeze shaking sugar-like particles of frost on to the frozen earth beneath.

I was staring out of the conservatory window, trying to block the image of my beautiful treacherous Leo from my mind, but my eyes kept returning to the woods and the patch of earth where she lay. It seemed that whilst I was at River House I'd never be free of her but somehow I couldn't face leaving. As I watched a robin hopping on the frozen earth, I became aware of a car drawing up on the gravel drive outside and of Mrs Bates letting someone into the house. I remained seated, lost in thought.

"Hello, enjoying your break from the office?"

It was Alan. He stopped in front of my chair admiring the view for a moment and then sat down opposite me, his back to the woods. I smiled; at least what passed as a smile these days. It was actually little more than a stretching of the skin at the side of my mouth.

"It's good to see you. Not bad news?" I said, beginning to fear that his visit was not just to find out how I was coping with my wife leaving me.

Taken at the Flood

"On the contrary, I'm the bearer of good news." His face stretched into a broad grin. "I had to come and tell you in person. We've found our saboteur!"

Chapter 30

I felt as if a weight was pressing down on my chest; the colour drained from my face and I gasped. I was dreading hearing what Alan had to say. "Quite a shock eh?" he said, lying back in his chair.

"Who?" My voice was barely audible.

"Chip Thornley."

The pain in my chest slid down my arm like ice melting as Alan continued, "Our security boys have done a grand job. They've been working away at this for weeks and at last they've cracked it. They found that Microbites had recruited our Mr Charles Thornley during his time at University and that he's been passing information to them ever since. I could kick myself for introducing you to him, I had no idea."

Alan hung his head. I couldn't speak, my voice dried in my throat. The minutes ticked by Alan looking more and more uncomfortable. Finally, I said, "No one could have known. I didn't doubt his sincerity, why should you?"

Alan relaxed but the effort of talking had taken its toll, the pain was radiating across my chest as I fumbled in my pocket and slipped a tablet into my mouth. He seemed not to notice and expanded his story.

"He was clever, I'll grant you. He must have been waiting for an opportunity such as *Gemini* to come along. Do you know, he memorised the safe code by listening to the sound the digits made on the keypad when we opened the safe? He could hear it from his office, if the vents were open."

"What about the key?" I asked, not able to understand how he could have opened the safe without it.

Alan shifted in his seat and his face reddened. "My fault again," he admitted. "It happened so easily. One morning I arrived at the office early, before the night staff had left. I needed an early start to finish tying up some loose ends and I thought I'd have time to work in peace before the rest of the staff arrived with their problems for me to sort out." He wiped his forehead with his handkerchief. "Anyway, someone had parked in my space and I had to drive to the office staff section and walk further than anticipated, so I was in a bad mood to start with. Then the programme kept crashing and I was getting nowhere fast when Chip arrived. I threw him my keys without thinking and asked him to move my car for me. He was out of my office before I remembered the safe key was on my key ring. My only excuse is that I had no reason to doubt his loyalty to the company."

"How did he copy the key without arousing your suspicion?" I asked.

"He must have been prepared for just such an eventuality. I suspect he carried some sort of

Taken at the Flood

clay device in his pocket, ready to take an impression of the key if an opportunity arose, because he was gone no longer than it would have taken him to move my car and return to the office."

He looked out over the frozen landscape and sighed, "At least we know our future projects are safe."

"He's gone, I presume?"

"Once he suspected we were on to him, he was off like a rat up a drainpipe. On the next available flight to the States and the offices of Microbites, I should imagine."

He stood up, "I can see this is all a bit much for you to take in. I shouldn't have come, not while you are still recovering from the news about Leo."

The pain was easing. "Nonsense, "I said. "I appreciate you holding the fort. It's good to know I can always rely on you." I was trying to appear normal. "I think this news calls for a celebratory drink. Come into the sitting room and I'll open the Remy."

Pouring the golden liquid into the brandy balloons, Edward Bentley's words going unheeded, the importance of our conversation hit me with full force. My hands began to shake uncontrollably as the realisation dawned that if Thornley was the culprit then Leonora was innocent of sabotage.

Taken at the Flood

After Alan left, I went into my study. I'd been so sure she was the one trying to destroy my company. Why else would she have been looking in my safe on her return from Tuscany on that fateful night? I remembered her looking over her shoulder secretively as she entered my study. I supposed she must have seen me open my safe on countless occasions and had memorised the code. I'd never felt the need to be cautious where Leo was concerned; I'd trusted her without question.

Crossing the floor to the safe, I tapped in the code and opened it. I hadn't had reason to open it since before Leo had gone to Italy. In fact, I'd forgotten the significance of her action that night until now. The weeks following her death I'd spent trying to exist, attending appointments, finalising my contract with Brockwell and Hansen and generally operating on automatic pilot; now as I stood in front of the opened safe, I feared what I'd find.

It lay on the shelf under a pile of computer discs, which were copies of partially completed programmes. I picked up the package, which was inside a paper bag with a clock face on the front surrounded by Italian script. Sliding it out of the bag, I saw a square box wrapped in silver paper with a gift tag attached by a thin silver thread. I carried it to my desk and laid it carefully on the highly polished surface then opened the gift tag and read;

Taken at the Flood

> ***To my darling Abe,***
> ***for loving me so long and so well,***
> ***My thanks and love, always, Leo X***

I removed the wrapping paper, lifted the lid of the box and saw it contained a gold watch. I lifted it up and saw the inscription in Italics on the reverse of the dial. It read, *Abe and Leo* and the date.

It had been a long-standing joke between us that I would never buy a watch until the hands fell off the existing one. I held it and felt my heart pounding in my chest. What was going on? Why would she buy such a present, was it another facet of her treacherous nature, or something else? The possibility that she hadn't deceived me with another man was something I refused to contemplate. The evidence of her infidelity lay shredded in the offices of Brockwell and Hansen. And there *was* no mistake. I'd seen it with my own eyes.

Chapter 31

Alan's news had a profound effect on me. Guilt seeped into me like damp into the walls of a derelict building and I spent less and less time in River House, the place where memories gnawed at my conscience. I saw Leonora everywhere, heard her laughter flowing throughout the house and could not tolerate looking out into the woodland. Every day that passed I tried to forget what I'd done but failed miserably.

The apartment in Mayfair became my refuge. Her presence was less obvious there and I was able to put her to the back of my mind for hours at a time. Softcell was ticking over and Alan was thrilled I'd made him a Director of the Company at last.

I became aimless and wandered around the city like a lost soul. My friends were sympathetic and understanding but none of them knew the truth. What would they say if they knew what I'd done? Would their generosity stretch to harbouring a murderer in their midst?

I spent my evenings in an alcoholic daze once more but this time the soporific effect was absent. Instead, I drifted into a sleep filled with haunting dreams, which failed to disperse on waking. Television became my constant companion. I watched daytime chat shows, soaps, news reports, dramas, cooking programmes, DIY and travel shows. One evening when I was watching a travel programme about Italy, I became aware that the image on the screen was familiar to me. I was half-heartedly watching the presenter's dyed blonde hair falling in her eyes as she walked up a cobbled street. She passed kerb-side tables situated outside cafes, each with an attractive array of tablecloths draped over them and then I watched her stride uphill towards a large stone tower looming in the background. Across the screen floated the words San Gimignano, Tuscany.

I sat up, suddenly remembering where I'd seen the place before. It was in the offices of Brockwell and Hansen and I was staring at a photograph of my wife with another man. Then I remembered a postcard Ian Hansen had sent me during his investigation, which was still in the drawer of my desk at River House.

The next day I went down to River House. I was feeling like shit, my drinking was having an effect. Stubble grew on my chin. I looked like a tramp and as far removed from the photograph of me in HI LIFE magazine, as it was possible to be. My hair had grown long and my skin had an unhealthy pallor.

The house looked deserted as I drove up. The shutters on the upstairs windows were closed, as were the blinds on the ground floor windows. I was surprised to see Josie walking away from the front door as I locked my car and went to meet her.

"Oh there you are. Henry and I were beginning to think you must have moved. We see far too little of you these days. How are things?" she asked, kissing my cheek and grimacing. "I can see you need taking in hand, my lad." She laid an affectionate hand on my shoulder.

I gave a rueful smile. "I know I look disgraceful; I promise I'll shape up some time soon. As for not seeing me, I can't seem to settle in River House for long, I'm too restless."

She looked at me and sighed. "I understand; too many memories for one thing. Look, one of the reasons I've come over to see you is, Henry and I are having an anniversary party at the weekend. We've been married for ten years and are celebrating with a few friends. We really would like you to join us. Say you will?"

I stroked my chin, felt the rough hairs dragging against my fingertips and hesitated. "I don't think….." I began then raised my eyes to her face. Dear Josie who had known Evelyn in her youth and had stayed loyal in spite of everything was trying to save me from myself. "I'll be there," I said, "but please, please, don't invite some unattached female on my behalf."

She laughed, called to her dogs and replied, "I see you know me too well. See you at eight on Saturday."

Taken at the Flood

She left me standing there and took the river path towards her house. I watched her go, saw the dogs run through the woods past the place where I'd buried Leo and waited with trepidation, but they just sniffed the ground as usual until she called them to heel, and continued along the path until she was lost from view.

Afterwards, in my study, I picked up the telephone on my desk and ordered flowers to be delivered to the Dangerfields' house for Saturday, then opened the bottom drawer and felt around until my fingers closed on the postcard. As I had thought, there in front of me was the small Tuscan town of San Gimignano its towers dwarfing the surrounding landscape. Picking up the telephone again, I dialled the number of Thomas Cook's office and booked a flight to Pisa for the following Monday morning. I also arranged for a hire car to be waiting at the airport. Deciding the time had come for me to go in search of Leonora's mysterious aunt and whatever else I may find in Tuscany had given me a sense of purpose. However, hovering at the back of my mind was the question, what if I was opening Pandora's box, and would it be safer to stay at home?

Chapter 32

Champagne corks were popping as Josie opened the front door to me. She looked very like she had on the night Evelyn and I had first visited her all those years ago, elegant, sophisticated and adorable. Henry Dangerfield was a very lucky man, I thought, but then Henry was aware of it and had told me so on many occasions.

The room was full of people but this time Evelyn, Leo and Lucas were buried deep beneath the ground and I alone had the knowledge that three bodies now lay beneath the soil.

The unattached female Josie had invited to 'make up the numbers' was a small mousy creature, who replied to questions with one-word answers and then waited expectantly for the conversation to continue. After failing to keep up the flow, I retreated to find Henry. He was in the billiards room at the back of the house puffing away on a sly cigar.

"I see you've found my hiding place, old bean," he said, swinging his chair around to face me.

"Still not allowed to smoke in the rest of the house I see, Henry."

"Josie'd have a fit if she could see me smoking at all. She's decided it's not good for me. I have to grab the odd puff whenever and wherever I'm able. I noticed she was in deep conversation with Sarah Jessop about cushion covers so sloped off here for a spot of indulgence. Glad you felt you could come tonight," he said, abruptly changing the subject.

"Can't bury myself away for ever, as a matter of fact I've decided to push off to Italy for a month or two. Soak up some sun and get away from the winter."

Henry looked at me and sighed. "Not trying to find her, are you?" His eyes narrowed in the smoke from his cigar.

"I suppose at the back of my mind there is always the possibility I might bump into her. But no, I've decided to close that chapter of my life. Josie did try to warn me and now I realise I should have taken more notice."

"She is very beautiful. I can understand your obsession," Henry said.

"Obsession?" I thought for a moment. "Yes, I suppose you could call Leonora an obsession, my beautiful obsession. But the letter she sent me put an end to all that."

Henry muttered some words of sympathy and I walked around the room towards the glass cabinet housing his polo cups and medals, aware that he was contentedly puffing away behind me. I noticed a small silver cup on a wooden stand dated the year before I had met Evelyn. The plaque read *To Henry L. Dangerfield,*

Captain and the date of their win against the Argentineans.

"What does the L stand for?" I asked idly inspecting a row of medals on the shelf beneath the cup.

"Leonard, my father and grandfather were both blessed with the name and it sort of got handed down to me but thank heavens only as a middle name, I don't think I can quite see myself as a Leonard, do you?"

We laughed together and Henry reminisced with me about his time in Argentina. "I was a different man then you know. What a time we had. I was young, successful and what they would call today a 'babe magnet'".

I spluttered into my drink, "Sorry," I apologised.

"No need to apologise. I can see it might be difficult to imagine now, but back then we had the world at our feet. Groups of girls used to follow the team around to different tournaments and if you won, well then, you were flavour of the moment and could take your pick. I had the time of my life, I can tell you." He looked down at his legs and the smile slipped from his face. I coughed in embarrassment not knowing what to say until he suddenly brightened. "Anyway that was then and this is now and I have Josie - the best consolation prize any man could have."

Taken at the Flood

It was my turn to look wistful and this time I sensed Henry's discomfort as the door opened and an autocratic voice announced.

"So this is where you are both hiding. Come on you two we're waiting to cut the cake. Put out that cigar you're holding behind your back first, Henry dear," Josie added, sweetly.

When I said goodbye to them both later that evening, I think I knew then it would be for the last time. I was glad I'd made the effort to go to their party and sorry our lives had taken such differing paths, theirs to happiness, and mine to despair.

When Monday arrived, I closed up the house. Mrs Bates had rung earlier in the week and advised me that she would be returning at the end of the following week and I told her I didn't expect to be back for quite a while. She didn't seem to think this was odd and, as I hadn't asked her to terminate her employment, seemed satisfied with the arrangement.

As I boarded the aeroplane, I felt a terrific burden lift from my shoulders. I was leaving the horror behind, I thought, unaware that I couldn't have been more wrong.

"Would you like something to drink, sir?"

The pretty airhostess, her dark hair tied up on top of her head, waited at my elbow for my reply.

Taken at the Flood

"Brandy, thank you," I replied leaning over to look out of the window from my seat in first class. It was a clear sunny day. There were no clouds to hide the view of the Alps as we soared high above them. Far below I saw snow-capped peaks rising up into the sky like giant coconut cakes and turned back to the pages of my paperback with a sigh of contentment. When I looked down again, holding a tumbler containing a large measure of brandy, it was to see the Italian landscape spreading out beneath me like a map, lakes and mountains giving way to fields dotted with red-roofed houses, stretching as far as the eye could see. Cars sped by on miniature roads like ants on a ribbon and I marvelled at the changing scenery with new eyes. I'd buried myself in work for too long and missed the pleasures of a relaxing holiday with nothing to worry about. I was kidding myself, trying to forget what had happened on that fateful night, trying to pretend it hadn't happened. Part of my brain succeeding in blocking out the horror of it all but far beneath the surface it was waiting to reappear, waiting to compromise my sanity.

The flight was smooth, as was the landing. Customs clearance was unusually quick and efficient for a country known to find haste an anathema. I found my hire car waiting at the airport terminal, a Fiat convertible that had seen better days, its white paint scratched and dented in places where previous drivers had conformed to the Italian code of driving. It was the kind of car that could be seen on any Italian street and as such I knew it would not arouse unwanted suspicion. As I sat behind the wheel and consulted the maps I'd brought with me, I wondered why I was pursuing something, which might have been better left alone but knew I had no choice. When I laid Leo to rest, she'd refused to remain beneath the soil and, although she was hidden from my sight, my soul was in turmoil. Ever since that day, she haunted my every waking hour, insidiously torturing my consciousness. I'd lost count of the number of times I'd thought I'd seen her shopping in the city or walking along a country lane ahead of me. At night, when I lay dreaming, she entered my head, her beautiful blue eyes pleading with me for forgiveness.

Alan's recent revelation had shaken me to the core. If she was innocent of sabotage, was it possible she could also have been blameless where Evelyn was concerned?

I clung on to the fact I'd had photographic evidence confirming my suspicions regarding her infidelity and her countless visits to Italy but I could feel the threads of certainty beginning to unravel and dreaded the outcome of my journey. Nevertheless, I was determined to discover the reason why she was so insistent that I shouldn't accompany her on her previous visits to her 'aunt'.

During the drive out of Pisa, I took the road leading through verdant countryside. To either side of me I saw fields of sunflowers nodding their large golden heads in the sunshine, colouring the landscape in a sheet of yellow. The road became steeper and narrower until I saw the towers of the small Tuscan town of San Gimignano in the distance; those same towers I'd seen on Leo's postcard and on the travel programme. I wound my window down and sniffed the warm fresh scented air, as I looked around for a place to park.

From what I could make out, it seemed as if most of the small town was paved for pedestrian use, accessible by foot or bicycle alone, but I'd noticed a tourist bus further down the road making for a car park, outside a large stone walled area and so headed in the same direction.

Removing my small trolley case from the boot of the car, I locked it and walked towards the outskirts of the town where I could see an information office in the distance. Fortunately, the woman behind the counter spoke excellent English and advised me to book into the Hotel Colligiata but after taking a cursory glance at the brochure, I asked if she could recommend a small guesthouse, as I was not sure how long my visit would be. She nodded and produced a card with F. Orsini, Proprietor of Santa Lucia guesthouse, written in green cursive writing on one side and on the other, a sepia drawing of a square stone building, which, I was assured, lay in a side street off the main cobbled square.

Climbing the cobbled incline, which gradually rose through a narrow street lined with gift shops, I stopped to catch my breath and noticed passageways at intervals traversing the main thoroughfare and caught glimpses of the hills, which surrounded the town. I picked up my case and walked on until I reached a side street down which I could see the sign of the Orsinis' guesthouse swinging on a bracket above the front door. The stone building was square and stood three storeys in height, wedged in-between a wine bar and a shop selling newspapers and magazines.

A middle-aged man with thick greying hair opened the front door as I reached it and held it open for me to pass through into the hallway. Behind a small desk in the corner stood a woman who smiled shyly at me as I approached her.

"I would like a room, please," I said, putting my suitcase down on the floor.

"Perhaps I introduce myself and my wife?" the man who had opened the door for me held out his hand. "I am Franco Orsini and this is my wife, Cecilia." The woman inclined her head in my direction.

"How long you'll be staying with us?" Franco asked, pulling a large register towards him and opening it with a flourish.

"I am not sure. It may be for some time."

"No problem, sir, the room is yours for as long as you like."

I thanked him and he added, "Now I show you the way," as he picked up my case and turned towards the staircase beckoning me to follow.

The room was on the first floor overlooking the street.

"Breakfast is at 9.30 and dinner 7.00 o'clock," Franco said, putting my suitcase down on the floor at the foot of the bed. As he started to leave, I handed him two large denomination notes and saw the spring in his step as he walked towards the staircase. His gaze lingering on the lira notes, he thrust them into the pocket of his cotton trousers and I knew I had only to repeat the gesture to gain his trust.

The room was clean and adequate for my purposes; it wasn't the Ritz but then if I'd wanted luxury I would have stayed elsewhere. There was single bed, its headboard resting against the middle of one wall, covered with a patchwork cotton quilt. Either side of the bed stood a side table, on one lay a telephone and on the other a lamp. A large dark wooden wardrobe with a full-length mirror set into one of the doors, stood opposite the bed and a small

Taken at the Flood

dressing table sat under a watercolour of the town on the wall opposite the window.

My reflection in the mirror startled me. I was overweight and dark circles ringed my eyes. Evelyn would have said I looked years older than my age and she would have been spot on. I walked over to the window to draw the curtains as the light was fading and then I saw her.

She was hurrying down the narrow street beneath my window, her pale blonde hair flowing behind her like a wave. At the corner of the street, she paused beneath a street lamp and I caught my breath as she turned her head and I saw her face. It was Leo.

I began to shake and wrapped my arms around my body. It was getting worse, before I had simply imagined I was seeing her passing by, only to be disappointed when a stranger turned to face me. Now I was actually seeing her. There was no mistake. The girl who had stood in the street beneath the lamp had Leo's face. I shuddered as I drew the curtain, opened my luggage and removed the flask of brandy nestling amongst my clothes. Never had I needed its solace more than I did at that moment. I feared for my sanity and as midnight approached, the image of what I had done shook me as forcibly as a madman shakes the bars of his cell.

I couldn't sleep but when I finally closed my eyes my dreams were troubled by half remembered moments that dissolved into a mist as the faint rays of morning sunshine crept through the thin cotton curtains covering the windows.

The smell of breakfast cooking surprised me. I suppose I'd thought a continental breakfast of rolls, coffee, ham and cheese was the most I could hope for. Ever since that night I'd had little appetite but the aromas wafting up the steep staircase from the Orsinis' kitchen made me ravenous.

Cecilia Orsini smiled at me as I entered the small dining room. She was wearing a striped blue and white apron and I suspected she'd had a hand in preparing the breakfast of eggs, bacon and large bright red tomatoes that she placed in front of me. "A nice hot day," she said, and I suspected her English was limited to a few basic phrases.

I complimented her on her cooking and she made the same facial responses that Mrs Bates would have done. The thought of River House made me shudder and I resolved to put it as far out of my mind as I could.

My subsequent days were spent searching the medieval town for anything that might lead me to Leonora. During this time, an idea occurred to me. In a small bookshop, I bought another blank notebook and decided to continue with the journal, which lay in the bottom of my suitcase. I hoped it would become an occupation that would eventually rid Leo's ghost from my memory.

I decided it might be a good idea to become known in the area as a tourist who was planning to stay for some time, in the hope that the locals would tell me as much as they knew about Leonora and her family.

I spent my days in the Piazza drinking coffee and watching the world go by, lunching on spaghetti and red wine and chatting to the café owners. I strolled into the gift shops lining the cobbled walkways, bought trinkets and souvenirs, passed the time of day with the shopkeepers and inspected the churches with what I hoped would appear to be an interest it the architecture.

The days were hot and at mid-day I often sought the shade of a large lemon tree growing in a field bordered by a low wall on which I sat and drank in the glorious scenery. If things had been different I could have stayed here and left 'Softcell' and the rat race for good.

It was at the beginning of the second week of my stay in San Gimignano that I met George Masters. The temperature had steadily risen during the day and I'd managed to escape the heat of the midday sun by finding shelter under a canvas awning outside a small restaurant with a great view of the surrounding countryside. I sat at a table covered by a red and white check tablecloth, ordered a pizza and a large glass of red wine, and then sat back in my chair to enjoy the view. In front of me lay a small stone wall about two feet high and beyond, for as far as I could see, were fields and trees in more shades of green and gold than I would ever have thought it possible to imagine. To my left sat a man with his back to me. He was sitting on a canvas stool, facing an easel. I watched him dip his brush into a pot of water, add a colour and transform the blank canvas in front of him into the scene that lay beyond the wall, skilfully converting blobs of paint into trees, flowers and rooftops catching the afternoon light. With each stroke of his brush, the canvas came alive. I was fascinated. Putting my glass down on the table, I strolled towards him and watched spellbound, as he put the finishing touches to the watercolour.

"That's really very good," I said, standing behind him. He turned a weather beaten face in my direction, a myriad of fine lines framing his eyes and mouth.

"Thank you."

"Would you consider selling it?" I asked

"Certainly but for the right price, of course."

"Excellent," I replied, holding out my hand and introducing myself.

"George Masters," he replied, "Although locally they call me Georgio."

"I wonder if you would care to share a bottle of wine with me whilst we wait for the paint to dry on my new acquisition," I asked, pointing to my table under the canvas awning.

"I think I can be persuaded, without too much effort," he replied, packing up his stool and easel and resting them against the wall.

We talked about art in general and the beauty of the Italian landscape in particular and as the wine flowed more freely he told me a little about his life.

"I was a young art student when I first visited San Gimignano," he explained. "I'd been travelling outside the town and was struck by the unusual light flooding the surrounding fields in the late afternoon. Today is a fine example - see there," he pointed in the direction of a gentle escarpment lined with trees. The sunlight filtering through the leaves turned each one to colours only a true artist would appreciate. I nodded as he continued, "I think I'd been in the town for as little as two days when I first saw my Maria. She was so beautiful, thick black hair, dark eyes and her figure!" His face softened as he spoke of her, "I fell in love with her at first sight and to my good fortune I found she held similar feelings. Afterwards, it would have taken an earthquake to uproot me from San Gimignano and my lovely Maria."

"Go on," I prompted.

"Well it took some time to persuade her family that she should marry a penniless English artist but I think they were able to see how much we loved each other and the rest is history as they say. I've managed to provide a decent living for my wife and family over the years and now it's just the two of us."

He raised his glass to his lips narrowing his eyes in the sunlight, then said, "Our daughter is married and living in Lucca and our son is studying architecture in Rome. I paint now merely for pleasure and if I'm able to make some money from the tourists so much the better, eh?"

He laughed and his face creased in good humour until his eyes almost disappeared amongst the laughter lines.

When we'd finished the wine, we agreed a price for the painting and George gave me his address.

"Maria and I would be glad if you'd come and visit us before you return to England," he said, as I shook his hand once more. Then he left carrying his painting equipment under one arm and a bottle of red wine to share with Maria, under the other.

I was beginning to see why Leonora had escaped to this place so often. The pace of life was slow to the point that I sometimes wondered if time had stood still and I found the longer I stayed I finally began to relax and to forget the reason for my visit.

I met George Masters often and became a frequent guest at his house. His Maria was still

Taken at the Flood

beautiful, although her hair was no longer black but threaded with fine grey strands. She welcomed me into their home and encouraged me to visit when the fancy took me.

"George, he misses his English friends. Oh, I know he would not say as much but I know him. It is so good he has found you. I'm glad you say you don't have to hurry home," she told me as she kissed my cheek.

I remember my visits to their home as being always filled with laughter and I could well imagine why George had forsaken England for his place in the sun.

It was the end of the third week and I'd become recognised by the locals who appreciated my faltering attempts to speak Italian and smiled encouragingly when I, more often than not, muddled up my sentences making little sense. It became usual for me to meet George most days, sit with him, and watch the world go by while he painted his pictures. I never asked him about Leo. I was afraid to spoil everything.

I'd been in San Gimignano for nearly a month and the tourist season was in full swing. The temperature had risen with every passing day and I was as brown as the locals. Buses loaded with pensioners arrived on Sunday mornings. I watched them walking unsteadily over the cobbles until they reached the Piazza

Taken at the Flood

then became dwarfed by the twin towers looming above them.

It was on one such Sunday morning that I saw Leonora again. This time I was sitting at a table outside Antonio's café, a favourite haunt of George's. The sun was beating down out of a clear blue sky, in the distance the Sunday morning peal of bells rang out and the usual line of pensioners, their sticks tap tapping on the cobbles, passed in front of me. I looked across the street, blowing the froth off the top of my cappuccino and saw a flash of blonde hair. She was looking straight at me and I felt as though the past six months had been a dream. I watched her, my heart thumping in my chest as she entered a confectionery shop and re-emerged carrying a small package. Then as she walked up the hill, I hurried behind her afraid she would disappear like a forgotten dream.

Chapter 33

Walking quickly trying to lessen the gap between us, the nearer I came I was certain it was Leo; there could be no doubt. Then she turned the corner and disappeared through a wooden door with rusty hinges. The two-storey house was badly in need of repair. Chipped masonry fronted the building leaving bare concrete patches showing through in places. Three small windows faced the street, two on the upper floor and one to the right of the front door. The larger of the upper windows led on to a rusty balcony where an old woman was sitting on a green plastic chair. She was knitting and I watched her pause to drink from a bottle of beer. Her long grey hair was matted and untidy and she was shabbily dressed in a black dress with a grubby white cotton collar. Transfixed, I saw Leonora appear at the upstairs window and hand the old lady the confectionery, I'd seen her buying a moment ago, then she disappeared once more into the depths of the house.

It was almost mid-day and the heat carried with it a pungent smell of drains and cooking. I was tempted to retrace my steps and head for the sweet aroma drifting out of the doorway of Antonio's but was rooted to the spot. There was no doubt in my mind that it was my wife I'd seen but either I was going completely mad and Leo had risen from her earthy grave or there was a reasonable explanation, neither of which I could fathom. Either way I had to make sure.

I stood hidden in a doorway for what seemed like an eternity, the sweat on my brow falling into my eyes like tears. However, I didn't see her again. I even thought about ringing the rusty bell but what would I say 'I just saw my dead wife and wondered if I could speak to her'? Frustrated, I retraced my steps to Antonio's café and waited for George to arrive. Surely he must know who lived in the shabby house and if I was to retain my sanity, I needed the answer to the question more than anything I could contemplate.

The day crept towards evening. I ate a sandwich sitting outside the café, watching the patterns of light drifting across the fields and wondering what had happened to George. He never missed our Sunday afternoon chats outside Antonio's. As the sun slipped over the horizon, I made up my mind to call at his house. Desperation dogged my every step - I had to see him.

The sound of church bells, drawing worshippers towards the church on the hill, rang in my ears as I arrived at my destination. Lifting the shiny brass knocker on the front door I heard a window open at the house next door, followed by Gina's head. Gina was an Italian student who was on vacation from her studies in Venice and I had met her several times during my stay.

"Hello, I saw you walking up the road but you won't find Georgio today," she said, leaning over the windowsill and peering at me through small black rimmed spectacles. "He and Maria 'ave gone to Lucca to visit their daughter."

"Oh, he didn't say he was going away when I saw him yesterday," I said, my disappointment showing in the tone of my voice.

"E didn' know then, 'e 'ave a telephone call from his daughter, her son 'as the chicken-pox. I think 'e and Maria be gone some time."

The worst possible news, I thought thanking her and walking despondently down the cobbled street to my lodgings. The likelihood of me putting an end to my nightmare, by an explanation from George who knew most people living in the town, would have to wait. Now it looked as if I'd have to be content with that, at least for the moment.

Knowing I dare not approach the girl who looked like Leo for fear of what would happen if I did, gripped my heart like a vice and I slipped a tablet under my tongue for some relief. My sanity fluctuated from rationality to periods where I thought I was going completely crazy as I tried to make some sense of it all.

During the time George was away, I saw the girl just once more, even though I spent hours at a time hovering in the vicinity of the house with the peeling masonry.

Taken at the Flood

The day before George returned, I saw my wife's lover. He was leaving the library as I was coming out of a gift shop with a pile of books under one arm. I almost walked into him and he muttered an apology without looking up then quickly hurried away. His fair hair and pale blue eyes were unmistakable. My heart skipped a beat and the familiar pain gripped my arm. I stopped, felt in my pocket and slipped a pill under my tongue.

Following him at a discreet distance, I watched as he came to the house where I'd seen Leonora disappear. I saw him stop, pick up a pebble and throw it at the upper window. Hardly daring to breathe I waited until she appeared briefly on the rusty balcony then hurled a key in the young man's direction, as he waited in the street below. I shrank back into a doorway and watched as he opened the door and went inside. Then I stood in the shadows until darkness fell, my body aching from inactivity but neither he nor the girl appeared again.

That night I couldn't sleep. I was afraid to close my eyes. Shaking with fear, I watched the darkness blend into grey and waited until the sun crept over the horizon. My head ached. Dragging my feet towards the bathroom, I stood under the shower and let the jets wash away the terrors of the night.

The following day, I was sitting outside Antonio's when to my amazement George appeared as if he'd never been away. He sat beside me, ordered a strong black coffee, and said, "Hullo, my friend, did you miss me?"

"More than you'll ever know," I answered ambiguously then added, "How is your grandson?" My hands were shaking as I lifted my cup.

"He's much better, thank you. It is always the way with small children, I'm afraid - they are poorly one minute and running about the next. Maria and I stayed to help our daughter because she developed the disease also and was feeling rough. It's always worse in adults apparently. Of course that wasn't the only reason; we enjoyed spending time with them all." He raised his cup to his lips and squinted in the sunlight before saying, "Now then, tell me what you've been up to since I've been away? I must say I'm very pleased to see you sitting in our usual spot as I did wonder if you would have gone back to England before I returned from Lucca."

He squinted through the sunshine and looked at me properly. "You don't look well, my friend." He called to the waiter. "A bottle of Chianti, please." Then to me, he said, "A hair of the dog, I think?"

Anxious to dispense with the small talk as soon as possible, I nodded. I was desperate to turn the conversation around to the occupants of the shabby house but George was in an expansive mood and continued to regale me with tales of his grandson's exploits well into the afternoon. Two bottles of red wine later, I eventually managed to seize an opportunity.

"George," I said, refilling his glass. "You seem to know most people in the town. I wonder if you know of a girl living in a rather run down property further up the street and to the left. I noticed her the other day, especially as she appeared so unlike most of the Italians girls I've seen locally. She had pale blonde hair and blue eyes. I wondered if she might be English."

George gave me a knowing wink. "Ah, so you have seen Laura Servini at last!" he said, smiling. "A real beauty wouldn't you say?"

I nodded, unable to trust myself to speak. Then after taking a deep breath, I said, "What nationality is she?"

"Italian. Her father is Claudio Servini, a real waster and her mother Petra was Swedish."

"Oh I see, that explains the colouring. I thought it rather odd." My heart was hammering against my ribs. The red wine burned my throat and I felt the contents of my stomach rebelling. Unwilling to make a fool of myself in front of my companion, I fled to the washroom at the back of the café and vomited into the toilet bowl. After washing my face in cool water, I returned to my seat knowing that what I was about to hear would shed some light on Leonora's past and I dreaded the outcome.

Taken at the Flood

Chapter 34

George sat back in his seat preparing himself for what I was sure was going to be a long tale. I tried to remain calm but my appearance was at odds with the pounding in my chest and the tension behind my eyes. To stop my hand from shaking, I gripped the edge of my seat.

"There's a sad story attached to that family, my friend," George began, as I shifted in my seat. He glanced at me for a moment then continued, "The father is a gambler, as fast as money comes into his hands it's gone. His habit is the reason the family home is in such a state. He broke his wife's heart. I remember her, she was a lovely woman who had stuck by him through thick and thin, until unable to take any more - she gave up. She died last year after a long struggle of trying to keep the family fed. It was very sad. They were a large family you see; Claudio was prolific, unfortunately for his wife and family and produced four boys and three girls. The family live with Claudio's old mother but the youngest girl died of whooping cough when she was two. As if that wasn't enough of a tragedy to hit the family, it was soon discovered that the youngest boy was handicapped."

George lifted his glass and I waited in the heat of the afternoon unable to move.

"The two elder boys left as soon as they could. They are living on a sheep farm in

Australia as far away as they could get from their father. Anyway, I know the family don't see them anymore. They never visit and I can't blame them. Their mother, Petra, pleaded with them not to leave but they had a violent row with their father and beat him within an inch of his life. I gather it was all because of Claudio giving Petra a black eye. The boys were furious and after attacking their father, escape seemed to be their only option. Claudio lives on the edge, always has and his family frequently has to bail him out one way or another."

"He sounds a charmer," I muttered, fearing a pattern was beginning to emerge. I was one step ahead of him.

"He is indeed," George conceded. "The girl you saw, Laura, and her sister Leonora spent their young lives handing any money they made over to Claudio as they feared he would land himself in trouble with 'the mob.' In truth it was for their mother's sake but Claudio was the one who benefited, poor Petra never saw a penny of it."

"What happened to the other daughter, Leonora?" I could barely say her name without choking.

"I don't know. I used to see her and her sister regularly then someone told me she was married to a doctor in London. She used to come home often and after her visits, Claudio always seemed to be 'in the money.' Lately I don't think I've seen her but I could be mistaken. It's difficult to tell the two daughters apart actually. They're very close in age; Petra was always pregnant in those days. I remember her pushing the pram with the two of them together, as alike as two peas in a pod."

The pain was starting again and getting worse, gripping my chest like a vice as I tried to remove the pills from my pocket.

"Are you feeling ill?" George asked, bending towards me, as I slipped a tablet under my tongue.

"I'll be OK, in a minute." I gasped, waiting for the pain to pass.

"Perhaps you should see a doctor?" George suggested. "You really don't look well."

"It's nothing." I replied. "But perhaps I could do with an early night.

I left George puffing away on his pipe, the smoke drifting high into the still, night air. My worst fears were taking shape. It must have been Laura I'd seen in Venice. So Leonora hadn't lied.

That night, again, I was unable to sleep. I knew now that Leo must have been visiting her family on those occasions when she'd pretended to go to her sick aunt. It also made sense now why she was not keen on either Lucas or me joining her on those visits. The family was a shambles, the father a rotter who lived off his children. She was ashamed of them – my poor

Leo. I shook my head. What was I thinking? She'd deceived me with another man and I was feeling sorry for her. My head began to swim; nothing was turning out to be as I'd thought. I clung to the fact that she was responsible for the deaths of my unborn child and Evelyn, in order to stop the threads, holding my sanity together, from unravelling still further. It was all that kept me from tipping over the edge. It wouldn't do to weaken now.

Two days later when George and I were drinking wine outside the restaurant, where I'd first met him, I saw the man again. He was walking in front of us, a preoccupied expression on his face as he hurried onwards and before he could disappear from view, I said, "George, quick who's that man, the one going towards the Piazza, with the fair hair, blue shirt and white shorts."

My companion turned to look where I was pointing and smiled. "You do seem to be preoccupied with the Servini family at the moment, my friend."

"What do you mean?" I asked, fearing the reply.

"That is Carlo Servini. He's Laura's brother, remember the girl you saw the other day?"

The colour drained from my face. That the man I'd seen in the photo-fax with Leo was her brother was a possibility that had never crossed my mind. Now so much of what happened was starting to take shape in my mind. Naturally Leo would have wanted her brother to be at her wedding. If only she'd trusted me enough to tell me the truth. If only I had known.

My hands began to shake as I poured a glass of wine from the bottle standing between us on the table. I couldn't speak until the alcohol had deadened my senses a little. Refilling my glass again, I managed to croak, "What does he do? I've often seen him walking through the town."

George looked bemused. He had already forgotten my preoccupation. "Who? Do you mean Carlo?"

I nodded.

"He's the local librarian, quiet studious sort of chap. Keep's himself to himself. He's always on his own, unless of course he's with his sister. Since his brothers left San Gimignano under a cloud, he has remained with his brute of a father. If it wasn't for Laura, I dread to think what he would do, poor chap."

I drank deeply and with each glass, my voice became strong enough to continue with my questions. "And Laura? Why is she still living in the house? With her looks I'd have thought she would have moved on, got married, raised a family, the usual things beautiful young girls do."

George sighed, "More trouble, in a family who have had more than their fair share, unfortunately. When Laura was seventeen and even lovelier than she is today, the son of a wealthy Venetian family who was staying in the town, fell deeply in love with her. They met in secret because of her father and eventually the young man managed to persuade her to go back to Venice with him. Once there, she wrote to her distraught mother telling her she was in love and would be living with her lover in a flat in Venice."

He was enjoying himself, as continued with the story, unaware of the effect it was having on me. I wanted him to stop – to ease the pain that increased with every syllable. For with each word, the structure of my world was melting into that sun-drenched street.

"Apparently, her father went mad and insisted on going to Venice in order to drag Laura back home but the stress of it all was too much for Petra, she became ill and one morning Claudio found her dead in bed at his side. Afterwards, Claudio lost interest in going anywhere and lived off the money his daughter Leonora managed to send him from England."

"Where was Leonora living at this time?" I interrupted.

If George thought my interest in Leonora's whereabouts was odd, he didn't show it.

"In London, working as a nanny I believe," he answered and then continued with his story. "But there was worse to befall that beleaguered family because the inevitable happened and Laura fell pregnant by her Venetian lover. Unfortunately, he acted true to type, rich, spoilt boy with no honour, and when trouble hit, he left the poor girl to fend for herself and ran back to his parents with his tail between his legs."

The sun burned the top of my head as the waiter emerged and lowered the sunblind. But even the welcome shade it produced couldn't stop the sweat of fear from drenching my body.

"She was desperate and had no option but to contact her sister in London. There was no one else who could help her. Leonora paid for her fare back to San Gimignano and came over from England to stay with her until her baby was born. I gather she smoothed things over with Claudio by ensuring he had a continual supply of money, which was all he was interested in anyway."

George narrowed his eyes.

"Laura and the young child live with the family now and she has her hands full coping with the old lady, her father and her child. If it had not been for her brother and sister's help, I don't think she would have managed. Since then she's lived in the family home, never leaving the town. She is like a horse whose spirit has been broken. It's as if her youth was left behind in Venice all those years ago."

George ordered another bottle of wine.

Taken at the Flood

"A tragic story," I muttered, hardly able to speak. It was Laura who had captivated me in Venice, not Leonora. The truth was stripped to the bone. I wanted to leave George and hide away with my past but for some reason I sat rooted to the spot, unable to move.

The days were shortening, evening coming earlier with each passing day. Antonio lit the candle on our table saying, "Winter will be here before I know it and these tables will be blown by the winds so I'll have to put them away in the basement." He looked at us and smiled. "But you gentlemen are to have 'special table' inside.

George laughed, "That's a hint if ever I heard one. I hope you will still be around to make his words come true."

I hesitated."Er, I'm not sure. I've stayed longer than I'd anticipated as it is."

"I know how that feels. Perhaps if you find a good woman here you'll stay." He glanced at me." There is always Laura Servini," he said.

A wave of pure terror swept over me, thankfully unnoticed by George who was discussing the wine with Antonio.

"I must go," I said, spilling the remaining wine from my glass in my haste.

"Same time tomorrow," George said.

I mumbled an assent and left as if the hounds of hell were nipping at my heels.

Following my conversation with George, I was faced with a range of conflicting emotions.

Taken at the Flood

Part of me wanted to leave and put as much space between myself and Laura Servini as possible but part of me was desperate to be near her, to hear her speak, to touch her and to re-live that part of my life when Leo had inflamed my senses.

I wandered the streets in the hope of seeing her, like a lost soul seeking redemption. If George noticed the change in me, he didn't comment. On the surface, nothing had changed, only I knew how misleading that was.

The seasons were changing. Autumn colours painting the trees in the fields surrounding San Gimignano with an ever-changing palate, yellows turning into vibrant reds then merging into russets before leaving the branches naked to face the winter.

Late one afternoon when a cool breeze sliced through alleyways like a knife through butter, I ran into her. I was leaving the warmth of Antonio's café, my head bent against the wind, when I collided with a figure hurrying in the opposite direction. Her face was half-hidden in the folds of a cream lacy scarf, her hair blowing around her head like a fan. I murmured an apology before I realised who she was but it was her reply sent the blood rushing to my face.

"Thank you but I was as much to blame. I admit to not looking where I was going," she replied. It was Leo's voice, as soft and sensuous, the slight hint of an accent in the coating the perfectly formed vowels.

I raised my head and found myself staring into the eyes that had captivated me one lazy afternoon in Venice, a lifetime ago. She smiled and passed me by without a backward glance. I was unable to move. My feet stayed rooted to the spot and I turned to watch her walking away in the direction of her shabby home. Then I began to shake, my guts turned somersaults; I had to see more of her. It suddenly occurred to me that Laura must find it odd that her sister hadn't been in touch with her.

I had to do something and act quickly, before she disappeared behind the rusty-hinged wooden door. I caught up with her at the top of the hill before she turned into the alleyway leading to her house.

"Excuse me," my breath was coming in short gasps. I stopped and rested my hand against the wall.

Laura turned around. "Are you unwell?" she asked, walking towards me.

"No, it's not that, just a little breathless and out of condition."

She stopped, "You wanted to ask me something?"

"Yes," my breath was steadier. "It's just… you remind me of someone I met at a party some time ago. She was married to a man who owned a computing firm."

Her face changed; she was excited. I felt her hand on my arm, "You met my sister, Leonora?"

I made as if to think about my reply. "Yes, I think that was her name. It was a pity about what happened."

"Pity?"

"About the marriage break-up."

"I'm sorry. I don't understand. What marriage break-up?"

I shook my head. "Look, it's none of my business. Maybe I'm confusing your sister with someone else. Forget what I said." I started to walk away but she rushed after me.

"Please, I need to know. You see I haven't been able to reach her for some time. I have no address. For reasons I will not concern you with, Leonora was not keen to give me her address in England. It's family business and involves my father, you understand?"

"I have no wish to pry into any family business," I said. "But I heard from a friend that Leonora Hope and her husband had split up because she'd met someone else. Apparently, she didn't want to be found, in case her husband followed her and tried to make her change her mind, and no one seems to have heard from her since."

She looked crestfallen. I placed a hand on her arm. "I'm sure she'll be in touch, once she's settled." Every shameful word ate into my soul.

"Yes, I expect you are right. Thank you so much for telling me."

Leaving me alone with my conscience, she hurried away and was out of sight in seconds.

Chapter 35

Later, it occurred to me that Laura's brother Carlo might recognise me as his sister's husband. I looked at the image staring back at me from the dressing table mirror. Would anyone recognise this haggard face as the one I wore on our wedding day? My eyes were puffy and a permanent haunted look lingered. The fine lines, once induced by laughter, now etched deep grooves into my brow and at the corners of my eyes; two deep furrows ran from my nose to my mouth making me look permanently miserable, adding to which, I'd put on weight and my skin looked sallow, even with a tan. But was there still enough of me remaining, to jog his memory? Could I risk staying a moment longer in this place?

I had to know more about Leonora but knew if I questioned Laura she would suspect there was more to my enquiries than simple curiosity. My inadequate explanation of my meeting with her sister had left me surprised that she'd accepted it without suspicion. However, I knew without doubt, as the months passed, her family would have to make enquiries as to her whereabouts. Surely her silence alone was enough to prompt further action on their part.

I opened the bottle of wine I'd bought and drank until the edges of my paranoia blurred. Sleep was elusive and punctuated by dreams.

Taken at the Flood

Leonora and Evelyn became one, each indistinguishable from the other, and I awoke in a bath of sweat believing I'd murdered an innocent woman whose only purpose had been to make life easier for her family. As daylight crept into my room, it brought with it a certainty that I'd misjudged my beautiful wife and I began to doubt whether she'd had anything to do with Evelyn's death or that of my unborn child. What if I was right? I began to tremble and wiped away the sweat trickling into my eyes. What sort of monster had I become?

Unable to stomach the prospect of breakfast, I left my room and the guesthouse and walked along the back streets until I found the house where the Leonora's family lived. I stood shivering in a doorway, out of sight, as a cool wind blew leaves into a pile on the cobbles. At half past eight, Carlo Servini opened the door. He was dressed for work, and walking in the direction of the library. I waited until the clock in the square struck ten o'clock and then walked towards the house. There was an urgent need in me. I had to talk to her again. But before I could summon up enough courage to cross the cobbles to her front door, she appeared. She saw me immediately.

"Hello again," she said, wrapping a scarf around her neck. She was pushing a child in a wheelchair.

"Hello," I stood in front of her and waited. She bent towards the child who I could see was not a child but an adult trapped in a child's body, and who spoke to her in Italian.

"I am explaining to Claudia that you met her aunt in England. She misses her dreadfully," Laura explained.

I gulped, "Actually, I was hoping to see you again. It's about your sister; some information I hoped you could supply."

She straightened up.

"I have to take Claudia to the day centre but I could meet you in the café on the square at eleven o'clock."

I agreed, watched her walk away and was again struck by her resemblance to Leo. She was my only hope. How could I live with myself if I had taken her sister from her for no good reason other than jealousy and mistrust?

The seconds turned into hours as I waited for her to arrive. There were no longer any tables arranged outside the cafés in San Gimignano and as I sat in the warm interior of Mario's café, I was surprised by my heightened senses. It was as if I was seeing the world in Technicolour before it seeped away from me. The bittersweet smell of roasted coffee beans and the cinnamon rising from the cakes lined up in rows on the counter cocooned me in a fragrant cloud from which I desired no escape; the colour of the chequered table cloths and the framed prints on the walls, their vibrancy making my eyes ache.

Then I saw her walking up the cobbles towards the café. The wind was blowing her hair into her eyes and she raised her hand and flicked it away just as I had seen Leo do a thousand times. She opened the door and brought with her a draught of bittersweet autumnal air then sat opposite me as I ordered coffee for us both, wishing it had been brandy.

"You said you wanted to see me, something about my sister?" she asked, leaving her coffee untouched in the cup.

"It's nothing really," I lied, "It was just that I remembered something after I'd left you the other day." I was breathing heavily but she didn't seem to notice being more concerned with the topic of my conversation than how it was delivered.

I took a deep breath. "I told you I met her at a party. Later, one of the guests told me your sister had been very close to someone called Evelyn, at least I think that was her name. I just wondered if you might be able to find out some more information from this Evelyn, as to the whereabouts of your sister."

Laura took a sip from the cup and sighed. "I wish that was possible. But the Evelyn, of whom you speak, died before my sister married her second husband."

"I'm sorry." Lying was beginning to become a habit.

"It was good of you to think it might be of help but I think you are mistaken - Evelyn was not really a friend of Leonora's."

I tried to hide my surprise but my voice was shaking as I asked, "Really?"

"No. You see my sister did try and befriend her neighbour. Leonora was married to Lucas at the time and lived very near Evelyn and her husband and, although they met frequently, Leonora was aware she had 'how you say' other fish to bake."

"Fry," I corrected.

"Of course. She told me Evelyn had a lover and as time went on my sister felt she was using her as a cover, by pretending to be her friend."

I choked on my coffee, spluttering and coughing, gasping for breath, as a fist gripped my heart. Somehow, I managed to remove the tablet from my pocket and slipped it under my tongue. Laura's concern was obvious.

"Are you unwell?" she asked and once again, I lied.

"It's nothing,"

When my heart rate slowed to something approaching normal, I spoke. "What made her think that?"

"Pardon me?"

"Why did she think Evelyn was having an affair?"

"She overheard her on the telephone one day. The housekeeper had shown Leonora into the house and Evelyn was on her mobile telephone in the garden. The conversation she unwittingly overheard left her in no doubt. Apparently, she was telling her husband she was meeting Leonora when in fact she was meeting her lover. She was using her as a decoy; that is the right word?"

I nodded; the muscles in my throat had tightened to the point where speech became impossible. Laura looked at her watch. "I really must go, I have shopping to do before I pick Claudia up from the day centre. Thank you once again for trying to help," she said. I started to tremble as she stood up and looked down at me through Leo's eyes.

Chapter 36

Lying on my bed in the Orsinsis' guesthouse, I watched the pictures on the television set in the corner without seeing them. My mind raced in circles. Evelyn with a lover was something I'd never contemplated, not even for a second. I was so sure of her love, certain she wouldn't betray me. Laura's words forced me to think about the possibility and the longer I mulled it over the more probable it became.

But I had to consider her diary entries. Her frequent absences were mention as time spent with L.B. or Leo. I'd assumed they were one in the same person. What if that were not so and Evelyn had been using some sort of code as protection should either Mrs Bates or I happen to chance upon her diary and read it. She must have known I would never stoop to such a thing but I doubted if Mrs Bates could have resisted such temptation.

I wondered what part Leo had played in the subterfuge and concluded that if her sister's account was to be believed, she was not involved. Why then would she have planted the spiders in the car that night? It just didn't make any sense. What did make sense was that Evelyn's death must have been an unfortunate accident. However, it still left the question of the identity of her lover unanswered. My tortured brain wouldn't allow me to speculate who it could be. It was bad enough I'd discovered that she had been unfaithful to me. The full implication of it registering in waves of melancholy whilst destroying my memory of her. Evelyn's image was tarnished and I couldn't face trying to discover who she had been seeing or why. As for my unspeakable crime, I would never forgive myself; it was something I'd have to live with for the rest of my life. My punishment, worse than any I could envisage, was the knowledge of what I'd done eating away at me, day after tortuous day.

If only Leonora had trusted me enough to tell me about it all. Now everything had turned on its head - I began to doubt her complicity in Lucas's death whilst part of me argued it would have made her a wealthy woman and as such would have eased her family's dire financial situation. It would also explain why she would have found me an attractive proposition in the marriage stakes, as my fortune was increasing and my business thriving.

My fevered mind had almost convinced myself that my explanation of her behaviour was a reasonable one, when I became aware of Josie's face looking back at me from the television screen. The programme was tuned into Sky News and the reporter was describing how the autumn rainfall during the past twenty-four hours had been more than was usually expected for the whole month of October. The river level was rising and had flooded the properties bordering the river path. The reporter looked windswept and beads of rain stuck to the camera lens through which I saw Josie. She was standing in her back garden dressed in wax jacket and Wellington boots, a headscarf covering her dark hair. Several inches of water covered the lawn and the path near the woods was under water. I sat upright in bed. Beads of sweat trickled down my brow and slid into my eyes. Damp patches prickled under my armpits. I had to return to London immediately.

Glancing at my watch, I saw it was too late to do anything today but first thing in the morning, I would arrange a flight home. Once more I hardly slept and at six o'clock I got out of bed and packed my suitcase.

Afterwards, I scribbled a note to the Orsinis enclosing a cheque, which more than adequately covered the cost of my accommodation and left some lira notes for their staff on my bedside table. Then I folded the rest of my currency, which was considerable, as I'd been gradually removing it from my account with my credit card, ever since I arrived, and placed them in an envelope. I wrote the name Laura Servini in large letters on the front of the envelope.

It was still early when I left the guesthouse and walked towards the shabby house where Laura lived. Squeezing the envelope and its contents flat, I managed to push it though the

Taken at the Flood

post-box attached to the crumbling wall. Before leaving, I looked up at the rusty balcony which was empty now and tried to imagine my Leo sitting there watching the sun going down on the cobbled street below, whilst she desperately tried to keep the family finances in order. My body was struck by a shudder, which affected every part of me. There was no way I could recompense for what I had done; the money was merely a gesture. My head sank low towards my chest, and with sagging shoulders I prepared to carry my burden for eternity, as I walked back to pick up my suitcase from the guesthouse.

Chapter 37

The sun was rising, shedding a clear golden light over the red, tiled rooftops as I made my way down the cobbled incline, through the narrow street towards the car park. It was seven thirty by the time I put my suitcase in the boot and glanced at the map. George and Maria would be awake now. I dialled their number on my mobile and waited.

"George, it's me. I know you're both early risers otherwise I wouldn't have rung. I'm leaving San Gimignano today; in fact I'm in the car park now. I wanted to thank you both for welcoming me into your home and to tell you how much I've enjoyed your company these past few months."

"Do you have to leave so early? We would love to see you one last time before you go." George's sleepy voice made me smile.

"I know, I'm sorry too, but an emergency at work means I have to beat a hasty retreat," I lied. "I want you to know I'll always treasure your painting and the memory of our pleasant days in the sun will keep me warm on dark December days."

I could hear the smile in his voice, "Farewell, my friend. Maria says God speed you on your journey," George said, as I finished the call and turned the key in the ignition.

Taken at the Flood

Driving to the airport, I realised I was going to miss George and Maria, friends, who like Josie and Henry made a difference and with a sinking heart knew that events would never allow me to make this trip again. Yesterday, the sight of Josie on television, amongst the devastation left by the weather, made it imperative I make plans before disaster struck.

My beautiful Leonora had resurfaced in San Gimignano in the guise of her sister Laura and I'd been allowed to see her lovely face for one last time. It was much more than I deserved. I dreaded to think how far the river had risen in my absence, fearful that my shameful past would rise up to meet me upon my return.

The airport was relatively quiet, the tourist season being over and luckily I was able to book the short flight to Switzerland without too much trouble. I could have driven but the quicker I completed my transactions there the quicker I could return to the UK.

As the aircraft took off for the short journey to Zurich, I began to formulate my plan in detail. The plan, I'd spent half the night agonising over, after I'd seen the television news report.

After the plane landed, I took a taxi to the business quarter. My intention was to stay in Zurich for as long as it took me to complete stage one, then I'd make arrangements to fly home to London. There was no problem opening a numbered Swiss bank account. The bank official completed the necessary paperwork and I arranged for a large transfer of funds from my UK accounts to take immediate effect. When all the transactions were completed to my satisfaction, I left the bank and went shopping.

I bought a large suitcase, some hand luggage and a complete new wardrobe of clothes, which I packed into the large suitcase. I knew there was no option for me now but to leave the UK. and disappear abroad but before that stage of my plan could be put into action, there were a few loose ends I had to tie up first.

As the door to my London flat opened, I drew in a deep breath and thought I could smell the lingering scent of Leo's perfume. The ghost of her hung around every corner now. I saw her in cafes, doorways and sitting opposite me in the taxi driving me from the airport.

The first thing I did, on entering the sitting room, was to open the top drawer of a rosewood cabinet, which stood against the wall, and remove a small black book. I ran my finger slowly down the index until I found the number of my solicitors then rang and asked for an appointment for the following day. I also made an appointment with my bank manager. Then I rang Thomas Cook and made enquiries about booking a ticket to Rio.

Chapter 38

My appointments for the following day being made, I unpacked the suitcase containing the clothes I'd worn during my trip to Italy. Then I threw the contents into a black bag ready to put out for the rubbish in the morning, with the exception of George's painting, which I placed at the bottom of the suitcase I'd bought in Zurich. Next, I filled the case with items I would require when I arrived in the heat of a Rio afternoon. The following day, I would visit the chemist's in Sloane Square, where my repeat prescription was held and collect enough Glyceryl Trinitrate to last until I could visit a doctor in Rio. I felt I had covered most eventualities, and with the exception of a few loose ends, I was making progress.

That night I lay exhausted on my bed and listened to the steady drumming of the rain on the roof until sleep overcame me. But there was no peace to be found in slumber. There never would be again. It was what I deserved and I accepted my punishment without question.

The next day, as planned, I visited my solicitor's office and waited whilst he drew up a deed of gift. I also instructed him to put into operation the sale of my Mayfair apartment and to forward the funds, less his fee, to an address in Tuscany. Then leaving his office, I crossed the street and, dodging the puddles and the traffic, walked towards my bank.

It was a relatively simple operation to arrange with my bank manager to keep an account open with an automatic transfer to Mrs Bates's account in Kings Datchet. I'd already allocated the funds necessary to keep such an account in operation for the foreseeable future and so it was just a matter of signing the forms. The manager was a young man who didn't query my decision to close my accounts, wind up my investments and transfer the funds to a numbered account in Switzerland, and completed the transaction to my satisfaction.

Afterwards, walking through the rain to the chemist's, I began to think it was going to be fine – I'd covered everything I could think of - Mrs Bates and Laura would be financially secure. Leaving the pharmacy with enough tablets to see me through the journey, I caught a cab to Thomas Cook's Head Office and concluded my business.

Later, back in my apartment, I picked up a photograph of Leo in a silver frame and packed it into my case. She would always be with me, haunting my waking hours, and filling my dreams but I was afraid time would dull her features and I owed it to her to remember

Before I left London, I rang Mrs Bates. "I'll be arriving later today but leaving again tomorrow." I told her. "There's something I need to discuss with you. I'd be grateful if we could have a chat later this evening, if you could keep some time free."

"Time is all I've got, sir and it's yours," she said, then had second thoughts. "Everything alright, is it?"

"I'll tell you later."

"Right. It will be good to see you again, Mr Hope. I hope you won't stay away so long next time."

The taxi driver drove through torrential rain towards River House. The river had burst its banks outside the village of Kings Datchet and the fields, through which Josie and I used to walk the dogs, were completely submerged beneath muddy water. The River Road where Evelyn had met her death was passable, as the council had reinforced the riverbank with sandbags, but I doubted whether they would hold for much longer, if the rain continued. The rooftops of the Bennett house showed through the trees, a grim reminder of the past, and I knew I'd made the right decision to leave.

Mrs Bates opened the front door when she heard the taxi draw up and welcomed me with open arms. "Am I glad to see you, sir." She took a step back surveying me. I could see she was shocked. "You need some feeding up, if you don't mind me saying. I can see you've not been looking after yourself. I thought as much, so

Taken at the Flood

I've baked your favourite steak and kidney pie, I expect you can smell it cooking. Tinker will be so pleased to see you," she chatted on, as I removed my mackintosh and put my suitcase in the cloakroom.

"Left the car in London have you? A wise decision if you ask me, in view of the weather!"

Her answer to her own question seemed to satisfy her without any input from me and so I followed her into the kitchen where Tinker was curled up in his basket beside the Aga. He raised his head when he heard our voices, stretched and flopped out of his basket but did not run to me with his tail wagging as he had in the past. Instead he sidled up to Mrs Bates, eyeing me suspiciously until she said, "You silly boy, it's your master, go on now."

Tinker was still not convinced and I didn't think it worthwhile trying to coax him, under the circumstances. I had a brief flashback to the time when I'd first seen him bounding into the hall with Evelyn and felt my throat tighten.

"Mrs Bates, after dinner I would like to have a word with you in my study, before you go to bed. Would nine o'clock suit you?"

"That will be fine. Coronation Street should have finished by then," she replied.

At five to nine I sat at my desk having collected my personal belongings and packed them in an overnight bag. At nine o'clock exactly, I heard a knock on the study door.

Taken at the Flood

"Come in, sit down, Mrs Bates," I said looking at her homely figure and suddenly realising I knew very little of her life other than that she had a sister living locally and had made friends with the new owner of the Bennett house. "I have something very serious to tell you and I want you to listen very carefully." The smile slid from her face and she nervously fingered the neck of her blouse

"I'll be going away tomorrow and I will not be coming back." I heard her rapid intake of breath but she remained quiet until I'd finished speaking. "I would like you to stay on here and look after Tinker for me. I can see he's become very fond of you. I will continue to pay your wages via automatic bank transfer into your account and of course there will be enough money to pay any household bills and expenses." Her agitation seemed to pass and I was glad I'd come to the decision about her future in the way I had planned. "As for River House, it is yours to do with as you please, Mrs Bates, providing you keep Tinker with you of course - until he dies, that is, then it's yours, naturally."

Her fingers flew to her face as she held her hands up to her reddening cheeks. "I don't understand."

"It's simple," I explained. "I can no longer live here. You must understand why. I need a new start so I'm going to live abroad for a while. I would like you to have the house and I know Evelyn would have agreed. She loved this house and was very fond of you." Tears trickled down her cheeks as I handed her a handkerchief, together with an envelope containing the Deed of Gift. "My solicitor will write to you concerning the formalities, later. I will give you his card but you need not worry, everything is in order. I spoke with him earlier today."

"I don't know what to say, sir." She rose from her chair and to my embarrassment hugged me, dampening my tie with her tears.

"It's my pleasure, Mrs Bates, now if you don't mind, I have some things to tidy up before tomorrow. Oh and if you could send any clothes etc to worthy causes, I would be very grateful."

"Don't you worry, sir I'll see to it. Do you want Morton Phillips in the morning?" she added as an afterthought when she was closing the study door.

"Yes, thank you. Could you have him call for me in time to meet the ten fifteen train from Kings Datchet, please? I'll be taking the train to London, which will be a relief to Morton I'm sure, as he hates driving in the city."

"I will, Mr Hope," she said, gently closing the door behind her.

I let my gaze slowly wonder around the room for the last time, remembering when Evelyn and I had bought the house. We'd thought it would become a family home with children floating their paper boats downstream on days filled with sunshine and laughter but it was not to be. I'd foolishly believed Leo had stolen my future and replaced it with emptiness and now she lay beneath the sodden earth in the woods at the bottom of my garden. Soon the river level would rise and she with it and I would be in a new country with a new identity far away from River House and my guilt.

Chapter 39

When I awake the next morning and open the bedroom curtains, I see my prediction is correct. The river has encroached as far as the bottom of the woodland and the rain is still falling in a torrent. Branches and debris litter the surface of the water as it creeps up the garden. The journal is finished and ready to be posted to Leonora's sister.

At breakfast, Mrs Bates is tearful and keeps thanking me for my generosity. When the time comes for me to leave, she throws her arms around my neck and kisses my cheek. "Keep safe and don't forget us," she says, wiping her eyes with the end of her apron.

"I will and thank you for looking after me so well all these years." I reply patting her shoulder and handing her the letter I have written to Alan Henderson and the journal addressed to Laura Servini.

"Perhaps you could post these for me after I've left, Mrs Bates?" I ask, realizing this is the last task she will ever carry out for me.

Sitting in the back of Morton Phillips's taxi, I look back as the car approaches the bend in the drive. Mrs Bates and Tinker stand on the steps of River House, their images blurred by the raindrops, which trickle down the car window. I sigh remembering it is always a mistake to look back.

Taken at the Flood

The train to London stopping at Kings Datchet at ten fifteen is half-empty and I find no difficulty in locating a seat. I lift my suitcase into the luggage rack and sit down as the train pulls away from the station.

Chapter 40

Arnold Simpson has been working for 'Constant Caterers' for six months; it's his first job since leaving school and his mother is proud of him, especially as he looks so smart wearing his uniform. She presses his black polyester trousers every morning and makes sure that the striped shirt, with the Constant Caterer's logo on the pocket, is crisp and freshly laundered.

Arnold likes trains, likes the excitement of watching people. Travelling is something Arnold hopes to do, when he has saved enough money. He likes to watch travel programmes on the television, imagining lying on an exotic beach somewhere, sampling foreign foods or exploring ancient buildings. He's a dreamer but has the sense to know his dreams will have to wait awhile longer. Until that day arrives, he lives vicariously through the lives of people using the trains. Most are commuters travelling to work, some, the lucky ones, are off on holiday. He often tries to imagine what it would be like to be able to travel in the first class compartment, along with luggage that looks and smells expensive. It's a habit of his to visualise where these people are likely to be going and what their lives are like. It helps to pass the time, whilst he pushes his trolley along the train.

Arnold's flights of fancy often run away with him as he contrives occupations and locations to

Taken at the Flood

suit the passengers. For instance, he has noticed a man sitting in the first class carriage and imagines he's an international jewel thief making his escape to the continent.

Arnold feels the train hit the buffers as it draws to a halt; he is used to it now and manages to stand upright without having to hold on to anything. Over the top of his trolley in the buffet car, he sees the passengers hurrying along the platform, heads bent against the wind, which is whistling through the station. He looks for his jewel thief but doesn't see him, so concentrates on squeezing a large spot that has appeared on the side of his nose instead.

"Jump to it, Arnold lad, them carriages need tidying up."

Fred Hopkins, Arnold's boss, calls to him across the bar. Wiping the tip of his finger on the edge of his sleeve Arnold pushes his trolley down the train, picking up empty drink cartons, crisps packets and cardboard coffee cups and putting them into the waste bin attached to his trolley. He whistles softly to himself as he enters the first class compartment and sees his jewel thief asleep, his head resting on his chest.

"End of the line, sir!" he gently prods the recumbent finger with the tip of the finger he used to squeeze his spot, earlier. The man slides sideways in his seat, his head slipping forward at an angle. Arnold takes a step backwards and gasps.

Taken at the Flood

It's the first corpse he's seen and the blood drains from his face leaving his skin the colour of putty as he staggers out of the carriage in search of Fred Hopkins who will know what to do in such circumstances.

Chapter 41

Henry Dangerfield is alone in the house. Josie is visiting Emily, the new owner of the Bennett house. In the distance, Henry can hear the sound of a mechanical digger as the council struggle to build up the riverbank with earth taken from the woodland in order to stem the rising water. He looks out of the window to the bottom of his garden. The river path is no longer visible due to the river having encroached half way up the garden. The level has risen throughout the day, as the showers have become heavier. Henry looks upwards at the leaden sky and realizes there is unlikely to be any improvement in the weather for the rest of the day.

He glances back to the newspaper resting on his lap and opens it. An item at the bottom of the second page catches his eye, it reads; - '**Man found dead on London train'**. As he continues reading the report, the paper slips to the floor. His good friend and neighbour has suffered a fatal heart attack on the ten fifteen train to London from Kings Datchet.

As Henry looks up from the paper, his gaze falls on the photograph on the top shelf of the bureau, which was taken at a polo match. He was seated on 'Desert Night' a beautiful black stallion with a coat as shiny as a maiden's hair. The image of a vibrant young man, at his physical peak, stares back at him. The photograph was taken when he'd captained the winning team against the Argentineans. It was a year before he had met Josie.

That was the year he met Evie. She was in the crowd watching him when the photograph was taken and had shouted out his name along with the rest of the fans. The night before she'd spent in his bed; one of the many girls who found his celebrity status and good looks an aphrodisiac; but Evie wasn't like the others, Evie was different.

Henry closes his eyes and the memories come flooding back.

*****

The South American sun beat down out of a cloudless blue sky, merciless in its intensity, as the mid-day temperature rose. Henry Dangerfield, Lewis Sanfield and Buster Norman headed for the shade of the bar in the centre of Buenos Aires, sweat trickling down the back of their cotton shirts. The bar was cool and, as the next match was two days away, they sank a few more beers than usual.

Buster saw her first. "Hey guys, check out the waitress, the one with the legs up to her armpits!"

Henry turned around. He was sitting on a stool at the bar. He locked eyes with the girl with short dark curls framing her elfin face. She wore a black mini skirt, which left nothing to the imagination and a white cotton blouse thin enough to outline the shape of her breasts.

Henry knew if he showed any interest in her whatsoever The Game would start. It was always the same and ended in the same way. The victor was the one who bedded her first. He turned back to his beer. "Bit obvious, I've seen better," he commented, raising his glass and ordering another. His friends soon lost interest and the conversation turned to the forthcoming final in two day's time. As the late afternoon sun set, they left the bar and headed back to their hotel. Sometime later, after dinner, Henry left the trio drinking in the hotel bar and caught a cab back to the bar they'd visited that afternoon. She was still working, serving drinks to the customers seated at the tables. Henry sat in a corner and watched her for a while. There was something about her that stood out from the crowd of other attractive women who caught his eye. This one was different.

"What can I get you?" she asked, notepad and pencil at the ready. She didn't look at him; her eyes were fixed firmly on the pad. A lock of damp hair curled on her forehead and she pushed it back impatiently.

"I'd like you to come and have a drink with me in my hotel room, after you finish here," Henry replied.

"I think you've got the wrong idea, sir." She looked up and hesitated as their eyes met.

"I'll have a beer," he said, keeping his eyes on her face.

He waited until she'd finished her shift then left. When she emerged from a side door, he was leaning against the wall waiting for her. "At least let me walk you home," he said

She hesitated, smiled then nodded and they walked together in silence for a moment then she stopped and removed a key from her bag. "Thanks," she said.

Henry looked up at the building, which was a hostel and laughed. "Not much of a walk home. Not much of a home by the look of it either. Look, I'm staying at the 'Excelsior' in town why don't you join me for a nightcap and a bite to eat?"

At first, he thought she was going to refuse but she narrowed her eyes in consideration, quickly popped the key back into her handbag and said, "Why not?"

It was a night he'd never forget. Henry had slept with his fair share of women, some beautiful, some not so but none had excited him like Evie Wallis. She was insatiable, and adorable. In the morning Buster Norman saw them leaving Henry's room together and whispered, "You sly dog. No one told me we were playing."

Taken at the Flood

Out of Evie's hearing Henry mouthed, "We're not," leaving Buster with his mouth hanging open.

Afterwards, she slept in his hotel room every night until the final game and the photograph was taken and then he was caught up in a round of publicity and lost contact with her. Soon after, the English team returned to London, amid a blaze of photographers and media interest and Evie Wallis became a memory.

He remembered that she'd mentioned she would be travelling around South America on a year out before she started her college course and he had intended to look her up but the team was now in great demand and his good intention evaporated. Then he met Josie. It was at the return fixture in Buenos Aires the following year that the accident happened, resulting in him ending up in hospital with legs that refused to move. It was the beginning of a new life - the end of an old.

From then on Evie Wallis became a treasured memory he would retrieve from time to time, when the result of his accident became too much to bear. It helped him to remember what it was like to feel the thrill of their lovemaking - his energetic days of sheer abandon when he'd lived for the minute. Lost in thoughts of her made him relive the pleasure of being young, fit and free. And it would all have remained a treasured memory had Josie not returned from a shopping trip in town one day and announced, "I know who the new owners of River House are and guess what? It's only an old school friend of mine, Evelyn Hope and her husband."

At first, Henry didn't associate Evelyn Hope with the girl he'd met in Buenos Aires. There was no reason why he should. But, shortly after Josie met their new neighbours, she organised a dinner party and the new owners of River House were invited along with Lucas and Leonora Bennett, the owners of the property adjacent to theirs. He recognized Evie at once, she had hardly changed and it was as much as he could do to greet Josie's friend and her husband impassively, without acknowledging their previous acquaintance. Fortunately, Evie's husband was good company and Henry was able to monopolise him for most of the evening in an attempt to avoid having to talk to her directly. He could see she'd recognized him by the way she glanced at him over the top of her wine glass, keeping her eyes fixed on his just a fraction longer than was necessary.

After dinner, his luck ran out. As he was returning from a sly smoke in the billiard room, she came towards him from the direction of the downstairs cloakroom. Standing in front of his chair, she leaned towards him and placed her hands on the arms of his chair. Then she bent forward so he could see the shape of her breasts beneath the top of her dress, and whispered, "Henry, we've got some time to make up, you and I."

He felt his cheeks burning as Josie walked towards them. "Isn't it amazing, darling; to have my very best school buddy living so close, I just can't believe the coincidence. Evelyn and I haven't seen each other for years." She linked arms with her friend adding, "Now let's sneak off to powder our noses and catch up on the gossip."

"Amazing," he murmured, through clenched teeth, when they were out of earshot.

Later that night, when he lay in bed alongside his wife, he began to think he'd imagined Evie's obvious suggestion. He knew, as far as he and Josie were concerned, there was no question that he was able to perform his marital duties in the bedroom without too much difficulty but it might not have been an obvious assumption for Evie to make at first glance, considering his injuries. He began to wonder whether another connotation might be placed on her words, as in themselves they were pretty innocuous but it was the tone of her voice, which had set his heart racing.

It seemed that, after the party, Evie took every opportunity available to call when he was alone. She watched Josie's movements like a hawk and used her friendship with Leonora

Bennett as an alibi with her husband. In less than a month after the party, they became lovers and she was every bit as insatiable as he remembered.

She was meticulous in her deceit, making sure their meetings were noted in her diary. Henry was shocked when she told him, "What if your husband finds your diary? How will you explain so many sudden departures?" he asked.

She'd laughed, eager to explain to him the full extent of her cunning. He noticed a gleam of satisfaction in her eyes and something inside him twisted.

"I remembered your middle name. Do you remember how I laughed when I saw the Polo Cup? It's simple Leonard dear. If I am meeting you then I write, *meeting Leo*. I've already started to call Leonora Bennett Leo, as a precaution, but when I'm meeting her, I write *L.B*. It's so easy; my darling husband doesn't suspect a thing. He doesn't like Leonora very much so I take every opportunity to feed that dislike. It wouldn't do to have them become too friendly with each other and compare notes about my non-existent shopping trips with her."

It was convenient too, that Evie cut off her association with Josie, although Henry did feel pangs of guilt whenever Josie became distressed by her friend's behaviour towards her. However, as time passed and in spite of his doubts, he became obsessed with her and longed for their meetings, which sometimes took place in a small hotel in London during afternoons when Josie thought he was visiting his Physiotherapist or calling in at his bank. These were the times when Evie used Leonora as her alibi.

But it was when she announced she was pregnant that alarm bells rang for Henry. She wanted to keep the baby. He tried to convince her that a baby would complicate their relationship but she said she knew the baby was his and it was why she wanted to keep it. Henry didn't believe her and later found out he'd been right to suspect her of lying; she was already in the early stages of pregnancy when he'd met her.

His liaison with Evie was now turning into something more than merely the feeding of a pleasurable obsession. It was becoming a nuisance, in addition to which he feared discovery. The last thing he wanted was for it to destroy his marriage. He was terrified she'd tell Josie. She hinted at it often,

"How would Josie feel if I told her about us, Henry?"

What if I told them all?"

Don't you think it's about time you made up your mind who you want, Henry?"

It was all getting too much. She wouldn't listen. But somehow, he'd managed to persuade Evie to get rid of the baby. Initially she said no but when he'd produced the pills she'd gone along with it, to please him, she said the obligation hanging in her words – look what she was doing for him – what she was prepared to do to strengthen their relationship. He was beginning to feel she would do anything to feed her obsession with him.

Fortunately, for Henry he'd still kept in touch with Buster Norman who was a consultant Obstetrician in Charing Cross hospital. Buster was not happy about providing the tablets but Henry knew about Buster's reliance on prescription drugs and could have destroyed his career should he haven chosen to do so. In the end Buster produced the pills, stressing that as far as he was concerned the transaction had never taken place.

The real trouble started after Evie's miscarriage. Leonora went to Italy and Evelyn was unable to use her as an alibi in order to see him. She took chances, ringing him at odd times and he began to be afraid she'd become so indiscreet Josie would find out. Her behaviour became so erratic he felt he could no longer rely on her keeping her mouth shut. She threatened to tell her husband she wanted a divorce. Henry felt the like a fly trapped in a web, the more he struggled to escape the tighter the web became.

The evening he and Josie visited River House for dinner had been the last straw. She'd flirted outrageously with him all evening and Henry began to be seriously concerned she'd wreck his marriage. He tried to think of ways to silence her but before he could decide what to do fate took a hand.

The weather was bad that night. Henry was driving home. He cut his speed and drove slowly down the River Road, taking care to avoid the ice. He could see patches of light glistening on the icy surface in the reflection from the overhead street lamps when suddenly in front of him he saw Evie's car turning out of the side road leading from the Bennetts' house. He followed behind her until the car skidded on a patch of ice sliding across the road and hitting the lamppost head on.

Darkness fell on the road, as the lamps went out. In the light shining from his headlights he peered through the darkness to where the car had come to rest, then drove slowly towards it and drew up alongside. The lamp post lay across the bonnet and had sliced through the windscreen just missing Evie's head, which was lying against the driver's side window, her face was bleeding from the shards of flying glass and he noticed her hair was strewn with particles of glass, glistened like diamonds.

He wound down his window as she opened her eyes. "Henry, help me, please, help me. I'm trapped, it's my legs." Her voice was weak. She was pleading with him, her dark eyes closing as she drifted into unconsciousness. Her voice was quite unlike the last time he'd spoken to her, when she'd taunted him, threatening to tell Josie about their affair.

Picking up his metal crutch, which rested behind the front seat, Henry ignored the gleaming hair and the pleading voice as he leaned through the window, smashed the remaining glass in the pane resting against Evie's head and using the rubber tip of the crutch pushed with all his strength until her head made contact with the lamppost.

When he was satisfied there was no possibility of her ever betraying him, he stretched across to her once more. It was fortunate he'd continued with his upper body exercises since the accident, otherwise he never would have had enough strength to force her over in her seat.

Afterwards, he put his car into gear and drove back down the River Road until reaching the turn off towards the lane leading to his house. His heart was racing and his breath rasped in his chest but he was safe, Evie was dead!

Chapter 42

Raindrops trickle down the windowpane as Henry picks up the newspaper from the floor, folds it and places it on the coffee table. The sound of the mechanical diggers increases in volume as they continue excavating the lower reaches of the woodland. A shiver runs down his spine, he thought he'd managed to erase the memory of the night he'd found Evelyn on River Road but it is still there begging to be remembered.

The noise from digger has stopped by the time Henry hears Josie's car coming down the drive. He propels his wheelchair into the hall to tell her about the item in the newspaper but before he can say a word Josie rushes towards him, "They've found a body, in the woods, at River House!" she says taking off her wax jacket and Wellington boots. Then Henry notices raindrops glistening in her hair like shards of glass, as she bends forward to kiss him.

Epilogue

The sun is sinking low on the horizon as Laura closes the journal and places it on the iron table. Claudia is spending the night at the respite retreat. Her father is drinking wine in the café on the square and she is alone, apart from the old lady who snores in the next room. The evening air blows through her hair and she shivers, afraid to move. Nothing has prepared her for this.

The Englishman with the haunted look has written it all down but it makes no difference, there is no solace to be found within these pages. She can taste the salt of her tears. She's spent months worrying. There was no one to call, no one to explain. Leonora told her once that she liked to keep her old life and her new one separate. It was the only way she could cope with family problems. She knew about Lucas and, although she'd never met him, she understood he was a kind and generous man. However, the man her sister married after Lucas's death was an enigma. All Leonora would say was that he was the love of her life and she would never let him know about her family – she was afraid it would change things.

Now, at last she knows the truth. The money is the Englishman's way of appeasing his guilt. But she has to accept the part she's unwittingly played in the events leading to

Leonora's murder also, she closes her eyes and gives way to her emotions. Anger mixes with sadness as she waits for her brother to come home from the library. Carlo will know what to do – whom they should inform.

It's little consolation to know the murderer will be found – life will never be the same again. She used to think that knowing what had happened to Leonora would ease the pain - now she knows that nothing ever will.

The End.

Taken at the Flood

Dear Reader,
If you have enjoyed Taken at the Flood, please spread the word. I would also appreciate you taking the time to leave a review on the Amazon site. With grateful thanks.
K.J.Rabane.

Details of all K.J.Rabane's books can be found by visiting. www.kjrabane.co.uk

Printed in Great Britain
by Amazon.co.uk, Ltd.,
Marston Gate.